"Do you open your door at night to just anyone?"

Zac's voice hit her like a fist. What was the etiquette for greeting a husband she hadn't seen in fourteen months? But here he was on her doorstep, ready to save...his immigration status.

"Obviously so," Grace answered. She backed against the arch that led into the living room. Then she turned and began snapping on lights.

Everything was bright. But she felt no safer. Instead she could see him better, and that was worse. He towered over her—the man who had walked beside her down so many streets. Her handsome defender. Her lover.

Grace searched for something to say. "Do you want a drink?" When he didn't reply, she suggested, "Water? Brandy? A cup of hemlock?"

Zac's dark-lashed green eyes crinkled to crescents. "You've missed me."

Grace's mouth twitched. She'd forgotten that Zac could dish it back—and it tasted good. She had missed him.

Dear Reader,

On the edge of the Colorado River, at the junction of U.S. 191 and state highway 128 near Moab, Utah, water pours from a natural spring in the canyon wall. Wherever moisture seeps, gardens of green fronds grow in sandstone crevices. This is Matrimonial Springs, and local lore holds that those who drink of its water will always return to the area.

This folkway took special meaning for me years ago when my husband and I decided to move from Moab, our home, to the Midwest. The change meant leaving deep friendships, a community we loved and a country whose surreal natural splendor was stamped on our souls. But our family went east…for a time.

Since then, the canyonlands—and perhaps some magic in the Matrimonial Springs water that sustained us through countless desert adventures—have been a beacon luring us back. We now live in Colorado and return to Moab often. Each visit is a reunion with a place we love, and it was a special pleasure to go back again, in every way, as I wrote *The Keeper*.

I hope you enjoy meeting Zac and Grace, seeing them reunited in Moab, and accompanying them down the Colorado River as they try to keep their marriage afloat in the wild, unpredictable river current of life.

Sincerely,

Margot Early

P.S. I love receiving your letters at P.O. Box 611, Montrose, CO 81402-0611.

Margot Early

THE KEEPER

Harlequin Books

TORONTO • NEW YORK • LONDON
AMSTERDAM • PARIS • SYDNEY • HAMBURG
STOCKHOLM • ATHENS • TOKYO • MILAN
MADRID • WARSAW • BUDAPEST • AUCKLAND

ISBN 0-373-70668-5

THE KEEPER

Copyright © 1995 Margot Early.

Printed in U.S.A.

For Doug

ACKNOWLEDGMENTS

My heartfelt thanks to David M. Good, M.D., P.C., to Beth and Ted Jacobs, Jeff "Flipper" Blacker, Bob and Mary Beth Dehler, Shirley Sowell and Jean R. Ewing, who generously answered my questions on subjects ranging from mental disorders to English tea and so helped make this book possible. All technical errors in this fictional work are mine.

Also, I am deeply grateful to my editor for her sage guidance and her support of this project, and to my family, whose love and countless sacrifices are help beyond measure.

CHAPTER ONE

Moab, Utah
Suddenly last winter
Separated...

HER FATHER WAS DEAD, her marriage was over, and she'd left a career she loved for *this?* Standing in gravel and sand just yards from the red-brown flow of the Colorado River, Grace Sutter clutched a bottle of Drambuie and gazed, stupefied, at the sign.

It read:

RAPID RIGG RS RIVER AND JEEP EXPE ITIONS
EXCITI G WHITE WATER RAFTIN .
SCEN C 4WD TOURS.

Watching the "T" in "EXPEDITIONS" rock back and forth on a single nail as though ready to cartwheel away in the blowing dust, Grace tried to suppress the disloyal thoughts penetrating her grief. She could not. Who would venture into the wilderness with an outfit that couldn't maintain even a billboard, let alone serviceable rafts and vehicles?

Beside her, Day was balancing on a patch of gravel in a pair of white high-heeled sandals, lighting a cigarette. Grace asked her, "Would it have been too much trouble to fix the sign?"

Day drew on her cigarette, expelled the smoke and tossed fluffy flaxen bangs out of her eyes. Gesturing at her aqua mohair dress and black tights, she answered, "Do I look like a woman who repairs billboards?"

Grace eyed her sister. Day was twenty-five, only ten months younger than Grace. For the past decade Day had worked nearly full-time as girl Friday of the Rapid Riggers outfit, but she would never look like a woman who fixed billboards. At the moment she didn't look like someone who had just come from a funeral, either, but neither did Grace. Anyhow, she loved Day, and right now she needed her.

Still, she couldn't help murmuring, "You look like a woman who could persuade one of the boatmen to fix a billboard." Grace lifted the bottle of Drambuie to her lips and took a drink, liking the smooth heat, not wanting to quit. She hurt like hell—and not just about her father.

God, make it stop, she thought. Make it stop.

Day glanced at her, and the cigarette floated to her mouth again. Stepping away from Grace to exhale the smoke, she answered, "Persuading boatmen is one thing. Persuading Dad to cough up money for paint or even a rusty nail is another." She paused. "Was another."

Grace nearly snapped back that Day could have taken some initiative, that *she* would have done something. This place mattered to her. The Sutters had been in Moab since the turn of the century, and Rapid Riggers was the oldest river outfit in town. Her great-grandfather had built the old River Inn, seven miles downstream, back when dreamers were running riverboats with paddle wheels on the Colorado and the Green, fighting sandbars and shallow water at every bend.

But Grace said nothing. After all, she could have stayed in Moab and helped her father. Before she'd gone to New York to become a chef, she'd been one of his best river and Jeep guides—and more. He'd treated her as both

partner and apprentice.... But she'd left. And now Rapid
Riggers was in the red, and the Sutter properties, which
had once dotted both sides of the river, had winnowed to
two parcels. Grace and Day stood on one—the river outfit on the north bank, just below the Moab Bridge, at a
place where the fault severing the river gorge had created
the expanse of the Moab Valley. The other was their father's house, which had once been the River Inn. Grace
knew the inn would become her refuge now. Home.

She frowned, disentangling a wisp of light brown hair
from one of the three earrings in her left ear. Her short
French braid was coming loose, and though it was February, she felt hot and dusty in the fitted denim dress and
cowboy boots she'd worn to the funeral. At the moment
she wasn't going to climb up onto any billboards, either.

She took another drink, and her gaze panned the surrounding area. Across the highway to the north lay
Courthouse Wash and the boundary of Arches National
Park, where rocks rose in strange and myriad forma-
tions, their colors ranging from beige to deepest bur-
gundy and black. To the east were the high walls of the
river gorge upstream of the Moab Bridge. The Colorado
swept beneath the bridge, broadening as it flowed past
Rapid Riggers. There were no rapids here, and the flow
meandered first to the west, then back to the east, disappearing in a forest of salt cedar and tamarisk. Come
spring, the tamarisk would be a mosquito haven. Now
dead branches folded into the river's current, catching
other debris flowing seaward toward the portal, where the
gorge began again. Beyond lay miles of wilderness—an
undammed river.

Seeing it all, Grace knew she was home and she was
glad, but also chagrined. When she'd left for New York,
reaction in Moab had been mixed. Some thought that any
river-running daughter of Sam Sutter's could show New

York a thing or two. Others thought that city people were untrustworthy and Grace Sutter would find out.

Grace had.

So why this sense of deprivation? She longed to be back on that lumpy futon with Zac. How could she still want him so much?

With no answer, Grace focused on her new existence—Rapid Riggers. Glancing around the gravel-and-dirt lot beside the office, she noted that the sign wasn't the only aesthetic problem. Trailworn Chevy Suburbans—two with the hoods lifted—sat beside the office. The logos had worn off the doors and their bright blue paint had faded to a dull gray.

Studiously ignoring another vehicle in the lot—the U-Haul—Grace thought of the events that had brought her home.

Her father's heart attack had come on Valentine's Day, and her sister had called her, worried. Sam Sutter needed surgery, but Day was afraid he wouldn't slow down afterward. Rapid Riggers was in trouble. Their best guide was on an expedition in South America, and... Grace had wanted to come home. Who else would cook nutritious meals for the crusty outfitter? Or take care of the defunct River Inn, which Day had forsaken years ago in favor of a home of her own in town? But Grace's place was in New York....

Not anymore.

She took another drink.

"You're going to get sick," said Day.

Day was a lightweight. Grace was a river guide. Grace said, "Good. If you'd been through what I have, you'd want to throw up, too."

From the corner of her eye, she saw Day stare thoughtfully at the U-Haul. They'd never had secrets between them. Even when Grace was in New York and Day in Moab, they'd remained close. Bad moments could be erased with a phone call from city to desert town. Instant laughter, instant love.

But she hadn't told Day everything this time, and now Day gave her a look that meant, *Since you brought it up...* "So what's going on with your husband?" She gestured at the U-Haul. "You've brought more than a suitcase."

Grace had brought everything. What was "going on" should be obvious. But Day, always fascinated by human drama, would want the blow-by-blow, the way Grace always wanted every detail of a recipe.

Okay, thought Grace. *How to make a Zachary Key. Take one seven-year-old younger son of a peer, dress him in an uncomfortable uniform and send him away to school to learn to be a perfect English gentleman. Then...*

She tried out the words. "Zachary married me for a green card."

Day made a choking sound.

A burst of wind lifted dust from the other side of the road and from the ground beneath them and swirled it up through the air. Both women turned their backs to the devil and started up the bank toward the two-story gray building that housed the Rapid Riggers office. As Day's sandals navigated a maze of yellow-blossomed goatheads growing among the gravel, she said, "Isn't that, like, against the law?"

Grace rolled her eyes. She capped the Drambuie and tightened the lid. Despite what she'd told Day, she didn't want to be sick. She said, "Well, in any case, it's a slimy thing to do to one's lover."

For a moment she saw Zac sitting on the bed that last day—Valentine's Day. They'd both been naked, because they'd been making love when Day called. It had made it so much worse somehow—their first fight right there on the sacred space of their bed. Zac had grabbed her by the shoulders...

Don't do this, Grace. I need that green card.

Green card.

It just slipped out, didn't it, Zac?

After four months of marriage.

Closing her mind to the rest of the argument—the careening emotions, everything—Grace climbed the steps and paused on the porch. She told Day, "You cannot imagine how it feels to know that a person I loved used me that way. Zachary asked me to marry him *the same day* he got a part in an off-Broadway play. He never mentioned that he needed equity and a green card. And I didn't think twice when on the day we were married—on the way home from the courthouse, no less—he wanted to stop at the INS office."

"INS?"

"The Immigration and Naturalization Service. You don't want to meet these people. Zac had to take a medical exam where they checked for everything from tuberculosis to insanity. Then we had this interview that was like a cross between "The Newlywed Game" and a Senate investigation hearing. They put us in separate rooms and asked us incredibly personal questions. 'What side of the bed does your husband sleep on?' 'What color is his toothbrush?' 'Does he wear boxer or jockey shorts?' "

Day blinked. "Which does he wear?" As Grace unscrewed the lid of the bottle again, she said, "Sorry. Just kidding."

Both sisters were silent while the wind beat at the international flags flying along the porch eaves.

At last Day said, "Well, no one could blame *you*. I mean, you sent me a picture. The guy's sexy."

Grace thought it was kind of her sister not to mention the words "whirlwind courtship." But Zac *was* sexy. Skin the color of honey, and beautiful lips and jaw and chin and the straight aristocratic nose that wasn't quite aquiline. Painfully Grace remembered her lover's body. Zac's washboard-hard abs and pecs and the swell of sinew in his thighs and calves—and her legs tangled with his. He'd been a rower at Eton and at Oxford....

Lost in thought, Grace remembered the intimacy of daily routine. Mornings they'd gone running together in the East Village before that world recovered from its nightly bacchanal. Zac loping ahead of her beside the river, then circling back to be with her, urging her on to their destination, the Brooklyn Bridge. On the way home, they'd always stopped for cappuccinos to go at a coffeehouse on Avenue B. From there it was five blocks to the turn-of-the-century hotel-gone-apartment building whose lobby smelled like cabbage. They would climb the four flights of stairs to their studio, strip off their clothes, and make love under the spray of the shower.

Grace shut her eyes as another gust of wind came, spreading red sand through the air, scattering it against her body and the never-clean windows of the river office.

Day said, "Grace, are you sure it was just the green card? I mean, I talked to him on the phone. He was so sweet and cute about that wedding gift I sent you."

The red leather teddy with peekaboo cups. He'd been sweet and cute, all right. A hundred and eighty-five pounds of excited male.

Day said, "I think he loves you, Grace."

Once Grace had thought so, too. Now one suspicion bedeviled her, and the green-card revelation told her she was right. Zac had been acting.

The possibility appalled her, but she knew he possessed the skill. On stage he had a cool riveting presence noticed by all the critics who'd seen him in *Leaving Hong Kong*. That play. The play that meant enough to lie for.

"He loves his career, Day. He's only twenty-six, but you can tell he's going to *be* someone. Nothing matters more to him."

But as she spoke, a wave of homesickness rushed over her, and she thought not of Zac the actor, the Zac who

was so very good and got a wild look in his eye at the
thought of being deported and losing this role. Instead,
she thought of Zac in waiter's black and white at Jean-
Michel's, slipping her notes between orders. Zac beside
her on the subway and walking her home from the First
Avenue station—past darkened doors of clubs that
wouldn't open till three, past people shooting up on the
sidewalks, past the homeless and the strange and the
scary. They'd fallen in love hard, Grace had thought.
Discovering each other, unable to get enough of each
other. Together every minute. Zac had made the squalor
and crime fade away. He'd introduced her to opera and to
smoky jazz clubs and to Greek plays that made her soul
ache, and he'd brought her not flowers but wheels of fine
cheese and specialized cooking utensils, a chef's dream.
In their walk-up, he'd dispatched colonies of cock-
roaches, replaced old baseboards, painted, constantly
fixed things to make it better—for her. He'd unearthed the
old hardwood floor so that they could dance in their bare
feet to scratchy music from the ghetto blaster, Ella Fitz-
gerald crooning their song, George and Ira Gershwin's
"Love Is Here to Stay." He'd risked eviction over a stray
cat.

He was easy to love.

When Grace had told him about her family's tradition
of making "coupons" for gifts, Zac had seized the idea
and taken it to new heights, creating beautiful, elaborate
IOUs that could be redeemed for housework or breakfast
in bed or...anything. Grace still had three she hadn't used.
With Zac, she'd seldom had to ask for what she wanted.

On his nights off, he'd ridden the subway to Tribeca to
meet her when she got off work. In faded Levi's and patterned thrift-shop shirts no one else could wear so well, he
was no longer the immaculate waiter with the Oxford
polish but just her lover—comfortable and familiar.
When she came outside he was always there, and he

hugged her tight under the streetlights, hugged her until they were both desperate to be home in bed....

For a moment, remembering, Grace imagined he *must* be missing her, needing her. But she knew she was drunk.

She told Day, "He won't return my calls. I've left about six messages on his machine." *Their* machine. "He doesn't even know about Dad. What am I supposed to do? Tell the answering machine my father died in surgery?"

Day looked at her thoughtfully. "If you do, he might call you back."

New York

WHEN THE PHONE RANG it sounded inordinately loud, and Zachary jumped as though someone had slammed a door. He stared at it for a long time. It was a red rotary instrument. Grace had called it the Bat Phone.

He waited for it to ring again, and after what seemed like a long time it did. He watched it some more. The click of the answering machine was like a gunshot in his ears, and he could hear the tape revolving on its spindles as his own voice boomed into the room. "You have reached the Key residence. Please leave a message."

The beep sounded more like a screech. Fingernails on a chalkboard.

"Zac, this is Grace. I guess you're not there.... Look, I apologize for leaving this kind of message, but you haven't returned my calls, and I want you to know— I've wanted to tell you in person . . . my dad died after his surgery. There were complications.... I want you to call me. Please." The sudden disconnection was harsh, amplified.

Swallowing hard, Zac stood in the middle of the room as he had for a long time. Had Grace spoken to him? Had the phone rung?

My dad died...

Had he imagined that? He stared at the blinking light on the answering machine. It seemed profound, a symbol of something he couldn't grasp. A message? The fan whirred in the window, and he heard it as he heard all the other sounds on the street. Sounds had never been so keen before.

Keen. Keening.

The words popped into his mind, uninvited and disconnected. They echoed. Keen. Keening. Keen. Keening.

He turned his head and looked at the picture on the milk crate beside the bed—the nightstand. The photo was of the two of them, a snapshot taken outside the courthouse the day they were married.

Zac tried to focus on her features, tried to see her mouth, tried to think what it was about her mouth that had been interesting to him, that he had always liked. But he couldn't concentrate on anything smaller than her whole image. A tall pretty stranger with mouse-colored hair and black eyebrows. *Hot,* he thought. In the photo, tights covered her long legs, but for a moment he remembered a bare thigh against his lips and his face.

Then the feeling and the flash of emotion went away.

He looked at the man in the picture. It was him, kissing her cheek, but he thought, *Is that me?* The photograph seemed fluid, as though the surface was liquid, a subtly moving liquid that made edges sharp. Alive.

Why was everything so noisy?

The noise made it hard to think, except for one clear wish. *Grace, come back.*

He almost reached for the phone. Had it rung? If he knew, then he could call her.

My dad died...

The sounds assaulted him, a cacophony. The fan, the cars, a child crying in number four, the refrigerator humming. Why had he never noticed that the electricity in the building was so loud? He could hear the bulbs in the light fixtures.

He remembered that he had a performance that night, but then the thought slipped away. It didn't seem important. There was something else important to do. Something he had to do. Something monumental.

He didn't know what it was.

He felt disoriented, frightened, confused. Everything had changed without Grace. Everything had new significance.

Everything seemed so . . . strange.

GRACE SET DOWN the phone, uncapped the Drambuie and wondered why her heart was pounding. *Because you're in love with him, stupid.* At least for four months you thought you were.

But her heart wasn't pounding the same way it did when she saw him or when she actually heard his voice, really him and not the machine. This was a different kind of pounding, almost as though she was afraid for him, which was ridiculous.

Afraid he'd be mugged or shot or . . .

Grace lifted the bottle from the reception desk and took a drink, thinking. Her address book was in the U-Haul. She could call a neighbor. *Excuse me, have you seen my husband lately?*

The plan was humiliating but sensible. What if something *had* happened to Zac?

Something *should* happen to him, she thought with a touch of venom.

The worst would not be learning Zac had been knifed in the subway or struck by a taxi. What she dreaded more was hearing that he'd been coming and going as usual— and ignoring her calls.

Why didn't he call her back? Was he hurt because she'd left? Did he really love her?

Had she made a terrible mistake?

At her elbow, the phone jangled, startling her. Grace blinked at it, then, barely breathing, lifted the receiver. "Rapid Riggers River and Jeep Expeditions. This is Grace."

There was a long pause.

Zac said, "Hi. It's me."

Grace shook. "Zachary."

The cultured English voice she loved said, "I'm sorry about your father, Grace."

She waited for him to say more—that it was a pity he'd never had a chance to meet Sam Sutter. But he was quiet.

At last she said, "Thanks. It was horrible, finding out." She brushed her hand across her eyes. Dammit, she was crying. She didn't want to start now, when he was on the phone and she was drunk. Things would get out of control in a hurry. She screwed the lid on the bottle.

The pause seemed endless, and Grace wondered what he was doing, what he was thinking. About her father's death? Or about her? Should she try to bridge the gap between them? No. Zac was the only one who could do that. He could say, *I fell in love with you. I wasn't even thinking about a green card when I met you.* He could say, *It was you I wanted.*

Instead, he said, "Do you hear that?"

"What?"

"That noise on the line—in the background. It's very loud."

"I don't hear anything," said Grace.

He made a noncommittal sound. Then in a rush he said, "Everything seems so different with you gone. It's all more *intense.* Even the textures. Every sound is sharper. Every color is brighter. Like Wordsworth's Margaret— '...I dread the rustling of the grass; The very shadows of the clouds have power to shake me as they pass....' I never liked Wordsworth." He stopped. "I wish you were here, Grace, so I could make love to you and feel what *that's* like now that everything's changed.''

Grace's brow furrowed, and she clutched the phone more tightly. "What do you mean? What's changed?"

He said nothing for a moment, as though registering her words, as though pondering them. Finally he said, "I just miss you. Grace, have you ever thought this phone might be tapped?"

Grace lifted her hand to her forehead, taking a small breath. *All he can think of is the INS!* She said, "I don't believe this. My father just died, and you're worried the immigration authorities have tapped the phone."

He said, "Don't yell."

"I'm not yelling." She wasn't.

"I find you deafening. Maybe it's the phone. Look— I'd like to come and see you if I can find a way."

Zachary? Miss a performance? Grace tried not to be cynical. "I'd like that." Together. Being held. Zac in her bed. Zac, with her.

"Good. We'll talk later. I love you."

He hung up, and Grace slowly lowered the receiver, wondering if he would really come, feeling how badly she wanted him, whispering his name in her mind. *Zac*, she thought, *don't break my heart.*

But for a time she stood at the counter, frowning, thinking how odd he'd sounded. Idly she wondered who Wordsworth's Margaret was.

ZAC UNPLUGGED the answering machine and waited alone in the apartment until dusk. Several times the phone rang, but he never answered it. Once, someone knocked on the door.

At seven he went out into the hall, leaving the door unlocked and his key behind, and walked down the four flights of stairs to the funky lobby that might have been elegant in another era. Then he slipped outside onto Avenue B.

He was assaulted by sound and sight. He squinted to block out the neon light from the gay bar across the street, and he almost put his hands over his ears to quiet the sounds of passing cars, their tires spinning through the residual slush left over from an early-spring snow. He had no reason to be outside, just a longing to be somewhere besides the apartment. Though he'd brought no coat and his breath rose in steam puffs from his nose and mouth, he didn't feel the cold.

Hours passed like minutes as he walked down toward Fourteenth Street, making his way through the Avenues—D and E, F and G. The area became increasingly seedy as he moved farther east, yet he felt invincible.

People tried to sell him crack, men offered him money for sex, and he ignored them. When someone stood in his path with a knife, he said, "Leave me alone," and the body moved. Clearly his power was more than physical, more than human.

He was chosen.

He was special.

Nothing could hurt him at all.

CHAPTER TWO

Moab, Utah
Fourteen months later
Reunited....

THE DAY the Ben Rogan jeans "I like to be close to my clothes" advertisements appeared, they were banned in Salt Lake City, in Phoenix and in Raleigh, North Carolina. In other cities where the brouhaha made the news, magazines flew off the stands, and women gaped at their television screens, asking, "Who is that *guy?*"

One woman who could have answered the question had never seen the ads, though she'd heard about the censorship. She gave it little thought. She was too busy running her deceased father's river outfit—and trying to find the husband who had vanished from her life after one strange phone call more than a year before....

AT FIVE O'CLOCK on the day Zachary reappeared in her life, Grace stood in the kitchen of the Rapid Riggers office, her hands caked with grease from changing the oil in Suburban number two. Through the dirty kitchen window, she could see three first-year boatmen, fresh off the river, engaged in a water fight. Hoses, buckets and the mud rapidly accumulating in the yard were all employed in the fray, and as a sloshing bucket of muddy water hit the window, Grace thought, *That's enough!*

She grabbed two paper towels in each grimy hand and used them to protect the frame as she unlatched the window and raised the sash. Seeing a boatman douse a nubile female guide with two gallons of filthy water, Grace yelled out the window, "You're making a mess! Cool it."

She slammed the window as a pair of high heels clicked on the linoleum behind her. Grace spun to see Day peering past her shoulder out the wet window. In a broomstick skirt and appliquéd vest, she looked as fresh and beautiful as she had that morning, and there was a copy of *W* under her arm. She said, "Lighten up on the boatmen, Grace. They're paid by the day, and they put in a long one. It's April. They've just got spring fever."

Grace used the two paper towels to wipe ineffectually at the grease on her hands, and Day helpfully snatched a bottle of heavy-duty liquid soap from the windowsill and squirted it on her sister's palms. Then she turned on the sink water.

Grace said, "Thank you." Day was right about the boatmen. Nonetheless, as she soaped her hands at the sink, Grace looked over her shoulder to say, "Well, if they have so much energy, one of them can wash the windows in this place tomorrow." As she spoke, she saw her sister's mouth tighten. Wheeling from the sink, she demanded, "Well, what's wrong with that?"

Day's blue eyes were sympathetic, and that alone sent the emotion crawling up Grace's throat. She didn't want sympathy. She just wanted— She didn't know what she wanted.

Day said, "Grace, this is a happy place. It has to be. We're serving the public, and we've got to be cheerful to make them feel good."

"I'm cheerful," Grace said. "As cheerful as I can be when my partner's been gone all afternoon working on the spring musical while I've been changing oil in two vehicles, painting a raft and waiting for that sinfully over-

paid Nick Colter to get his handsome rear end back from
Cataract Canyon. Where is he?''

Day restrained a sigh. "He's not that late, Grace. Anyhow, I just passed him downtown. He had a flat tire on
the way back from Hite Marina, and now he's dropping
two passengers at their hotels. As for his salary, you and
I both agreed it was worth it to hang on to him. He's our
best guide, and he doesn't need this job. He does it because he likes it. He's got money in the bank, and if we
don't watch it, someday he'll walk out of here and start a
river outfit of his own.''

"Good riddance," Grace murmured, not meaning it.
They couldn't get along without Nick.

Day said, "And I'm sorry about the rehearsal. They're
usually at night. How about cutting everyone some slack,
Grace? Ever since you've come back from New York,
you've been a full-time killjoy."

It was more than Grace could stand. She snatched at the
roll of paper towels and pulled it off the holder. Catching
it as it threatened to tumble to the floor, she exclaimed,
"You mean, ever since I've been in business with you?"

"I mean, ever since you left that jerk who hurt you!"

Grace gasped, and the paper towels slipped from her
hands and rolled across the floor, unraveling sheet after
sheet as she clutched the end tightly in her fingers. It came
out then, though she'd intended to keep it a secret until it
was over. "I'm getting a divorce."

Day's face changed. She stared for a moment, and then
she said, "Oh, Grace, why didn't you say something?"
She grabbed her, and Grace was enfolded in the only embrace she knew these days, the comforting arms of her
sister.

Her brow creased in deep lines as W dug into her back.
Remembering her greasy hands, she pulled away. "I'm
sorry." She retrieved the paper towels, then pulled several off the roll to dab at the spots on her sister's vest.

"It's just water, I think." She couldn't meet Day's eyes. "You're a great business partner and a great sister. I didn't mean anything."

"Maybe you meant you'd rather be a chef," said Day comfortingly. She changed the subject. "Since you brought up the unmentionable, I have some news. Maybe you already know. Guess who likes to be 'close to his clothes'?"

Close to his clothes? Grace recognized the infamous slogan for Ben Rogan jeans only because the designer's racy advertisements had recently been banned in Salt Lake. But before she could make sense of Day's words, a horn sounded outside the office, and a blue Suburban hauling a twenty-foot raft pulled around the side of the building and into the yard.

Grace glanced at the clock. "That's Nick."

The river guide was hours late returning from the outfit's first white-water trip of the season, a four-day float down Cataract Canyon. Even though she'd grown up in the business and was an experienced guide herself, Grace had imagined the worst. A flip in Satan's Gut, a boat wrapped on a rock or the most serious—orange life vests laid out in a giant X on the beach, signaling air traffic to send a chopper with a medical team.

Day was right. She needed to get used to things not running like clockwork. This was a wilderness-tour outfit, not a restaurant kitchen.

Day said, "Anyhow, about Zachary—"

"I don't want to talk about him." The last thing Grace wanted now was to entertain questions about her missing husband. They plagued her without Day's help, but she tried not to brood about Zac while she was at the office. A Colorado River outfitter couldn't afford to be that preoccupied.

Hearing tramping feet on the scarred wood floor of the reception area, Grace hurried out of the kitchen, following the sound. In the front office, Nick Colter—shirtless, suntanned and silty from four days on the Colorado—was accepting tips from three dirty passengers who told Grace how much they'd enjoyed the trip. Grace returned the pleasantries, but as she helped them separate their belongings from the Rapid Riggers sleeping bags and tents, her mind was on the river.

Two weeks earlier the snowmelt had begun to trickle down from the mountains and into the Colorado River. Precipitation in the eastern Rockies had been high that winter, and throughout Moab river guides were rubbing their palms in anticipation of big rapids.

Like them, Grace knew the thrill of navigating massive waves and guiding rafts around treacherous "keeper" holes, whose hydraulic turbulence could capture boats and bodies alike, sucking them under the surface and churning them like the agitation cycle on a washing machine. But she also knew what high water meant to a river outfit—danger, bad press and canceled trips. Each day as she drove along the Colorado from her home at the old River Inn to the Rapid Riggers office, Grace watched the swelling river with apprehension. Fortunately, both buildings were on rises of land high up the banks. Neither had ever flooded. That left only the white water to worry about.

When the passengers were gone, she asked Nick, "How's Cataract?"

Long black hair swinging below his shoulders, Nick made a face of mock terror, then sobered. Unlike the outfit's less experienced boatmen, he understood the impact of water level on business. "The waves were bigger than the boat. There's a mammoth whirlpool in Capsize and a boat-eating keeper in Satan's Gut. And I think we can look forward to, what, four more weeks of runoff?"

In other words, the rapids were big—and getting bigger. Grace tossed the sleeping bags in a corner to be taken to the cleaners and began pulling tents from their stuff sacks to check and repack them for the next trip. "How are we going to manage that movie?"

Since the days of John Wayne, the red rocks of Moab had attracted filmmakers hunting for showy scenery. Grace had been thrilled when Rapid Riggers landed a contract to provide technical support on *Kah-Puh-Rats,* a feature film about the nineteenth-century exploration of the Colorado River by Major John Wesley Powell. But could she ask her boatmen to guide historically accurate wooden dories through Cataract in extreme high water?

Nick grinned. "Don't worry, Grace. Rapid Riggers has the best. *Me.*" He blew a kiss to each sister as he disappeared into the kitchen with a cooler.

Day rolled her eyes. "Let's just hope we don't have to cancel on the movie. Saga Entertainment is big time. And speaking of big time..." With the air of a woman who would not be pushed aside again, she turned to her sister and proffered a tabloid-size ad supplement from her copy of *W.* "Have you seen this?"

Grace abandoned the tents and came over to look at the insert. On the cover was a black-and-white ad for Ben Rogan jeans. At least, judging from the words on the ad—"I like to be close to my clothes"—Grace assumed it was for the jeans. But the model wasn't really *wearing* them.

His body had more ripples than a rapid, each as familiar as a river she'd run a hundred times. But what got to her were his hands—though only one, his left, showed in the photo. A long-fingered, strong, masculine hand—hanging on to those jeans that were sliding either up or down his thighs, it wasn't clear which. She would know his hands anywhere.

Drawing her eyes away from his fingers, Grace stared at the long dark hair pushed off his forehead. As always, a stray lock angled forward toward one corner of that generous, sensuous mouth. Her eyes froze on those of the model, and she wavered on her feet. *Zac.* She had found him. "I've got to call my lawyer." Moving toward the phone, only half-aware she was shaking, she told Day, "I haven't been able to trace him. We haven't been able to serve him—"

Trailing after her, Day said, "Boy, you really meant it when you said you were getting a divorce. I didn't realize you'd actually filed."

Grace couldn't look at his picture again. *He was fine.* Dammit, he was okay. "Do you think I want to spend the rest of my life married to an illegal alien who doesn't call, write or answer the phone? Especially when we don't even live together?"

Day studied the ad at arm's length, as though considering.

Rolling her eyes, Grace moved toward the telephone, just as it rang. She lifted the receiver. "Rapid Riggers River and Jeep Expeditions. Grace speaking."

It was her lawyer, and the conversation was short. He, too, had found Zac.

And Zac had been served.

As Grace hung up the phone, the pain came. It was a surprise. She'd known this was happening; she'd set it in motion herself. But she hadn't expected it to hurt so much. Divorce. This was what it was like.

What hurt most was that Zac, alive and well in Santa Monica, had never bothered even to call or write. It was a cruel end to fourteen months of waiting. Empty nights, empty bed, aching and scared...for him. Embroidering fantasies in which he returned—with an explanation for his absence. And proof he really hadn't married her for a green card.

But prosaic life had just handed her the facts. Zac did not love her.

Grace resisted taking home the Ben Rogan ad at the end of the day, but when she reached work the next morning, after a long night, she saw it lying discarded on the couch in the inner office, and temptation was too much. She picked it up and took it to her desk.

I like to be close to my clothes.

Zac looked sexy and his half smile was inviting. His body was smooth and hard and indecent. But when all was said and done, this was an advertisement.

Grace set aside the ad, opened her center desk drawer and wriggled her hand into the back. Her fingers touched a snapshot, and she pulled it out. Casual and handsome in a peacoat and muffler, snow floating down on his hair, Zac smiled at her from the steps of the Metropolitan Opera House. They'd just seen *Aida*. Grace had never been to the opera before, and she'd cried while Zac sat beside her with a quiet, still expression that had made her want to own his heart. That evening, they'd made love for the first time.

The photograph hurt, like the memory. She put it away.

Hearing a vehicle in the lot, Grace glanced outside to see a Federal Express van arriving. She went into the reception area and saw that Day had already come in with the package.

Reading the shipping label on the square box, Day lifted her eyebrows slightly. "It's for you."

Grace's stomach rolled with foreboding as she took the package from her sister. It was from Zachary Key, on Ocean Street in Santa Monica.

"Obviously, he's a man of action," said Day.

He'd been served only yesterday. Trembling, Grace set the box on the reception counter and opened the pocket knife on her key chain. As Day perched on a stool and watched her take a gift box from the carton, Grace's heart thudded hard. The box was wrapped in paper made from a grocery bag, on which Zac had painted peace signs and hearts and pictures of himself and her together, pictures to be explored later. Along with the card.

Day said, "It's hard to hate a man who makes his own wrapping paper."

Grace said nothing. This box was her first communication from her husband in fourteen months. Later she would explore motives. Now she just wanted to absorb what he was trying to say. Now, for one moment, she wanted to believe. Carefully she opened the paper, her eyes catching an image he'd painted of the two of them on a subway seat, hugging. Not great art, but Grace could feel that bear hug.

Lifting the lid of the plain white box, she saw an object wrapped in tissue paper and carefully pulled it out. A music box. Custom-made.

"Oh, look," said Day. "It's you two."

Indeed, the music-box figurines were Grace and Zac, dressed for their first date. Recognizing her retro minidress and black tights, his black shirt with large red polka dots, Grace remembered the occasion and how badly she'd wanted to go out with him, like she'd die if he didn't ask. They'd stayed out all night—dancing, talking, never running out of things to say, and they'd watched the sun rise from the roof of an old theater. Outside her apartment, they'd kissed like two people who'd been waiting their whole lives to kiss. To find each other.

The figures on top of the music box were dancing cheek to cheek against a stage set made to resemble the East Village apartment she and Zac had shared.

Day said, "Wind it up, and see what it plays."

"I know what it plays." Grace's emotions boiled in her throat, volatile, threatening to erupt. Torn between hope and distrust, she gathered up paper and card, leaving the music box where it sat. Avoiding her sister's eyes, she said, "You can wind it, if you like," and went into the inner office.

At her desk chair, she tore open the card, which showed movie-star footprints at Mann's Chinese Theater. Inside was Zac's writing, still familiar, and Grace felt anger and pain and hope and excitement as she read.

Dear Grace,
I am coming to Moab to work on a film. Your river outfit is a technical consultant on the picture. I would like to spend time with you and discuss what happened between us. I'm sorry it's taken so long. You are never far from my mind.

Love,
Zachary

Grace was stunned. Zac was coming to Moab? He had a role in *Kah-Puh-Rats?* And he knew Rapid Riggers was involved with the filming.

She read the card twice, then pored over the wrapping paper, the pictures he'd painted. One showed her and Zachary in a dory on the river.

Zac. He was coming to see her.

Because of the movie.

Of course. Acting had always mattered more to him than she did. *As a matter of fact, Sutter,* Grace reminded herself, *it's why he married you.* And he was coming back for the same reason. To save his green card, now that a movie role was on the line. He'd sent the music box by overnight courier, undoubtedly after being served with divorce papers.

But Grace disbelieved her own explanation. The music box had been specially made. The time and care the artist had taken showed in the workmanship. This wasn't a dozen roses ordered on the spur of the moment.

You are never far from my mind.

Her hope scared her, because the pain of the night was still fresh. Raw. Grace tried to harden her heart, to be as strong and insensible as steel.

But from the reception area came the tinkling sound of the music box playing, "Love Is Here to Stay."

ZACHARY KEY stood at the window of his room in Moab's Anasazi Palace and stared out at the dusk. The gaudy new Santa Fe-style motel was one block off Main Street, close to a restaurant and a bicycle shop with an espresso stand in front. The stand was closed now, and Zac considered walking somewhere to find a cup of tea.

He'd left Santa Monica at six the night before, just hours after the process server had appeared at his door. After sending the music box, he'd packed in a hurry and gone, driving straight through, possessed. Twelve hours in darkness, then six more as the day began, the lights rising on a wonderland of rock like he'd never seen. Miles and miles of desert landscape so strange and exquisite it seemed unreal. When he'd reached the hotel, he'd fallen on the bed and slept for four hours. Now he was up, showered and shaved. Ready to see Grace.

But the urgency of his cross-country chase had died.

Zac stared bleakly at the gutter below. Letting the curtain fall against the glass, he turned from the window and his eyes caught the manila packet lying on his bed, the envelope containing the divorce papers.

A familiar fear settled upon him, and he lay down on the bed, overcome by an agony of indecision.

He shouldn't be trying to do this. He'd never even seen a doctor after that episode in New York. How could he go back to Grace not knowing what had happened or why?

But he was fine now.

Fine, and working as an actor again. Deliberately he focused on that. His career. He'd virtually destroyed it during that month after Grace left. Reflecting on the details, Zac closed his eyes. *I just lost control.* Things were hard after a breakup. Everyone knew that.

But it had taken a year to repair the damage. If Grace divorced him now, if the immigration authorities began investigating him . . .

He tried to think rationally. Even in the worst-case scenario, he was unlikely to lose his green card. He made too much money, paid too much tax, for anyone to want to deport him now. That wasn't why he was here. Nor was the role in *Kah-Puh-Rats*—his *only* role in more than a year—the reason he'd come.

He was here to see Grace. Grace, who thought he'd married her to legalize his resident status.

Hadn't he?

He hadn't denied it fourteen months earlier, the day her sister had called, the day she'd asked, *Is that why you married me, Zac? For a green card?*

To say no would have been at least partly a lie, and lies had a way of sticking in his throat. So he had said, *I love you.*

That's not what I asked.

If she'd believed he loved her, she hadn't cared. And now she wouldn't believe. He'd waited too long. He'd had to wait.

Zac envisioned an unpleasant scene—explaining to Grace. He wasn't ready for that. *She'd* left *him*. And even their both working on the movie was no guarantee she'd have anything to do with him. Zac held no illusions about what the music box might have accomplished. He'd had it made for love of her, but it wouldn't make her love him back.

Lying on the bed, Zac stared at the smoke alarm on the ceiling and tried to construct a plan. If only he had some leverage, some means of persuasion. A promise. A contract. A—

He sat up and grabbed his wallet from the nightstand. Flipping it open, he fished in the slot behind his driver's license.

Oh, God. There were *three* of them, scrawled on the backs of register receipts from Jean-Michel's. Not works of art like the coupon book Grace had given him on Valentine's Day, which had been full of pictures from magazines and sprinkled with glitter. Just quick coupons, dashed off generously, like kisses, one night at the restaurant when they were both so hungry for the shift to end, so hungry to be alone.

Coupons. Those promises they'd made as gifts, words on paper that meant, *I love you. Let me help you. Let me make your life better.*

Aside from their marriage, which Grace wanted to dissolve, the coupons were the closest thing to a contract Zac could wish for. With anticipation, he unfolded each slip of paper to see what she'd promised him.

1 Five-Course Dinner by Grace.
1 Anything of Zachary's Choice.

And one clearly defined sexual favor, the thought of which made him hard. Seeing that coupon, Zac thought of a half dozen like it in his sock drawer at home in L.A. He'd never had to cash even one with Grace, nor she with him. A cynical friend had told him he should hang on to them until they'd been married longer.

Redeeming that coupon now sounded like food to a starving man, but Zac knew it wasn't the place to start— nor, speaking of starving, was asking her to cook for him.

But the other...

An *Anything* coupon.

He lay back on the bed, dizzy with relief. He had found a way.

SOAKING UP to her shoulders in lemongrass bubble bath, Grace leafed through a chef's magazine, watching for recipes that could be prepared in advance and kept chilled in ice chests to be eaten on the river. Or recipes that could be cooked in a Dutch oven or fried over an open fire. When she was attending the Culinary Institute, she'd never anticipated such uses for her skills, but since she'd returned to Rapid Riggers the outfit had become famous for its gourmet river meals.

As Grace dog-eared a page showing an unusual orzo salad and a recipe for black walnut bread, the doorbell tolled through the house. There was a clock on the edge of the sink and she squinted at it. Nine-thirty. Who could be at the door? Day sometimes dropped in late, but she never used the doorbell.

Trying not to slosh water onto the floor, Grace stood up and reached for a towel, then climbed out of the tub as the bell rang again.

She toweled herself swiftly and slipped into her brown sand-washed silk lounging pajamas. Grace had ordered them by mail the day she filed for divorce. It wasn't that she anticipated finding a lover. She still couldn't imagine even kissing anyone else after Zac. But his charade had violated her femininity, and she'd wanted it back.

She hurried downstairs and into the foyer. Filmy, slightly yellowed curtains covered the glass panes of the front door, and all that showed through was a tall, dark shape. Undoubtedly it was some boatman low on cash, asking if there were any late-scheduled trips going out the next day.

She twisted the handle and opened the door.

At the sight of the man on her screened porch, illuminated only by the dim table lamp in the foyer and the moonlight flickering on the river behind him, Grace felt the world sway. Zachary.

He said, "Hi."

Her response to the sight of him, a desire to hurl herself at him, was leashed by doubt. Zac... Here. Despite the music-box gift, she hadn't expected to see him so soon. Filming wouldn't start for two weeks, but here he was on her doorstep, ready to save...his immigration status.

Zac didn't wait for her to speak, either to ask him in or order him gone. Brushing his hand at a mosquito whining near his ear, he stepped into the foyer and asked, "Do you open your door at night to just anyone?"

His voice hit her like a fist. It was low, striking, the voice of a man who'd grown up in a manor house in Kent and been educated at one of England's oldest public schools. A voice meant to ring through a theater, to linger in people's souls after they left a performance.

Was he questioning her living alone by the river, in a grand old house that had once been an inn? *Did she open her door at night to just anyone?*

She said, "Obviously so."

Fighting a smile, Zac shut the door behind him.

Grace backed against the arch that led into the living room. Then she turned and began snapping on lights. The living room sprang into sharp relief. The chandelier in the foyer blazed. Everything was bright.

She felt no safer. Instead, she could see him better, and that was worse. He towered over her five-foot-nine-inch frame, and old reactions shuddered through her. Here was the man who had walked beside her down so many streets. Her handsome defender. Her lover.

Grace searched for something to say. "Do you want a drink?"

Zac didn't answer at once. He was looking at her. The brown silk pajamas clung to every contour of her body. She was as hot as he remembered, with an earthy sexiness that reminded anyone who saw her that she was female.

And an exterior toughness that hid a vulnerability he loved.

Her damp hair hung loose about her shoulders, its fairness a contrast to her dark lashes and flushed cheeks, and her brown eyes were serious. Seeing her mouth, Zac knew what had eluded him about it for so long. When she spoke or smiled or laughed, the left side moved more than the right. It had made him want her the first time she'd spoken to him at Jean-Michel's, before he even knew her.

As he studied her now, Grace returned his scrutiny and said, "That's an ugly shirt, but it looks good on you." It was red, with a ghastly floral print. Silk, worn with faded Levi's. *Only Zac,* she thought, glancing at his face. He must have just shaved, but she knew where his beard grew, the sexy line of mustache that looked like it belonged to a bandit chieftain, the brush of stubble on his chin and jaw. His dark hair—longer than when she'd seen it last, longer than in the ad—was damp, pushed back from his forehead and eyes, but a few strands still crept forward. Sexy. Everything about him was.

Creep, Grace thought, trying to forget the music box on her armoire upstairs, the box that had so charmed her when she heard the song—their song—and saw the figures dancing. The box she hadn't been able to keep from playing again and again. It made up for nothing.

Finally she asked again, "Would you like a drink?" When he didn't reply, she suggested, "Water? Brandy? A cup of hemlock?"

Zac's dark-lashed green eyes crinkled to crescents. "You've missed me."

Grace's mouth twitched. She'd forgotten that Zac could dish it back—and it tasted good. She had missed him.

Lost for a response, she turned and moved toward the dining room. He followed more slowly, examining her home, eyeing furniture and pictures on the wall, the black-

and-white photo of her parents on the credenza. Her mother had been dead since Grace was a baby.

As she crouched beside an antique liquor cabinet and opened the doors, Zac admired the house, noting the French doors, the molding along the edges of the ceiling. Outside he'd seen the silhouettes of ornately carved balustrades rimming wide semicircular verandas, dormers with steep gables, and several chimneys stretching toward the sky. Now, as he surveyed the interior, the contrast between Grace's house and the flat on Avenue B made him ashamed. Yes, they had lived in New York, and the walk-up had been the best they could afford. But still...

He thought of Oakhurst, his family's home in Kent, which he and his brother, Pip, and his father had worked to convert to a hotel, to pay the upkeep.

Grace interrupted his reflections. "Well, if I can't talk you into Socrates' last drink, how about..." She faltered, staring at his left hand. His ring. He was wearing it. She had put hers away when she filed for divorce. A memory shot at her. *We have to go to Tiffany's, Grace. It's romantic.*

Grace peered into the liquor cabinet again, so that she wouldn't have to look at him. "Well, I have brandy."

"Thank you."

The words were laced with subtle humor, and Grace vowed to say nothing else caustic. In a battle of words, Zac could cut her to the ground if he chose, but she'd never seen his dry wit descend to sarcasm. He was too basically kind.

Grace removed the brandy bottle from the cabinet, shut the door and went into the darkened kitchen. Using only the light above the stove, she took two snifters from a cupboard and poured the brandy. She turned to offer him a glass.

Their fingers brushed as he took it, and Grace tried to avoid meeting his eyes. But then she saw there was no need; his were focused on her stove, the restaurant range she had brought with her to their apartment when she moved in with him. Zac had installed a special exhaust system to let the extreme heat escape... Uncomfortable with the recollection—not to mention the memory of their loading the stove into the U-Haul together just a few months later—she said, "Shall we go back in the other room?"

He didn't reply but followed her through the house to the brightly lit living room, where they sat at opposite ends of the velvet sleigh-back sofa.

Zac's eyes swept the room, taking in everything. The closed double doors opposite the foyer with a plaque overhead reading Princess Room; the paneled walnut bookcase; the baby grand piano; a print over the hearth— John Waterhouse's *Ophelia*. Lines of Shakespeare invited themselves into his mind: *Is't possible a young maid's wits Should be as mortal as an old man's life?* Bothered, he looked away from the picture.

The room was nice, the decor vastly different from that of their New York apartment. In fact, he didn't recognize a single piece. Had Grace put everything in storage—or sold it?

And where was the music box? Did she like it?

At last he turned to her and lifted his glass. "To potable beverages."

Grace returned the salute, telling herself he wasn't funny. He deserved to be poisoned.

They drank, and the liquor burned her mouth. It sloshed against her lips as she drew it away. She could feel his eyes on her, that steady gaze, his sable eyebrows drawn toward the bridge of his nose as he watched her.

Glancing out the translucent curtains at the river, he said, "You're isolated out here."

Was he implying that it wasn't safe? Sipping her drink, Grace remarked, "Don't start worrying now. You've been gone a year. I could be dead, and you wouldn't know."

Zac thought he would have to step outside. *I could be dead...*

He could read the questions in her eyes: What had he been doing for the past year? What had been more important than getting back to her?

He knew the answer and didn't want to explain. It wasn't just his pride, though he couldn't have faced Grace the way things were. There were other reasons. Time, for instance. Time to make sure it wouldn't happen again. And now he had money, and he was putting it away. Just in case...

Just in case it did.

He told Grace, "I'm glad you're not dead. I'd never have gotten over it."

Grace heard him soberly. Was he sincere? Once she'd discovered he'd lied to her, every action had become suspect. And Zac had never been easy to read. He didn't show his emotions like other people she knew. Granted, in bed...well, things had been intense. Good. But he'd stayed away a long time.

Grace put her glass on the table. "What do you want, Zac? The music box is lovely. Thank you for the thought." And the warning about *Kah-Puh-Rats*. The hint that he might appear at her door. "You said you want to discuss what's happened. Does that mean you have some explanation for why in fourteen months you've never tried to see me?"

Zac looked pale. Silently she begged him to speak, to say something, anything, that would make it all right. That he'd been in jail. That he'd been in an accident. That he'd been in a coma.

That he'd wanted to see her and couldn't.

But he said nothing, and at last she exclaimed, "You know, Zachary Key, I deserve a life—not to be used by you. Has it never occurred to you that I might want to marry and have children? That I might want a real marriage?"

A real marriage?

Zac's reaction was visceral. In a breath he was back in New York City, back in time. Running beside her before dawn, stopping for coffee, getting quarters for laundry—*he* had washed the clothes and shopped for groceries and changed light bulbs and fixed things they knew the landlord never would. He remembered long subway rides to meet Grace after work, to see her home, to keep her safe, just to *be* with her. They'd kissed on the platform while they waited for the train; and when they came home to their walk-up, they'd hardly thought to close the door or lock it before they began tearing at each other's clothes. Her hands parting his fly...

He set down his glass. "We *had* a real marriage, until you left me for your father's business."

"I left because our marriage was a lie."

He wanted to shake her. *"I loved you."*

"And that's why you've called and written so faithfully?"

He tensed. Silence fell, and they both heard the rustling leaves of the cottonwood trees outside and the tick of the grandfather clock in the foyer.

Grace waited. *Please,* she thought. *Say something that will make it all right. I'll forgive you if you just have a reason.*

When she realized he had no answer, her heart fell. Sitting back from him, she said, "Fourteen months, Zac. That's how long it's been since we spoke. When we talked on the phone after my father died, you said you might come out to see me. I would have loved that. I needed you."

Zac listened, afraid. What she was describing was something he couldn't recall, and a familiar question needled him. *What had happened to him after Grace left?* That period of his life, a month or more, was a blur of fragmented memories, all strange. Afterward, everyone treated him differently. People said he'd done things he couldn't recall doing, things he *wouldn't* do. But his few vivid recollections also involved things he wouldn't ordinarily do.

Grace said, "You told me we'd talk again, but you never called, and when I phoned you the machine was disconnected. You never answered my letters—"

She stopped speaking, as though recollecting something strange, and Zac thought, *What did I do?* If he was responsible for the behavior other people had ascribed to him, what might he have done to Grace? What might he have said during this phone conversation he couldn't remember?

"I even called your parents, and—" Stopping, she reddened.

"And what?"

"A servant answered. Your father wasn't there, and your mother wouldn't talk to me."

Zac drew a breath. He knew why his mother hadn't come to the phone, and he should explain. But how? Grace had probably never seen anyone too depressed to get out of bed.

But she was still talking. "I've faced some facts about our so-called marriage, Zachary. A man who loves his wife does not lose touch with her for a year. He does not virtually ignore the death of her father. He doesn't marry her for a green card, and..."

Leaning forward, Zac put his hands over his face. He had done those things.

Grace exclaimed, "Stop acting! I'm a real person. I really loved you! Stop doing this to me."

Zac sat up and grasped her shoulders, feeling her slender woman's bones through the thin shirt she wore with no bra. The silk clung to his fingers, and the feel of her made his throat swell with emotion, so that he could hardly speak. "It's not an act, Grace." He caught his breath. "I was a good husband."

Grace stared at him, her eyes connecting with his. Zac's hands were warm on her shoulders. She put hers on his chest and shoved.

He moved his hands.

Grace wrapped both arms around herself. "I want you to leave."

"I'm not going anywhere. I want to hear you say it. 'Zac, you were good to me. Zac, I know you loved me.' *Say it.*"

No, thought Grace. He was pretending. Zac always said the right things—like an actor who knew his lines. "A loving husband would understand when his wife's father is ill and needs her."

"You didn't leave me for your father."

"I left because you married me for a green card."

Zac's hand slid over hers and closed around her fingers. As she shuddered under the touch she'd cried for, as both his hand and hers suddenly clung more tightly, he said, "Grace, I was twenty-six. I'd known you two months, and we'd been sleeping together for two weeks. You want me to say I would have married you even if I hadn't needed a green card, but it's not true. I loved you. But no, I wouldn't have married you so quickly in other circumstances." Then, as though realizing what he'd just admitted, he dropped her hand and put his own over his face again.

Grace felt ill. "Would you ever have married me?"

Zac jerked his head up. "I did marry you. I loved you. I promised to spend my life with you, and you promised to spend yours with me."

"You didn't answer my question."

"*I don't know*. It doesn't matter, Grace. We were in love."

"You deceived me!"

"That wasn't my intention."

"Oh, please," she said with disgust.

They fell quiet.

After a long time he broke out, "I loved you, Grace. I lived with you, I worked with you, and I played with you. We made love together." There was vulnerability in his eyes. "You're my wife and I want you back."

Grace's heart raced wildly. Panic filled her. He seemed sincere—but she was sure he was lying. "Get out of my house."

"Will you have dinner with me tomorrow night?"

Grace gave him a look of disbelief. "No."

He felt a thrumming in his chest. He had one chance. It had to work. Carefully he reached into his pocket, pulled out a piece of paper and pressed it into her hand. "Please."

Grace looked down. She recognized the narrow strip of paper at once.

Her eyes watered.

She resisted reaching for her brandy glass and gulping the rest of it; instead, she unfolded the coupon and read what she'd promised:

1 Anything of Zachary's Choice.

She stared at it for a long time, then lifted her gaze. "Do you have any more of these?"

Zac glanced at the coupon. "I have two more with me. Not just like that," he added, wondering why she'd asked.

She sat up very straight. "I have three, as well. Let's just...trade."

Incredulous, Zac snatched the coupon from her hand. "I think not!"

Grace sat back. "It's sensible, Zachary. I mean, we're getting divorced. I'm not going to owe you all kinds of...coupon things."

Was it his imagination, or had her color heightened? Zac said, "Well, whatever coupons I gave you are still valid, and—" he considered the register receipt "—I don't see any expiration on this, either." He withdrew two more pieces of paper from his shirt pocket, examined them and held them up for her inspection. "Nor on these."

Seeing what one of the coupons was for, Grace opened her mouth, then shut it. Surely he couldn't imagine she would— Blotting out memories of when she *had*—lovingly, eagerly—Grace disciplined her eyes not to drop to his lap. She said, "I'll buy them back from you."

"Buy them?" Zac lifted his eyebrows, then bent his head for a moment to inspect the coupons. "Hmm..." His eyes narrowed, and he lifted his chin, as though calculating. "Let me see. The value of a five-course dinner from a woman who attended the Culinary Institute and worked under the great French chef Gilles Guignant..." He tossed the coupon in her lap. "I'll let it go for two hundred dollars."

"Two hundred—"

"Ah, this, though—" he held up another "—very dear. The street value of this particular service...well, it's probably only about fifty dollars, but it's priceless to me."

"You swine." Grace grabbed the receipt from his hand, crumpled it in a ball and threw it into the cold fireplace. "That's what I think of you and your—"

"Well, we both think a great deal of you." As Grace glared at him, cheeks scarlet, he eyed the wad of paper in the hearth. "Just for the record, I don't consider that coupon void, but in any case, I have another. And it

says—'' he studied the slip in his hand, then her body
"—anything.''

Grace leaned against the back of the couch, crossing her
arms under her breasts. "You're living in a dreamworld
if you think I'd even kiss you.''

"That's academic, since I don't plan to try at the moment. Don't look so disappointed, Grace. Actually I'll
forgive you the sexual favors you owe me—and by the
way, I have a stack of those coupons in Los Angeles—''

"I do not owe you—''

"—if you'll just honor this one.'' He held up the Anything coupon.

"Oh, anything you want!'' said Grace. "I suppose
you're going to ask me to rip up those divorce papers and
let you go on your way.''

He shook his head, moving nearer. Suddenly his scent
was in her nostrils, and Grace remembered how strong
desire could be. She didn't breathe.

"I want you to let me court you.''

CHAPTER THREE

I WANT YOU to let me court you.

He was too close. Grace stood up. "You're good, but you're not that good."

Zac leaned back on the couch with a groan. "I'm not trying to be *good*. I'm just trying to..." He looked profoundly frustrated. "I'm trying to save our marriage."

"You're trying to save your green card. Believe me, I've had time to think this through. You've got a movie role, and you're afraid of the INS."

Zac was on his feet in a second, diminishing the space between them until she was crowded between an end table and the baby grand.

Grace didn't breathe. Their bodies were so close....

He said, "You're calling me something worse than a whore. I don't need to be married to keep my green card, Grace."

That stopped her. Her thoughts were wayward. Making love, Zac holding her so tight she could feel his heartbeat and his breath. This man holding her. She said, "What do you mean?"

"Well...my employment. I have a job that pays very well, and I could make a strong case to the INS that it's a job no one else—American or otherwise—could do."

Realizing he must mean being "close to his clothes"—in other words, barely wearing them—Grace burst out laughing.

"It's true."

Humor gone, Grace shook her head. His argument was nice, but it wasn't the whole picture. "Maybe. Maybe not. Still, I doubt you want to deal with the INS again, and I don't think you want them looking at our marriage.

"Remember, Zac, I was there. I brought you hot tea in Federal Plaza at three in the morning while you waited in lines just to get the forms you needed. I was the woman who sat in the next room and told the men with the crew-cuts that you prefer cappuccinos to lattes and that you shave the right side of your face before the left. And I know those same men would have loved an excuse to snap a pair of handcuffs on you and put you on the next paddy wagon to wherever they take people like you."

Stepping around him, Grace escaped to the center of the room. "You know, I have this picture in my mind of what happened after I left. First you spent a few days worrying if you were going to be deported and lose the greatest role of all time in *Leaving Hong Kong*. Then you probably decided the INS might go years without noticing we no longer lived together. So you went on with your life." She shrugged. "Just like that."

From his place beside the piano, Zac stared at her, his features forming those sober, almost too-perfect lines. Grace could detect little emotion in his expression, but his gaze was unnervingly still.

"Grace, if you never hear anything else I say, hear this. When you left me, I was devastated."

Grace watched him distantly, wondering why she was shaking so hard, listening so hard....

"I lost my job. I lost the role you just mentioned so glibly. I lost my agent. I lost our apartment." He stepped toward her and looked down into her eyes, his own showing a familiar detachment. Grace had once suspected it hid his deepest feelings. Before she'd found out he'd lied.

"I loved you as much as a man can love a woman. I loved you. I needed you." His eyes searched her face, and she watched the pulse in his throat, the constriction of muscles, the apparent stifling of emotion. He whispered, "And I begged you not to leave."

Then he left, and the sound of the front door closing behind him was final and empty and lonely.

LYING AWAKE, Grace watched the shadows from a cottonwood tree outside her window play over the ceiling. She wished she could sleep. But she kept thinking of Zac and five words he had spoken, words that had carried the desperation of truth ignored.

I was a good husband.

No, you weren't, Grace thought. You were a great husband.

With a moan, she rolled onto her stomach and buried her face in the pillow, remembering the things he'd said, the expressions she'd seen on his face. Remembering the past. Real feelings. Separation had blurred her perception. Seeing Zac, touching him, brought it back into focus. What they'd had was complicated. Many layers deep.

When you left me, I was devastated.

Devastated.

Zac said he'd lost his job at Jean-Michel's. He had lost the part in *Leaving Hong Kong.* He had lost his agent and lost their apartment.

Grace couldn't see it, couldn't believe it. Zac never failed.

But obviously he hadn't made this up.

She should have been there for him after he'd lost that role. But Grace recalled the larger crisis *she* had faced alone—her father's death. The memory of Zac's response killed any sympathy she felt.

Still ... how had he lost the part? How had he lost his job? He never used drugs, and he drank little. He'd barely touched his brandy tonight.

I was devastated.

What did he mean?

Grace lay in bed, frightened, remembering the times she'd called him in New York and listened to the phone ring and ring. Once she had called in the middle of the night, and no one had answered....

Let me court you....

I loved you.

If that was true, why had he waited so long?

And how could she trust him now?

ZAC LAY BACK on the bed, trying to forget what had happened at Grace's. Why had he told her those things? She wasn't going to be impressed that he couldn't hold a job.

Things were better now, thanks to Ben Rogan—and to a casting agent who'd seen Zac at a photo shoot and said, *If that man can talk, he's got the part.*

It was a good part—Seneca Howland, one of the nine men who had joined Major John Wesley Powell in his 1869 exploration of the Colorado River. Zac had never wanted to be in films; he loved the stage. But the role of Howland in *Kah-Puh-Rats* was a godsend, and the film's being shot in Moab had seemed like fate. A chance to reconcile with Grace.

Her divorce suit had changed everything. He'd hoped the film would bring them together; Grace saw it as one more reason he couldn't afford trouble with the INS.

After *Leaving Hong Kong,* Zac had other troubles. His agent had said, *No one will touch you, Zac. Look, maybe you need to get some help. I'm hearing some pretty wild stories.*

Stories more bizarre than the one Grace had told him tonight—that they'd talked on the phone after her father's death. He'd known her father was dead. But how had he found out?

Nothing. No recollection. Of that. In a flash that came and went like a falling star, he saw the shadows of an alley and the overly bright red eyes of wrinkled, sun-baked men whose faces had looked so... wrong.

He swallowed.

The chaos of that period of his life was undeniable.

His agent. His career. His wife. In the space of a month they were gone. It had taken a whole year to even begin to undo the damage. Now, after a year, he once again had the first. And a chance at the second.

But what he wanted most was the third.

He wanted Grace.

THE NEXT MORNING, Grace awoke with feelings that reminded her of when she'd first fallen in love with Zac. As she dressed for work at the river outfit, her mind was full—with him. When will I see him again? Where is he now? What is he thinking? Is he serious about "courting" me?

They would be seeing each other on the movie set. So far, Grace had resisted trying to get a cast list to see what role he played. But she couldn't help imagining their being together on the river during filming. What would happen?

While she dressed, she played the music box, watching the figures dancing in front of the stage set; and as she drove to the Rapid Riggers office, she found herself humming "Love Is Here to Stay." *Our love,* she thought. Zac.

When Grace arrived at work, her sister was in the reception area opening a box of new brochures. Day was turned out in a powder blue linen shift and angora sweater. She was the only outfitter in Moab who wore stockings and heels to work, and she hadn't been on a river trip in more than a decade, but first-year boatmen soon learned that Day knew an oar from a paddle. She *was* a good partner.

After she and Grace checked the new brochure for pricing errors, Day lit a cigarette and began putting the pamphlets in a rack on the counter.

Grace examined her nails, found a trace of automotive grease. She and Zac had held hands.... Checking the adjacent doors to make sure she and Day were alone, Grace announced, "Zac's in town. He came to see me last night."

Turning, Day put down her cigarette. "That was fast." Her expression reminded Grace of the past fourteen months. It was a loyal sisterly look that meant, *You spit in his face, didn't you?* But even Day had liked the gesture of the music box.

Grace told her, "He said he wants to get back together." It didn't sound too good when she said it out loud. It sounded like Zac was scurrying to hang on to his green card. "I don't know. It's just interesting." Interesting? She had fantasized all night.

Looking like someone who hated to burst a bubble, Day asked, "Did he happen to say why he never called or anything? Was he abducted by aliens? Living with Elvis?"

Grace laughed hollowly and shook her head. That was what Zac hadn't said. What she needed to know. Concealing her hurt, she shrugged. "He just wanted to have dinner. And I nixed it. It probably won't amount to anything." Coupons. Courting. She glanced toward the kitchen. "Coffee time."

As she stepped around the reception counter and started to push through the swinging bar-style doors to the kitchen, Day's voice stopped her. "Grace?"

She looked back.

"I shouldn't have joked. It's okay to still care about him. You were married. It's a big deal."

Grace met her gaze. The words came without thought, but she knew they were true. "We *are* married. That's a bigger deal."

ZAC SHOWED UP later that morning when Grace was on the phone. Nort Stills, a coproducer for the Powell movie, had called to say the film crew had arrived in town; the call had come at a bad time, while Grace was preparing lunch for a women's club. The ladies would dine in the picnic area at Hittle Bottom, then set off on a half-day raft trip down a stretch of the Colorado known as the Daily. *If* the meal was ready.

While Day typed reservation confirmations into the company computer and Nick lurked in the doorway waiting for instructions on preparing the custard for asparagus tarts, Stills asked Grace the dozen or so questions no river guide can accurately answer. How deep is the river? How cold is the water? How big are the rapids?

"What kind of nightlife do you have out there?"

That was a new one. Grace echoed, "Nightlife?"

"Yeah. On the river. I mean, we've checked out the bars in town. This place is pretty up-and-coming, kind of like Taos or Telluride. What's there to do on the river? Where are the best spots? Any good bands?"

Struggling to contain herself, Grace resisted answering that the Doll's House was a beautiful section of sandstone monoliths and that sometimes, after a day on the river, the boatmen started mud fights for entertainment. Clearly Stills did not realize the vastness of Utah wilderness, and that was unsettling. How many hours had she spent on the phone with the studio coordinating the logistics of this venture?

In a level tone she said, "Mr. Stills, I think you have misperceptions about the terrain. Let me clarify some things so you won't be shocked by, well, the rather rustic conditions on the river."

As she spoke she heard tires on gravel outside, and Day rolled her chair backward from her desk so that she could see out the window.

"What a pile of junk!" Day said. "The car, not the man." She looked at Grace. "Guess who."

Zac? Grace peered out the dusty pane but saw only the tail of an old sports car painted with primer. The front of the vehicle was hidden by a banner hanging along the porch railing.

Quaking inside, she tried to focus on her phone conversation. The studio knew they were going into wilderness. Hal Markley, the producer, had told her he'd applied for a filming permit from the park service.

Grace told Nort Stills, "For example, Cataract Canyon, where you plan to film part of your movie, is 120 miles from here. It's a three-to seven-day trip by river—"

Nick walked over to look out the window, blocking the glass. As footsteps sounded on the porch, he told Day, "That's not junk. It's an Austin-Healey."

Into the receiver, Grace said, "Accessibility by land is two hundred miles and strictly by four-wheel drive or helicopter. There are no hotels or gift shops—"

The bell sounded as someone entered the front office, and Nick and Day tripped over each other and several river bags as they tangled their way out the door.

"—no bars and no bathrooms," continued Grace, unrelieved by their departure. Obviously they wanted to gawk at Zac. "We sleep in tents and cook in Dutch ovens we bring with us. Our river permits require that we operate under strict conditions, carting out all waste—"

"Oh, my God!" Stills exclaimed.

Grace put her hand over her face. When she could speak, she said, "Mr. Stills, I'm sorry if anything I've said has fostered a false impression. Given the film's topic, I just assumed that everyone had some idea what it's like on the Colorado and the Green.''

"No, no, that's all right," said Stills. "Just let me recover from the shock. I mean, my idea of camping out is, like, the Holiday Inn. Y'know? But I'm sure Hal must know... Yes, I'm sitting in the office, and apparently everyone here knew we were going into no-man's-land. Everyone but me.''

Grace would've smiled but she wanted to get off the phone and see Zac. Stills said, "Miss Sutter?''

"Grace, please." *Mrs. Key,* she thought. Stills must know Zachary....

"Grace, then, and it's Nort on this end. Grace, we've set up offices down here on, ah, what is this—Mill Creek Drive. Used to be a uranium company or something. The Uratomic Building, Hal says. Is there any chance you could come down here and talk to the director about what to expect in the white water?''

Grace agreed to come to the Uratomic Building in an hour. Hanging up, she listened for sounds from the front office.

Day was saying, "Um...I think she just got off the phone. Grace?'' She stuck her head in the door. "Zac's here.''

He appeared behind her sister. The room felt ten degrees warmer.

Standing, Grace glanced from Day to Zac. "Did you two meet? In person, I mean.''

"Your sister introduced herself,'' said Zac. It had been awkward. All he could think about was how Grace looked in that wedding gift Day had sent. He could like any woman who sent his bride a red leather teddy with naughty cups, but he didn't think Day liked him now. He'd hurt Grace.

Day said, "Grace, I'm driving Dirty Bob downtown to pick up his new boatman's license.'' Seeing Zac's puzzled look, Day explained, "All our guides have special names. Dirty Bob. Fast Susan. Cute Nick." She paused. "Amazing Grace."

The jab was hard to miss. Zac said, "I've always thought so myself."

The moment Day left, he stepped into the office with Grace and shut the door. They were alone.

Grace forgot her sister's skepticism—and her own. Zac stood before her in blue jeans and her favorite of his shirts, red polyester with grizzly bears on it. Grace felt as if she was scouting the Big Drop in Cataract Canyon. Nervous enough to babble.

While he surveyed the office, she said, "You never knew I liked squalid surroundings, but I do. We invite the boatmen to come in here after trips and shake out their dirty socks. The sand rises off them in clouds, and we get this ambience of filth. The tourists really go for it. It's cowboy stuff."

Zac laughed, his eyes sweeping over her. Her worn-out Rapid Riggers T-shirt gave him ideas about her breasts. *Want you,* he thought. *I miss you.*

He looked elsewhere. At the computer, the fax machine, the life vests piled in a corner beside the filing cabinets, the old brown couch with the springs popping through, the waterproof "dry" bags on the floor and an oar hanging on the wall. The last made him think of another river, the Thames, and another kind of rowing. He'd never seen white water. He'd never seen a desert like this.

Grace said, "I guess you'll be spending some time on the river with the movie."

"Yes." Zac looked at her. "Will you?" Or would she stay behind in the office to avoid him?

"Oh, yes. I'll be rowing." The movie required too many boatmen for her to skip out.

Zac studied her. *One more time.* "Grace, please say you'll have dinner with me tonight."

It felt like a long time since she'd said no, although it was only last night. A long night. She'd met too many of those. "Okay."

One moment Zac was looking hard at her eyes, and she was looking at his. The next they were in each other's arms, holding tight. His head pressed against her hair as he drew her closer. The embrace felt much deeper and more serious than what Grace had held in her mind for a year, than the travesty she joked about with Day so she wouldn't cry about it, instead. Wouldn't cry the way she had those first few weeks she'd spent alone. This felt good.

Grace was afraid to feel.

Zac tilted back her head, made her look at him.

His eyes probed hers. Watching his gaze move just slightly, Grace knew he was exploring her face. As she was his. His hair grazed her cheek, and she felt his fingers near her temples and on her jaw, and his thumb touching a side of her mouth.

She whispered, "Don't kiss me."

"All right." His cheek brushed her hair, her skin. Grace's eyes burned with memory and longing.

A rustling near Zac's foot startled him. It was a piece of paper sliding under the door.

Grace moved out of his arms to pick it up, and Zac read the words from over her shoulder: *How do I make the custard?*

The tarts. Telling herself the interruption was timely, Grace grasped the doorknob. "Nick and I have to make tarts. And then I have an appointment at the other end of town."

Nick? *Cute* Nick undoubtedly. Day had introduced them, and Nick Colter had not taken his hand—only looked at him coldly.

Zac stared down at Grace. "You're making tarts with another man?"

Was he joking? "It's not quite adultery."

"It's practically foreplay. You're very exciting in the kitchen. You were cooking the first time I saw you. At Jean-Michel's," he added, as though she might have forgotten.

She hadn't. She never would. Grace had turned at the stove, and across the kitchen, dressed in black and white, was the most beautiful man she'd ever seen. She'd known he was the new waiter everyone said was so gorgeous, but she hadn't counted on that immediate meeting of eyes or on the jolt that had gone through her, straight to her toes. She hadn't counted on his looking at her so long. Seconds. While nothing else happened. Just eyes.

She had thought, *I want that man.*

That man was now saying, in a low, private voice, "You're very sexy when you cook. It makes me hard to think about it."

Grace bit her lip, trying to figure how her hip had come to be situated against his. Yes, he was hard, and he was easing her back against the door, easing himself against her. It felt familiar and warm and intimate. So did his breath as he asked, "Have you changed your mind about being kissed?"

Grace tried not to look at the dark places where his beard grew, nor at his lips. She said, "Um . . . yes, as a matter of fact."

Zac smiled.

His eyes were on her face, and then his hands were, too. His mouth touched hers. Grace's lips trembled, and he tried to soothe her as he tipped her head to the angle he wanted. But he was shaking, too.

Grace tasted him and felt his beard stubble, and her breasts remembered warm, tight embraces inside his wool coat in the winter. She could feel his heart beating as fast

as hers. She moved her lips against his, with his, and then
she opened her mouth and his tongue came in, stroking
hers. Grace pressed against his erection because she
couldn't help it, and in her mind she saw a picture too
much like that jeans ad. But it was her hands unbuttoning, and she could hear his low moan, hear him saying,
"Gracie..."

He was hers.

Because he'd needed a green card.

He'd never been hers.

Grace dragged her mouth away, but his followed. He
nuzzled her cheek, traced her jaw with his lips, and she
dodged kisses she wanted and whispered, "We have to
stop. Stop, okay?"

He did, about as fast as a freight train stops.

Then he was hugging her tight, one of those bear hugs,
a never-let-go hug. His voice came through her hair. "Let
me help you in the kitchen, all right?"

Grace remembered other kitchens. Jean-Michel's. Their
own. She said, "Sure."

SHE SENT NICK outside to finish rigging for the afternoon's trip and to supervise two first-year boatmen
patching rafts. While Zac finished the asparagus tarts, she
put the chilled parsley-and-tarragon soup and the spring
artichokes into containers for transport to the river and
began assembling everything else to go in the coolers.

As Zac poured the custard over the tarts, he asked her,
"Do all the river outfits in town offer meals like this?"

"No." She put silverware and napkins in a paper bag
on one side of the cooler. "But seeing that I went to
cooking school..." Drawing Zac's attention to her restaurant range and the salamander or overhead broiler
above it, she said, "I had a friend ship them to me last
summer. Serving gourmet meals on the river is challeng-
ing. There are some interesting limitations."

Zac recalled her frustration cooking in their old apartment before he'd installed the exhaust system for her stove. Grace was a chef; he couldn't imagine that the limitations she'd mentioned were any pleasure to her. But she talked as though they were. Was Grace really committed to this place? Zac hoped not. He couldn't work as an actor in Moab, Utah. *Kah-Puh-Rats* was an exception.

He asked, "Business is good?"

Grace shrugged. "Moab has changed a lot in the last few years. More people are visiting and moving here, which is good for the economy. But a lot of our competitors have rich, out-of-town backers, which gives them an edge. When our equipment breaks down, we have to rely on ourselves—and any help we can get from the bank." She admitted, "Day wants to sell the house I'm living in—my father's house—and put the money into this place, but I don't want to. It might not have looked like much to you, but it's actually sort of historic. It used to be an inn."

Zac lifted his eyebrows, interested.

"My great-grandfather had a riverboat business, taking people from Moab to Green River and back. Some of them stayed at the inn. The steamboats back then were too big and unstable for these rivers, so that business went under. But my grandparents kept the inn going. So did my folks for a while. They even served meals. There's a big dining hall off the living room." Grace removed four loaves of bread from the racks where they were cooling and wrapped them in foil to take to the river. "But I guess the inn was too far off the beaten track. Finally my dad decided white water was the way to go."

Despite himself, Zac was fascinated. He knew what it was to belong to a place, to know that one's ancestors had lived and breathed and walked and loved within its walls. To know that someone before you had worked to keep it because they felt it was worth having—and worth your having.... Zac had been born five years too late to have Oakhurst. When his father died, it would be Pip's.

He asked, "You haven't thought of selling this place?"

"No way. That would be like...like selling my father." Hoping to make Zac understand, Grace crossed the kitchen and removed a framed photo from a nail on the wall beside the back door.

Zac came to her side and looked down at the faded eight-by-ten. It showed a man in a life jacket and Rapid Riggers hat rowing a six-foot inflatable boat through a torrent of white water. The waves were fifteen feet or more.

"That's my dad in Lava Falls, in the Grand Canyon. He was fearless. He was a world-class boater, and he'd run anything. He made three first descents."

Zac heard the pride in her voice. Curious, he pointed to the lower right corner of the photo. There, the white water became brown and scooped out a smooth, deep depression in the river flow. "What's happening here?"

"A hole. There's a huge lava block right there." Grace pointed to a spot just outside the photo. "The water pouring off it collides with the flow from river left. You can see the big wave starting to rise and break back on itself. Anything that big isn't really a keeper—not for people, anyhow. It's the kind of thing that sucks you under and spits you out fifty feet downstream."

No big deal. Zac stared at the massive hole. "A keeper?"

Grace explained. "Some holes will trap a person or a boat for a long time. You get churned around a lot—or Maytagged, as the boatmen call it."

Like a washing machine. Zac would have smiled at the expression if not for a disturbing vision of Grace in a keeper. Eyeing the Grand Canyon photo, he asked, "Have you run that rapid?"

"Yes, in a dory—more than twice the size of that boat."

This was a side of her Zac didn't know—the river runner. He wanted to know that side; without it he'd never know her. He should have suggested a trip to Utah a long time ago, after he and Grace had gotten married. But he'd been too busy with his career. And when Grace's father had died...

I should have come out for the funeral, Zac thought. Disturbed, he again tried to recall the phone conversation Grace had mentioned the night before. After she'd left him and come to Utah and learned of her father's death in surgery, she had called to tell him. And he had talked to her. *Why couldn't he remember?*

But he knew why—basically. He just didn't want to think about it.

As Grace stepped away and hung the photo back on the wall, Zac returned to the oven. He checked the temperature and glanced at the tarts. "Shall I put these in?"

"Sure. They look great." She went back to the counter and stared through the grimy window over the kitchen sink at the river beyond. Somehow Zac's presence stirred old dreams she had thought she'd put to rest...of being a chef again.

Thinking of *his* dreams, she turned and asked Zac, "What about you? What's your role in this movie?"

Zac slid the tarts into the oven and closed the door. "Cast member four. His name is Seneca Howland."

That was good billing. Grace thought for a minute. "Wasn't it the Howland brothers and William Dunn who left the expedition early and climbed out of the Grand Canyon?"

"Yes. I'm to be killed by Indians."

Grace smiled. "Where did they get the title?"

"It's what the Utes called Powell. It means 'rat miss-ing an arm.' He lost an arm in the Civil War."

Grace remembered. As a Colorado River outfitter and guide, she knew Powell's history well. "Who's playing him?"

"Martin Place."

Grace was surprised. The fortyish actor had won two Academy Awards. *Kah-Puh-Rats* was a big-budget film.

The phone rang in the next room, and a moment later Day appeared in the doorway. "Grace? It's Bill."

Her lawyer. Grace had tried to reach him that morn-ing, hoping to tell him Zac was in town and to get some advice. What would her lawyer say when he learned she'd agreed to have dinner with Zac.

Excusing herself to take the call, Grace tried to think it through again. Had the marriage really mattered to him? He'd said the green card had been the deciding factor in his marrying her. But he'd also said that he'd loved her. So why did he want her back? His green card? Love for her? Or both?

Grace thought the last might be hardest to accept.

WHILE SHE TOOK her phone call, Zac sat on the porch steps studying the rocks across the road, trying to iden-tify the strata. Campers and four-wheel drives sped past on the highway, some headed north out of town, others across the bridge to Moab. The traffic was steady, but even the roar of the vehicles as they passed seemed quiet compared to New York or L.A. Overhead, the interna-tional flags waving from the eaves made a gentle flapping sound, the sort of sound one never noticed in the city be-cause of the constant noise. Here Zac heard the distant drone of a lawn mower and the nearby buzz of a fly till it paused on the leg of his jeans. Quiet.

A semitrailer on the highway rumbled past, wheezing as it slowed to go into town, but Zac didn't amend his perception. Although there were many tourists here, Moab's small-town feeling reminded him of Belden, the village near Oakhurst. The thought made him feel rootless. And restless. Where was Grace, anyway? Still on the phone?

The screen door slammed behind him, and Zac glanced up. As Grace crossed the porch and sat down beside him, he said, "Who's Bill?"

"My attorney."

Divorce attorney. Another eighteen-wheeler roared past. Zac asked, "What's this costing you?"

"Between the detective and my attorney, almost fifteen thousand dollars. So far."

A detective? thought Zac. He hadn't intended to hide from her. He'd just wanted to get his life back together and figure out what had happened to him during that month after she'd left. The lost month. It had never occurred to him that she was looking for him—and that it was costing her money. A lot of money.

He said, "I'll pay it."

Grace stared at his profile, partly hidden by his long hair. "I'm not ready to drop the suit, Zac."

"More's the pity." He looked at her. "But it's my fault this has gone so far. I'll take care of it."

Grace was stunned. He was being...chivalrous. Actually, when she thought about, he had always been chivalrous. Except about his green card—and her dying father. "I'll have to ask my attorney."

"Fine." He paused. "Tell me where to book a table for tonight. Is there a good restaurant?"

Grace thought of the advice she'd received from her lawyer on the phone. *Sure. Find out what he has to say. But don't let him pull the wool over your eyes.* The warning didn't seem to cover the melting feeling deep inside her. She said, "The Moenkopi Café has a good chef."

"Wonderful. Shall I pick you up at seven?"

She should keep some distance. Letting him bring her home was risky. If he kissed her like he had in the office, she'd be touching him in inappropriate places and suggesting unbright schemes. *Let's go to bed....*

"I'll meet you there." Standing, she said, "I need to go. I have an appointment at the production office." And she needed to see that everything was set for the half-day excursion. Mentally she was already making a list of things to tell Nick. *Don't forget to take the tarts from the oven. Send someone to nab picnic tables at the beach....*

Zac leaned back on his hands and looked up at her. "Want a ride?"

Distance, Grace thought. She said, "Sure. Thanks."

A few minutes later they left in the Austin-Healey with its sheepskin seat covers and gray-primer paint job. As Zac headed the car across the bridge and south into town, Grace asked, "Where are you staying?"

"The Anasazi Palace." He raised his voice over the wind and the rumble of the engine. "I drove out to your house this morning, but you'd gone to work. I was going to talk you into running with me."

Running.

Memory attacked, and Grace remembered running with him in New York. Showers afterward. *Sex.* She said, "Oh."

"Do you run anymore?" he shouted.

"Sometimes." Alone. Alone on the River Inn Road, on the northwest side of the river. The Colorado, instead of the East River.

Zac decelerated as they drove into town. Businesses crowded both sides of the road. River outfits, realtors, hotels, trading posts, T-shirt shops, restaurants, pubs. All were in gear for the tourist season. Pedestrians with cameras strolled the sidewalks, while cyclists in spandex shorts sped up and down the roadsides, the fat tires of their bikes caked with red desert mud.

Slowing to stop at a light, Zac said, "I like your house."

Grace stared at him. She'd seen pictures of Oakhurst, Zac's family home, with its leaded-glass windows and Elizabethan chimneys and manicured gardens. But he liked the River Inn? Grace loved the place, but the condition of the property made her blush. Thinking of the weeds choking the yard, the porches that needed paint and new screens, the peeling plaster and water-damaged floors upstairs, she said, "It's a wreck right now. Dad never had much time for it. He was busy with Rapid Riggers."

The light changed, and Zac eased the car forward. "I have some time. Tell me what to do." He winked at her. "You're good at that."

Grace ignored the allusion to past domesticity. A man was offering to work on her house without bidding on the job first. Zac had always done that kind of thing around their apartment, but... "Are you sure you want to?"

"Yes." *I'm your husband,* he wanted to say. *That's something I do for you. I fix things. And you make wonderful meals, and we make love together....*

His willingness to help touched her. He'd even offered to pay her legal bills. Thousands of dollars.... *I was a good husband.* Had she been a good wife? Was what Zac had done bad enough to justify leaving him?

And had Zac really been so upset by her leaving that he'd lost his job and a role and—well, everything? If things were that bad... It wasn't like her husband, the son of an earl, to show up on her doorstep when he was down on his luck. He wouldn't want her to see him unemployed, wouldn't want to risk being a burden to her in any way. He would get himself together first.

Grace was still thinking of that minutes later when they reached the Uratomic Building. The parking lot was busy, and through the opened door of a warehouse, Grace saw people constructing sets. There were vehicles everywhere, and a row of expensive automobiles with California plates stood near the front door.

Zac parked the Austin-Healey between a Porsche and a Jeep Grand Cherokee, got out and came around to open her door.

Surprised, Grace said, "You're coming in?"

"I have business here."

The sunlight caught his wedding ring. His hand. The sight seemed sexual to Grace, a reminder of all they'd shared. The ring had always been a nuisance for him. He'd had to remove it for performances. But he was wearing it now, though they were separated.

Which didn't mean she had to wear hers. Not when she wasn't sure what it signified. She asked, "Does anyone ever ask who you're married to?"

"I don't talk about it. If you're worried about our working on the film together, don't be. In this business, everyone's related to everyone else."

As Zac opened the glass front door of the Uratomic Building and they went in, Grace heard voices from rooms up ahead. Near the door, the craft service had set up a refreshment stand, with an espresso machine and other drinks and snacks. Zac asked, "Would you like something?"

Grace shook her head and looked down the corridor at the clock.

Pausing at the stand to get some tea, Zac told her, "Go ahead, if you need to make your appointment. I'll find you."

Grace nodded and wandered down the hall, seeking Nort Stills.

Like the parking lot, the production office was busy. A woman stepped out of a door on the right and hurried past Grace with a smile, and a trio of technicians carrying lights and cables emerged from a double door at the end of the hall. They interrupted their talking to say, "Hi," as they passed Grace. Looking back toward the front door, Grace saw Zac had disappeared, probably into one of the rooms she'd already passed.

As she continued down the hall, voices reached her ears. The conversation was coming through an opened door on the left, and Grace recognized one of the speakers as Nort Stills. "I'm telling you, Hal, people are talking about him. Let's take advantage of it."

A woman's voice cut in. "Enhance his role?"

"Why not?"

A third voice—probably Hal Markley's—sounded dubious. "He's new."

Grace lingered in the hallway wondering how to interrupt. There was a sound of riffling pages, and a phone rang in another part of the building.

"Here, scene twenty-five," said the woman in the room. "He's saying goodbye to his wife. Let's make it hot. Does he do nudity?"

"I guess you've never seen those Ben Rogan ads," answered Stills. "Does Zachary Key do nudity? I should say so."

They all laughed.

Grace felt faint.

CHAPTER FOUR

WHEN HALL MARKLEY first offered her a seat, it had been all Grace could do not to say, *Wow, this is a really great chair.* The studio's temporary digs and hastily purchased office furniture would have been a face lift for Rapid Riggers, and the executives matched their surroundings.

Though dressed casually in slacks and polo shirts, Nort Stills and Hal Markley had the sleek, well-groomed look Grace associated with wealthy people from the city; co-producer Carrie Dorchester wore a tailored suit, stockings and heels. Only the director, Meshach Stoker, seemed different. He wore rumpled khaki trousers, a pile cardigan that looked as though it had actually seen some camping trips, wire-rimmed glasses and a full beard. Nonetheless, he seemed less relaxed than his clothes—running on creative energy, obsessed with making the film.

Grace and Meshach had been poring over a river guidebook together for twenty minutes, reviewing campsites and possible shooting locations, when Hal Markley removed his black horn-rimmed glasses and polished them as he said to Grace, "Maybe you have an answer to this. We've found a restaurant to cater for us through most of production, but no one will do the job down in Cataract Canyon."

Grace wasn't surprised. Leaning forward in the awesome chair, she explained, "It has to do with cooking equipment. Everything we eat hot on the river is prepared in a Dutch oven or over an open fire. It's tricky to turn out interesting meals."

In the past weeks she'd learned enough about moviemaking to be relieved when Hal Markley had said he'd hire a caterer to feed his crew of a hundred and fifty. Grace had cooked for big church groups on Rapid Riggers river trips in the past; but whoever provided meals for the movie crew would have to meet the demands of the filming schedule—which could change without notice. So why was she opening her big mouth? "If you'd like, we could do the meals in Cataract Canyon."

Carrie Dorchester, who half-leaned, half-sat against a stout table near the windows, exchanged a skeptical look with the others. The coproducer was the woman Grace had overheard asking if Zac did *nudity*.

Forget about it, Grace told herself for the twentieth time. *You can find out later what she meant.*

Hal Markley was shaking his head. "The cast and crew expect a lot of variety from the caterer. Anyhow, you'll be busy on the river."

Grace knew what he feared—a week of cowboy coffee and chili seasoned with river silt. "Mr. Markley, I am a graduate of the Culinary Institute, and we routinely serve gourmet fare on our river trips. If you're interested, I'd be happy to work up a menu for you."

Carrie's lined lips curved into a smile of surprise. "You're a chef?"

"I was sous-chef at a four-star restaurant in New York." For a moment Grace thought of Zac—and the simplicity of those days.

Nort Stills, a wiry man whose hair stood up around his head like the white seed tuft on a dandelion, shrugged at Hal. *Why not?*

The producer looked dubious. Replacing his glasses on his nose, he asked Grace, "But can you feed eighty people?"

That was the size of the "skeleton" crew they would be taking down Cat—half the regular crew. Grace said, "I've done it before."

Hearing a sound behind her, she glanced up to see Zac in the doorway.

Carrie Dorchester saw him, too, and pointed a finger in his direction. "We need to talk."

Nudity, Grace thought. What did they have in mind?

In the doorway Zac answered, "Fine." With a quick glance at Grace, he told the others, "By the way, this is my wife."

The sudden silence in the office was made more pronounced by the sound of hammering from the warehouse across the lot. The three producers exchanged uneasy glances, and Meshach, the director, stared at Zac. "You're married?"

Hal Markley burst into a wide, politic smile. "I had no idea."

Carrie Dorchester glanced at Grace, gave her a small smile, then continued smiling strangely as she stared at some distant spot on the floor.

Obviously they were all shocked that Zac had a wife in Moab, Utah.

He asked Grace, "Do you know how long you'll be?"

Hal looked at his Rolex. "Give us a half hour. And Carrie's right. We should talk."

Grace's appointment finished on schedule. Leaving Zac with Hal and Carrie and Meshach, she followed Nort Stills across the parking lot to the warehouse to inspect a new fleet of custom-built wooden dories. Though Powell's expedition had used only three, Saga had built a dozen to interchange during the filming.

Grace and Stills spent thirty minutes in the warehouse, and then the producer suggested that Zac would probably be free. He wasn't, so Grace waited outside the closed door of Hal Markley's office, thinking about the weeks ahead. This Cataract Canyon expedition would not be the usual river trip. She had seen the producers' reactions to the prospect of sleeping in tents and using the rustic, mobile bathroom facilities. And Hal Markley had assured her that *his* cellular phone would work in the desolate Cataract Canyon section of the Colorado River gorge.

Not a chance, Grace thought. Cataract was a long way from anywhere.

How would Zac behave on the river? Part of her wanted to believe the worst—that he would hop off the raft at the end of the day, grab a beer and try to coax a female guide to set up a tent for him...then share it. But honesty intervened. When they'd lived together, he'd more than pulled his weight, in every way.

Finally the office door opened. Someone inside was still talking, and Grace heard Zac say, "I will," before he stepped out. Seeing her, he smiled tensely. "I'm sorry. Were you waiting long?"

Difficult meeting? Grace wondered. "No, just a few minutes."

Together they walked out to the parking lot where the midday sun had warmed the sheepskin seat covers in the Austin-Healey.

As Zac opened the door for her, Grace sensed the fine strain in him, just under the surface. "Is something wrong?"

"No." But it would be—as soon as he told her. The producers' offer was the worst thing that could have happened. And the best. Stills had said, *You're an actor. She'd better get used to it.*

Zac knew he was right.

As he started the car, Grace remarked, "You know, I'm a little surprised you're in a movie. You've always done stage."

Zac put the car in gear and turned to look over his shoulder as he backed out of the space. "Acting is acting." And a role was a role—especially when he hadn't had one for a year. Grace wasn't going to see it that way "The Ben Rogan ads have helped me, actually. I've been asked for several media interviews, even a television appearance." He braked at the parking-lot exit and checked for traffic. "It's a chance to promote the film, so the producers want to expand my part. A new contract, everything."

Grace tried to feel happy for him. But as he turned the convertible out onto Mill Creek Drive, she recalled the producers' conversation she'd overheard. *Nudity. That* was why he'd looked tense. "How are they going to expand your part, Zac?"

He glanced at her. "Several ways." He looked back at the road and tried to sound like he was talking about something as uncontroversial as the weather. "For instance, there's a scene in which I say goodbye to my wife before leaving with Powell. It's supposed to be poignant because I'm going to die."

Grace knew what he was going to say. *Yes,* she thought. You're going to die. . . .

"They're going to turn it into a lovemaking scene."

Dazed, Grace pictured Zac in bed with some beautiful starlet, maybe one of those European actresses with no cellulite and with poreless white skin, instead of tan lines from working on the river in a bikini top and shorts.

She felt a craving for Drambuie.

Holding her blowing hair back from her face, she asked, "Who is she? Anyone well-known?"

"No." They reached a stop sign; Zac slowed the car and looked over at her. Vulnerable brown eyes. *Gracie*, he thought. I want *you*.

Grace stared out the windshield. Zac didn't blame her for being upset. He was sure she'd be more upset when she saw Ingrid Dolk, the nineteen-year-old Swedish girl who would be playing Seneca Howland's wife. But Nort Stills was right. Grace had to understand that a bed scene was just acting. Not the easiest kind, but part of his job.

Still, it rankled that the producers wanted to expand his role not because they liked his acting but because the Ben Rogan jeans ads had been banned, and suddenly everyone from Hal Markley to his own agent thought he was going to become . . . a sex symbol.

The irony was that he'd been celibate for more than a year. The love scene he wanted was a private one—with his wife.

He forced his thoughts back to the film, to what he had to do. "What they're offering is significant. More money. More exposure."

"I'll say. Not that you're shy."

He would have smiled, but he knew what underlined her words. She'd never liked it that he was an actor. The light changed, and he put the car into gear. "They're taking a risk, Grace. I've never worked in film, and it's my first role in more than a year."

A year? Grace thought. Zac had always had plenty of roles. All but *Leaving Hong Kong* had been off-off-off-Broadway—no pay—but what had been important to Zac was the acting.

As they passed the Moab visitor center, she asked, "Zac, what happened with *Leaving Hong Kong?* How did you lose that role?"

One hard heartbeat struck the wall of his chest. "I was upset about you. I told you that."

Upset enough to lose a role? "What do you mean? Were you drinking?"

The light ahead turned yellow. Zac slowed the car. *Drinking,* he thought. *That* sounded normal. "I did some of that, but it wasn't the problem." He needed to tell her. If she was going to remain his wife, she should know. But for now... He glanced her way. "I've been thinking about your house. What would you like done?"

Grace blinked at him. "We were talking about *Leaving Hong Kong.*"

Zac's eyes were on hers, and she sensed he was trying to communicate something he couldn't say. His lips were parted as though he *wanted* to say it...but the words that came out were "What would you like me to do on your house?"

For a moment they just looked each other. Again Grace sensed things unspoken. Something had happened.

Reminding herself that losing the role must have been humiliating for him—knowing he wasn't ready to tell her in any case—she let it go and thought about his question. What she'd like done on her house.

She didn't want to make requests. That would seem as though they were...married. Confused, she said, "Zac, it would take a year to get that place in shape."

Zac had thought the same thing. Slowing the car to stop at another light, he stared out the windshield.

He couldn't be in Moab for a year.

Pushing the thought from his mind, he looked at Grace. "Shall I start with the screened porch? And the yard?"

Grace smiled at him, the left side of her mouth twisting a little higher than the right, and for a moment Zac saw a look he remembered in her eyes. A look that was like the words *I love you.*

She said, "Thanks. Want to borrow a truck?"

THEY SWITCHED VEHICLES for the afternoon. Leaving the
Austin-Healey at the Rapid Riggers office for Grace, Zac
borrowed one of the Suburbans and drove out to her
house to assess what materials and tools he'd need.

As he nosed the truck down the drive, a small gray
shape darted from the tamarisk and into the road. A dog.
It trotted clumsily, weakly, holding its right rear paw
slightly aloft. Slowing the Suburban, Zac watched the dog
limp back into the tamarisk.

Easing the car forward until he could see the animal
again, Zac braked and stared out the opened driver's
window. "What are you doing out here? You're just a
puppy." He hadn't realized at first. The dog looked about
half-grown, but was so malnourished its ribs showed under its muddy gray fur. Quivering in the brush, tail between its legs, it stared at Zac through one brown eye and
one blue, then escaped through the tamarisk.

Zac whistled softly, but the dog didn't look back. At
last Zachary put the car in gear and went on, but he was
disturbed. The puppy must be lost, and it had to be hungry.

He was still thinking about it when he parked under the
cottonwoods and got out to inspect the porch and the
yard. As he made mental notes of what to buy in town, his
mind kept returning to the dog he'd seen. Limping.

Starving.

Zac turned away from the house and started back up
the sandy drive, peering into the tamarisk, whistling for
the dog.

BACK AT HER OFFICE, Grace called her attorney and
reached his paralegal, to whom she explained Zac's offer
to pay her bills. The paralegal said it sounded like no
problem, but she would check. Someone from the office
would call Grace in the morning.

All afternoon, Zac was on her mind. He was relieving her of a huge debt. He was working on her house.

But that love scene. Unwillingly Grace envisioned him in a bed with another woman, cameras and technicians all around. Fake lovemaking, but Zac would be sensitive to the actress, thinking of her vulnerability in front of the camera. They would be naked together....

It reminded Grace of his marrying her for a green card. No compromise was too great for his career. Granted, she couldn't think of a serious film actor who didn't do love scenes—but could she live with it?

If she remained married to Zac, she must.

At four-thirty Grace headed home. The sun was lingering in the sky, resting against the tops of the red cliffs, as she drove the Austin-Healey along the River Inn Road. The car seemed like a toy compared to the Rapid Riggers Suburbans. As the dry spring wind whipped her hair about her head, she glanced a few times toward the river, checking the water level. High.

The road meandered past sheer rock faces where rock climbers with ropes and harnesses were ascending difficult cracks, just feet from where others had climbed centuries earlier to carve petroglyphs, rock art, in the desert varnish. She passed a sign pointing out dinosaur tracks, another designating a trail to a natural arch, and eventually she reached her sandy driveway.

Zac had been busy. The tamarisk encroaching on the drive had been cut back; the area under the cottonwoods beside the house had been cleared; and the path leading down the long grassy bank toward the concrete boat ramp was visible for the first time since Grace had returned from New York. Zac had accomplished more in an afternoon than she could have in a month.

She parked his car under the trees beside the Suburban and got out to look for him. He'd mentioned repairing the porch, but there were two—a spacious deck curving from

the southern, river side of the house all the way around the
east wall and another more intimate, enclosed area on the
northwest corner. A sprawling stone patio with a low wall
traversed the west side of the house, linking the two
porches.

Wading through sagebrush and wild desert grasses,
Grace walked around the outside of the house. In her father's old room hung a faded photo of guests at the inn
sipping cocktails on the front screened porch, and Grace
enjoyed imagining those days. But now the porches were
cluttered with junk—retired river gear, rotting furniture.
Circling the house, she tripped over a boat trailer rusting
in the grass at the foot of the patio steps.

Zac was down by the river, looking like something any
woman would want to take home. Shirtless, he crouched
in the weeds near the old boiler and rotting paddle wheel
from the *Moab Princess*, her great-grandfather's riverboat, petting a strange dog. As he scratched the animal
behind its pointed triangular ears and pulled sticks and
leaves from its matted gray-and-white coat, Zac asked,
"Do you know this dog?"

Crouching beside them, Grace shook her head. She
didn't know the dog, but she could guess its story. Abandoned by tourists. "Looks hungry."

"Yes."

Something about the way he said it, his eyes avoiding
hers, sent Grace's gaze sweeping toward the house. At the
foot of the steps were two bowls and a twenty-pound bag
of dog food. Grace bit her lip, uncertain whether to smile
or frown. Zac and strays. That tabby, Chloe, for instance. It might explain how Zac had lost their apartment. Another cat.

I was upset about you...

Grace laid aside the recollection of their conversation
in the car.

Now Zac had found a dog.

Determined not to become as smitten with the sickly mutt as he obviously was, Grace stood up and cleared her throat. "So... going to take it back to your hotel?"

Zac was gazing down at the dog, his face hidden, but Grace knew the expression he was wearing. The figuring-out-how-to-persuade-Grace look. It felt like old times. Good times. Standing, he bent over to give the dog a last stroke and waded out from the weeds to join her. The animal followed him, and Grace saw how skinny it was and how its tail drooped. The poor thing was starving.

Beside her, Zac smelled wild, like dirt and sweat. Grace tried to keep her eyes off his chest and corrugated stomach. Beard shadowed his cheeks and jaw and upper lip, and his skin looked smooth and brown as honey.

"I thought I'd call the pound. Put an ad in the paper. Try to find the owners." His green eyes searched Grace's face. "If I could keep her here for a few days..."

"What if you don't find them?"

Zac looked down at the dog. Mismatched eyes gazed up at him. Part Siberian husky. He thought he could detect faint markings in the puppy's muddy coat. "Someone will be looking for this dog. If no one turns up, I'll find a home for her." He'd done it before, with Chloe. She was still living happily with friends on Long Island. Of course, he'd love to keep this animal, but he wasn't home enough. Dogs needed attention. Besides, his apartment didn't allow pets.

He told Grace, "I'll come by and take her for exercise. Feed her." The dog had devoured the food he'd put in her bowl. Starving. He'd used Grace's phone to make an appointment with the vet for the next morning. "Really, she won't be any trouble to you."

The dog wouldn't, thought Grace. But what about Zac? He'd be around every day.

He was crouching again, rubbing the dog behind the ears. Those hands. His wedding ring... A little breathless, she said, "Okay." As Zac stood up, she told him, "You're working on my house. It's the least I can do. And by the way, I'll reimburse you for materials."

He shook his head.

Grace opened her mouth to argue, but his eyes said the subject was not open for debate.

I was a good husband.

Avoiding his gaze, Grace looked about the property, scanning the shoreline and the house. He'd replaced several of the porch screens, and there was so much more he could do here. She remembered his penchant for fixing things in their apartment. Good handyman. Good carpenter.

Good husband.

Zac told her, "I'll have more time tomorrow. I have a one-o'clock call, but I can come here early. Now, I should go back to town, though." He needed to call his agent about Hal Markley's offer. The afternoon working had given him time to think about everything that was happening . . . and everything that had happened before.

Tonight he'd spend with Grace.

Would she ask again how he'd lost the role in *Leaving Hong Kong*? At some point he would have to answer. Tell her.

God. What would she think?

He squatted beside the puppy, petting her.

Grace stared at his fingers—and his wedding ring. At Tiffany's, she'd told him she didn't want a diamond because she didn't want anything to get in the way when she cooked. Zac had said she could wear it on a necklace. But in the end, he had bought her an earring with a heart and a diamond on it. *Engagement earring,* he'd said, kissing her neck beneath it. As affectionate with her as he was with that dog.

His hands— A terrifying realization swept over her.

She still loved him.

BEFORE HE LEFT, Zac made a bed for the dog from a cardboard box, and Grace lined it with an old blanket. They put it on the screened porch, and when Zac had gone, Grace brought the puppy food and bowls up there, as well. She held the door open, and at last the dog came limping in, tail down.

Observing, Grace felt indignant. She was sure some tourist had brought the puppy along on vacation and lost her. It happened all the time. Occasionally, Rapid Riggers passengers embarking on the Daily asked her and Day to look after their pets at the office. Grace didn't mind that. But there were too many people who left dogs in hot cars or tied up at camp in the sun or set them loose in the unfamiliar desert.

As Grace poured herself a glass of wine in the kitchen, Zac's waif sat down beside the table and watched her. When she took a seat, the dog flopped down on the floor, tail limp, as though she'd never learned how to wag it.

Grace said, "I'll feed you again before I go out." Was the puppy housebroken? She would shut her in the porch when she left for dinner with Zac.

Zac...

Seeing him with the stray had been a graphic reminder that he was not the two-dimensional villain she'd painted in her mind for fourteen months. He was a complicated man she'd never fully understood. A man she'd adored anyhow, for the four happiest months of her life.

What if the things he'd told her were true? What if she'd really hurt him when she'd left? Today he'd said, *I was upset about you.* That was why he'd been sacked from two jobs and lost his agent and—

Upset how? wondered Grace. She'd been upset, too, but she'd stayed in control. Burying her dad. Running his business. *What did Zac mean?*

She had to find out, and it might as well happen tonight.

Eyes on the dozing dog, Grace drank down her wine.
It might as well happen now.

ZAC HAD ALMOST FINISHED shaving when he heard a
knock at the door of his hotel room. He gave his jaw two
last swipes before he wrapped one towel around his waist,
grabbed another to wipe his face and walked out of the
bathroom to open the door.

He expected to see someone from the studio, maybe
Nort Stills. But it wasn't Stills at the door. It was Grace.

Her hair was in a loose braid, and she was wearing a
dress he'd bought her in New York, a sheer powder blue
silk with a small point collar and nineteen-inch skirt. The
thin straps of the lining gave it a sexy, gossamer look, and
the way it clung to her breasts made him remember her
naked. Remember how deeply in love they'd been.

The towel about his waist stirred, like a snake charm-
er's bag containing a cobra, and he grabbed the white
terry cloth and released a breath between his teeth.
"Come in."

"Thanks."

Grace stepped inside. He pushed the door shut and
stared down at her. "Let me dress. I didn't expect you."

As he moved toward the suitcase lying open on the hotel luggage rack, Grace glanced about his room. The
clothes he'd been wearing earlier lay heaped in a corner,
and his script was on the bed.

He went into the bathroom to pull on a pair of black
Ben Rogan jeans. He didn't close the door, and Grace remembered what she'd said to him earlier about being shy.
He wasn't. Somehow his going into the bathroom to dress
emphasized both the intimacy they'd once shared and the
fact that they no longer shared it.

But when he emerged from the bathroom, he came
over, took her chin in his hand and kissed her mouth.

Grace swallowed hard. Electrified.

Dropping his hand, he gazed down at her. "You're sweet to come early." He went to the closet for a shirt. Indicating his pants, he asked, "Will I be all right for this place?"

"Yes." She watched him pull a shirt from a hanger and slide it on. It was red silk and patterned with black silhouettes of Mickey Mouse in various guises. The Sorcerer's Apprentice. A film director. She wondered if the shirt had come from a thrift shop or Rodeo Drive.

She sat on the edge of one of the two queen-size beds and thought of the reason she'd come. "So, Zac..."

Tucking in his shirt, he glanced at her.

"What happened to you in New York after I left?"

She knew he'd heard, but he showed no reaction. He continued to dress without answering. Grace watched him take some black socks from his suitcase and sit down on the edge of the other bed to pull them on. Then he got up and retrieved his black walking shoes from the closet. Returning, he sat down beside Grace. She could smell the hotel shampoo in his wet hair and the soap on his skin.

Zac could smell her, too. Lemongrass. Grace. The scent resurrected old feelings. Closeness. Love. Betrayal.

They had to forgive each other. They had to trust.

He had to answer her question.

"Do you even have a green card? I left before you got it."

Seizing the brief reprieve, Zac got up and grabbed his wallet from the desk under the mirror. Sitting beside her, he showed her the card.

The photo was a three-quarter profile of his face, with the right ear exposed, his long hair tucked behind it. The address was that of their New York apartment.

Grace stared up at him. His mouth was an immobile line, his face just as still. She didn't know why she felt afraid. "How did you get the card?"

"The INS mailed it to our apartment."

"When?" said Grace. "I sent a letter to our apartment six weeks after I left you, and it was returned to me. They said you weren't at that address."

She felt Zac's slight start beside her. He looked at her. "You wrote to me?"

"Of course I wrote to you! I was married to you and I loved you, and then you dropped off the face of the earth. I called you and we talked that once, and after that you didn't answer the phone, so I wrote to you. I told you that last night."

"I'm sorry. I didn't catch it." He said, "The card came a short time after you left. I lost the apartment sometime later."

"How?"

He'd dreaded this moment for a year. *Talk*, he thought. *If you just start talking, you'll get it out. Then it'll be over.*

But he didn't believe it.

He knew Grace. She wouldn't let this go. She would wonder and she would ask questions. Grace always asked questions.

But doesn't it bother you that your brother will get Oakhurst?... What does that mean, your parents "put you down" for Eton before you were born?... They sent you away to boarding school when you were seven?

She always sounded horrified, which was ridiculous. It wasn't fun to be separated from one's parents at that age, but there were worse things in life. Anyhow, all the men in his family had gone away to prep school when they were seven, then to grammar school and then to Eton, which was a great privilege. But the tradition offended Grace's maternal instincts. She *would* make a good mother.

Immediately Zac jerked away from the thought, trying to forget that she'd mentioned children the night before. Trying to forget everything that meant.

Grace stood up, impatient.

He looked into her eyes. "All right. I'll tell you what happened. I've wanted to tell you, but it's a very private matter."

Grace stared at him, astonished. "I'm your wife."

"I know. And you're trying to divorce me."

She felt the implication. He didn't trust her.

But he was talking.

"The day you left, I began feeling . . . strange. I don't know precisely what was going on, and my memories are unclear. It's like a dream, a very bad dream." Remembering, Zac searched for words to describe what had happened to him. He knew the right words. Precise words. But they would frighten her.

They frightened him.

He used layman's terms, instead. "I had all sorts of wild feelings, and my senses were overacute. I could hear things going on three blocks away, and there were...there were voices in my head to drive anyone mad." Rushing past it, he said, "Initially I was very confused. I missed a performance, but they accepted me back with a warning. About that time, I began to entertain the most florid delusions imaginable of persecution by the INS. I was afraid to go to work at Jean-Michel's. I was afraid to go to the theater.

"During a performance about a week after you'd left, I became convinced that there were INS agents in the theater, that they had wired my clothing with microscopic recording equipment to monitor my most private conversations, and that they planned to arrest and execute me. So during intermission I went upstairs, removed my clothing and left the theater by a fire escape."

He glanced at Grace. Her eyes were unblinking, her brow drawn into faint lines. Concerned? Perplexed? Aghast? He went on, aware how rehearsed his speech sounded, though he never had rehearsed, never had quite believed this moment would come. "There were people outside looking at me—theatergoers—and finally the director came out and— Anyhow, I didn't finish the performance, and everything got worse from there. I went home and cut a hole in the wall of our apartment and disassembled the plumbing, looking for wiretaps. I know it makes no sense. I was not in my right mind." He realized it felt good to be telling her, to be telling someone, anyone, but especially her. Not to bear it alone. "These kinds of things went on for a month. I was rude to everyone I knew, accusing friends and acquaintances of plotting against me, and I took up associations with homeless people of unhappily like mind with whom I lived in condemned buildings.

"When I awoke one morning in such a place, groggy but more myself, I remembered enough of what had happened to know what kind of hell I was in, and I hurried home to learn I'd been evicted. Surprise, surprise." Numbly he thought of the following days and weeks and months. Coming back to himself. Trying to put his life in order. *Trying to find out what in hell had happened.*

Not wanting to go into that, he said, "Perhaps all this can make you understand why I was reluctant to approach a woman I loved and admired. A woman who had already rejected me once." The last sounded bitter, and he laid his hand across his face. "I'm sorry."

Grace didn't move. She didn't want to think about the things he said he'd done or what it meant. All her reactions seemed wrong. Because, in a way, Zac's story was an answer to her long prayers, that he would have an innocent excuse for his long absence. Innocent, but...

She thought of what she'd been doing while he was imagining plots involving the INS. While he'd been having this...breakdown.

She'd been burying her father.

Wanting space of her own and knowing he must need some, too, she said, "Thank you for telling me. I'm going to have a glass of water."

Zac nodded, eyes remote.

Going to the desk, Grace selected one of the hotel glasses, then went into the bathroom and shut the door. She turned on the tap and filled the glass. As she drank, she stared down at the vanity and Zac's shaving kit, the same one he'd had when they lived together. His razor was still out, lying on a crumpled towel, as though he'd set it down in a hurry when she came to the door.

The details of his story came crashing down on her. Delusions of persecution. Zac standing on a fire escape naked.

It was beyond reason. Sure, he'd always been a little obsessed about the INS. What alien waiting for a green card wasn't?

But microscopic recording equipment . . .

A chill swept over her.

It sounded—well, sick. But it also made a painful kind of sense. She, the person closest to him, had walked out of his life. And it had hurt him enough that he'd unconsciously created an alternative reality.

Or, rather . . . unreality.

But I didn't react that way, thought Grace. He hurt me, too. And I went on with life. I buried my father and comforted my sister and revived a failing business.

Zac couldn't have been wounded more deeply than she was.

Could he?

The night before she'd left him, they'd slept together because there was no second bed but the floor, and Zac had held her tight in the night, saying, *Grace, don't do this. I love you. Please . . .*

A horrible realization swept over her. Her doubts . . . the decision she'd made to leave Zachary. He really had loved

her. *I promised to spend my life with you, and you promised to spend yours with me.* Even their song had promised lasting love. Staying love. Though the Rockies could
tumble and Gibraltar crumble...

But she hadn't stayed. Zac had loved her.

And she had left.

IN THE OTHER ROOM Zachary put on his shoes, then sat
on the edge of the bed with his forearms on his knees and
his head in his hands.

He'd told her.

Feelings bombarded him. Relief. Exposure. Doubt.
What was Grace thinking? This wasn't over. He'd been
right as rain for more than a year, but what if it happened again?

He'd been right to tell her. He should tell her more.

When she emerged from the bathroom, Zac stood up
and met her eyes, half expecting to see revulsion in her
gaze. But she was only frowning slightly, watching him as
though she didn't know what to say.

Zac spared her the trouble. There was only one balm for
times like this. He said, "Shall we go find a cup of tea?"

CHAPTER FIVE

WHEN THEY STEPPED outside, it was dusk and cooling off slightly. The whine of mosquitoes in the air was a reminder of the rising water in the river and the onset of spring. The Anasazi Palace had switched on its No Vacancy sign, and Grace saw many California license plates in the lot. The movie crew.

As they walked down an outdoor staircase to the street, Zac asked, "Do we need a car or can we walk?"

"It's four or five blocks to the restaurant."

They walked slowly, admiring the fading colors of the slickrock skyline to the east. Because their dinner reservation wasn't for an hour, they stopped at a deli on Main Street, got two cups of tea to go, then continued down the sidewalk, walking and window-shopping. Everything was open late, for the tourists.

Everywhere, women stared at Zac, and people who knew Grace looked curious. She was embarrassed, wondering if anyone noticed his ring and thought she was running around with someone else's husband. Her own ring was home in the bottom of her jewelry box with the coupons Zachary had given her last year on Valentine's Day. The day that had changed their lives.

As they walked, Grace pondered what Zac had told her in his hotel room. She'd never known anyone who'd done the kinds of things he had described. But Zachary wasn't like anyone else she knew. Sent to boarding school when he was seven, obsessed with acting ...

Together, they perused the art and jewelry and pottery in the windows. Nearly all the merchandise reflected the locale. T-shirt designs depicted rafting, mountain biking, natural landmarks and figures copied from petro-glyphs—the rock art of the Anasazi, the Old Ones who had built homes in the canyon cliffs centuries before, then mysteriously left the area.

Seeing Zac studying the primitive images, Grace vol-unteered, "If you'd like to see some rock art, there's a great pictograph panel across the highway from Rapid Riggers."

Zachary glanced down at her in the light from the shop window. "I'd like that." He put his arm around her and Grace hugged him, and they walked to the restaurant that way. Grace realized she was happier than she'd been in fourteen months.

Despite the disturbing things Zac had said.

At the Moenkopi Café, they sat at an intimate corner table lit by a candle in a Southwestern-style metal lan-tern. Over a bottle of chianti and food to satisfy any chef at the Culinary Institute, she and Zac talked about the puppy at her house, then about Rapid Riggers and *Kah-Puh-Rats* and his career. Zac told her how a modeling agent had approached him at a New York coffeehouse where he was waiting tables. He'd been in Europe several times in the past year doing Ben Rogan ads, and he'd spent Christmas at Oakhurst with his family.

Grace asked, "What do your folks think of your mod-eling? Have they seen any pictures?"

"One of the Rogan ads. My father didn't speak for several hours afterward, but my mother said she was glad I had a job." Zac thought of what he'd wanted to tell Grace the other night at her house. He said, "When you phoned Oakhurst looking for me, and my mother wouldn't pick up..."

Grace raised her head. "Yes?"

"She has spells of depression. It's bad sometimes."

Grace listened, hoping he'd say more. Zac seldom opened up like this.

Eyes on hers, he said, "You must have called during one of her spells. I'm sorry." And angry. But it was his fault, for not giving his wife a way to find him. For giving her a reason to leave him.

"She didn't answer the phone because she was depressed?"

"I'm sure of it. It keeps her in bed for days at a time. She won't answer the phone or the door." *Or her family.* How many holidays had he spent alone at school? *Your mum's going through a rough patch, Zachary. Try to understand.* He'd understood enough to be terrified.

He told Grace, "I think it's beyond her control." That was something he'd discovered only recently. Only since he'd begun looking into what had happened to him.

Of course, the two were unrelated. He'd never behaved like his mother.

Watching him closely, Grace asked, "Zac, did you tell them what happened to you?"

"I haven't told anyone. Just you." Biting his bottom lip lightly, he wanted to say more—to share the things on his mind. But why worry Grace when there was no need? He was all right now.

Grace sat lost in thought. *He'd told only her.* Even though she'd left him. But any guilt she felt was lessened by her reason for leaving. Nothing had changed that.

How could a man who lacked the integrity to tell a woman he was marrying her for a green card resist the temptations Zac would face in Hollywood? Their marriage was doomed.

Grace thought of the love scene, but she didn't want to bring it up. Instead, she asked, "Did the producers say anything about your announcement this morning? That we're married?" She doubted Zac would want the studio—or the public—to know why he wasn't living with his wife.

"Yes." His eyes made a quick pan of the room. "They fished, and I told them we've been estranged and are working on getting back together." Again he looked about the restaurant, assessing their privacy. Deciding they could talk, he asked, "Grace, would you like to discuss that scene?"

The love scene.

Grace watched a couple at a nearby table. They were laughing as people do when they've known each other for years and are having a wonderful time together. Looking back at Zac, she asked quietly, "How would you like it if I took off my clothes and got in bed with another man?"

Zac's abdominal muscles tightened. "I've pictured that scenario." He'd been picturing it for fourteen months; he'd also thought about it in relation to the film. How would he like it if Grace were in his shoes? He wouldn't. He didn't want her to share her body with anyone else—in any way.

He leaned closer to her over the table. "Men and women are different. Men are visually aroused, and any man would get an erection in a second seeing you naked."

It was gratifying he thought so, but... "And you're not going to get hard over Miss Whoever?"

"It's not an exciting situation."

"You just said it was."

"I said that *you* are exciting. I'm an actor, Grace, and a model. My body is public. Not sexually, of course. But visually."

"Zac, I don't mind your being 'close to your clothes.' I mind you being close to someone else's skin."

Zac wanted to be close to *her* skin—not just her cheeks and throat and arms but the paler skin that never saw the sun. He remembered her breasts against him and how it felt to run his hands over the backs of her thighs. How it felt to kiss her there. Everywhere.

Grace said, "I could name a dozen celebrity couples who met working on films together. Who, when they met, were married to other people."

Zac spoke quietly but with great intensity. "I have always been faithful to you, Grace. Even this past year. We covered this ground before we were married. Infidelity is anathema, and marriage is for life. You're the one who's trying to divorce me—not the other way round."

Her heart thudded as though nothing else mattered, nothing but commitment. Maybe her heart was right.

But she said, "If you want to be faithful, why tempt yourself?"

"Any temptation I feel is the result of sleeping alone for a year."

Grace's chest constricted. "You could have come to me."

"I told you why I couldn't."

How had the conversation begun to feel so sexy? Under the table, one of his long legs nestled against one of hers. As his hand found hers on the tabletop, his ring shone dull gold in the candlelight. Slender ring, ring from the time when they'd gotten by on two paychecks from Jean-Michel's.

"Grace, I'm telling you that what I have to do is just acting. Acting. It's not real. If you'd like to watch, I'm sure you can be on the set."

It was all Grace could do not to exclaim, *Thanks, I always wanted to watch you with another woman.* She remembered the feel of his body, the crushing weight of him on her, his hard thigh muscles straining between hers.

She didn't want to be on the set.

His ankle rubbed against hers, an under-the-table caress. Her heartbeat wouldn't slow down and she knew why. She was in love with him. She looked down at the marinated artichoke hearts and mushrooms on her plate. "Let's try and enjoy our food." *Let's forget about that damned scene.*

THE REST OF THE MEAL passed pleasantly. Afterward they were too full, so they walked for a while on Main Street, then down a side street to the Robber's Roost Tavern, Moab's most authentic cowboy bar. A band was playing, and Zac paid the cover and they went in. They each had a watery Utah beer—3.2 percent alcohol, because the state's Mormon heritage was still felt in its liquor laws—and they danced on a dance floor hazy with smoke and played two games of pool. When Grace looked at the clock, it was midnight.

She excused herself to go to the ladies' room, and when she came out Zac was reading flyers stapled to the wall near the phones. They advertised coming events—a concert, the spring musical, evening slide shows. When Grace joined him, he nodded at the poster for *Oklahoma!* and said, "That's coming up next weekend. Would you like to go?"

Another date. Grace felt absurdly thrilled. "I wouldn't miss it. The spring musical is an event around here. Anyhow, Day's in the chorus. We've got a good theater group. This fall, they're doing *Suddenly Last Summer.*"

Tennessee Williams. Zac was impressed. It was a great play. Wistfully he remembered working with small theater groups on projects like that. It would be fun to see the musical with Grace.

They left the bar. As they walked back toward his hotel holding hands, Zac asked, "Are you all right to drive?"

"Yes." After a moment she added, "Thanks for dinner. I had a nice time."

"Good. That must mean you're going to let me court you."

Grace smiled, heart shaking. "I have an Anything coupon, too, you know."

Zac remembered when he'd given it to her.

Valentine's Day.

He'd made her a card with three heart-shaped promises inside.

That fast, the pall of the day, the bleakness of her leaving, slipped over him. He saw himself in the weeks that followed, and there was a feeling like a ball of snakes in his chest—the things he hadn't told her.

I told her the facts.

When they reached the Suburban in the hotel parking lot, he opened her door, planning as platonic a good-night kiss as he could get away with. Memory had made him cautious.

But Grace didn't get in the car. She stood in front of him, her breasts almost touching him, and asked, "When are you coming over tomorrow?"

Thinking of the obligations he'd made—to the dog and the house—he met Grace's brown eyes. Their expression made his chest tighten and blood rush to his groin. He said, "I'll come at six-thirty. We can go for a run." Then his hand went to her waist, and he pulled her against him, aware of her body beneath the blue silk dress dress he'd given her.

It wasn't platonic at all. Couldn't be.

Grace felt the demand of his arms, of his whole body. They stood just inside the open door of the vehicle, in the shadows away from the hotel lights. The spot was secluded, and the things happening between their bodies seemed deeply private. The fact that the warm hard bulge at the front of his jeans was not a mystery but familiar and dear to her intensified Grace's response. It would be so easy to go up to his room with him.

Zac's hands explored her shoulder blades, all the small places on her back, as he kissed her, tasting her with his tongue. He pressed closer, wanting to be inside her, to feel like her husband again.

The sound of laughter and clicking heels penetrated the stillness of the parking lot, and he blinked alert, then untangled himself from her. Some of the film crew walked by, returning from night revelry. Instinctively shielding Grace's body with his, Zac smoothed the back of her dress and tucked her into the driver's seat.

Making a sound of deprivation, Grace clung to his arms, then to his hand, then to the steering wheel as he pulled away. He leaned into the car, and they kissed some more before he said "Good night," and moved away and shut the door.

Grace caught her breath, then put the key in the ignition and started the car. The V-8 roared. As she backed out of the space, her headlights caught Zachary, watching her. His eyes were sober. With a jolt of awakening, as though she'd just rammed into a post, Grace remembered what he'd told her that night. What had happened to him in New York.

Her heart raced in another way. Scared.

Taking a last glance at him as she turned the car, Grace wondered if he, too, was thinking of what had happened to him. Because it *was* strange. It was troubling. And Zachary was a highly educated man, someone who thought deeply about things.

Oh, God, Grace thought. *How have you stood it alone?*

THAT NIGHT IN HIS BED in the Anasazi Palace, Zac's own cry awakened him, and he lay rigid in the dark, breaths shallow, the sheets damp and cold around him. The images that had recently filled his mind—the paneled Tudor-style door, the Karastan carpet, the bed—faded away, and he saw the hotel drapes, the light from a street lamp shining around them.

He knew where he was.

Hotel. Anasazi Palace. Moab.

Moab.

Grace.

She seemed far away now. Irrelevant. The nightmare had locked onto him, making everything dark. As the sheets clung to the light sweat on his skin, the dream images were replaced by memory. A blackened ceiling overhead. His shoes filthy. His body stinking.

Zac got up, resigned to the routine. Shower. Read a book. *That* book. *DSM-IV,* the book in his suitcase. The diagnostic manual accompanied him everywhere. He read it as though it was a religious tome, as though if he studied it long enough answers would emerge—and he would know if there was something wrong with his mind. Of course a doctor would have answers—but Zac didn't need a doctor. The problem had been stress. Grace.

Zac got up to look in the bathroom mirror. His skin was wet and clammy, his hair damp and limp with sweat. Seeing his reflection, he felt emotions so powerful and negative he couldn't examine them, and he dealt with them the only way he'd ever learned.

He ceased to feel.

GRACE MOVED the dog's bed into the kitchen for the night and encouraged her to lie in it. No dice. The puppy would not be left alone. She slept on the floor of Grace's room, and Grace found her presence comforting. Even more than the music box, the stray was a reminder of Zac. Almost as though he was there.

In the morning when the alarm went off, the first thing Grace saw was the gray dog, looking at her. Tail limp on the floor.

Grace took her downstairs and filled her bowl. The dog didn't let the food land before she snapped at it hungrily. Glad Zac had found the animal before it starved to death,

Grace set the door of the porch ajar so the puppy could get out, then ran back upstairs to dress.

When Grace had moved back into the inn after her father's death, she'd begun sleeping in the spacious front room that had been her parents' before her mother died. Now the plaster walls were peeling and the floor was scuffed and in need of refinishing. But an antique fan hung from the ceiling, and an enormous hearth warmed the eastern wall. To the south, French doors led to a wide patio balcony. It curved out over the screened porch downstairs, offering a view of the river and the mesa called the Amasa Back on the other side.

Grace opened the doors, and stepped out onto the terrace. It was still the charcoal light before dawn. But overhead, the sky was heavy with clouds, and already the river flowing past hinted at dusky red. She knew it would rain.

Returning indoors, she played the music box and dressed in a sports bra, tank top and shorts, then went downstairs to stretch. She heard Zac's car; heart racing, she hurried through the kitchen and out the side door to meet him.

It was raining. Zac had raised the top on the Austin-Healey, and when he got out she saw that he hadn't shaved. He was wearing black running shorts and an old blue T-shirt, and he seemed sleepy as he smiled at the dog limping up to greet him. He stooped to stroke the animal, but the smile didn't reach his eyes. When he straightened, he didn't quite look at Grace.

She remembered the night before, the way he'd kissed her, everything. *Maybe he was drunk,* she thought. They'd just had one bottle of wine, but he looked as though a hangover might be the problem. She said, "I fed the dog."

"Thanks." Again his eyes skirted hers. He felt disconnected—flat. Not enough sleep. He had come to Grace's only because of his obligations there. The dog. The promises he'd made.

And because running helped.

After he'd stretched, they set out in the rain. The dog followed, hobbling, and Zac led her back to the house and shut her in the porch, saying, "When your leg's better, you can come." Then he joined Grace.

The rain was falling hard, sending russet water cascading off the canyon walls, cutting paths in the rocks, staining the river the color of blood, filling the air with the smells of wet plants and ozone and evaporation.

Grace was tour guide. She told Zac how the river was coming up, showed him where the water had swallowed familiar boulders. After a detour to show him dinosaur tracks beside the road, she headed up a footpath in a rocky talus slope.

Following cairns, she led him on a narrow trail high over a canyon. Sage, juniper and scrub oak poked between rock outcroppings. They ran until the trail merged with sandstone, which seemed to roll endlessly in all directions as the canyon widened. There, Grace stopped.

Turning in the rain, she said, "We shouldn't go any farther. When it's dry, you'd never know why they call the stuff slickrock, but on a day like this it's like walking on banana peels." She shrugged at Zac. Wet strands of hair, loosened from her ponytail, stuck to her cheek. "I just wanted you to see this. It's called Sutter Canyon."

It was spectacular. The rocks sprawled out in the distance, all the way to the mesa top. They stood before a wide natural bowl. Above it, on the opposite cliff wall, was an alcove, and Zac could make out toeholds worn in the rock leading up to it—and the ruin of a structure built of sand-colored rocks.

He asked, "Is that an Anasazi ruin?"

"Yes. You can climb up there, but it's too wet now. Let's go back to the road a different way, and I'll show you the spring and my grandfather's still."

"A bootlegger?"

"Oh, yes. He used to ferry moonshine on the river."

Grace's family history was here, Zac realized, as his was at Oakhurst. It was an unsettling thought. He shouldn't take her away.

As they returned to the Potash Road and finally slowed to walk down Grace's drive, Zac felt better than he had earlier. Tired, rain-soaked, breathing hard. Alive. He noticed the small round indentations the rain had made in the sand and the shades of green in the dripping tamarisk corridor around them. As they neared the house, Zac studied the lines of the gables and the chimneys and balconies. It was a graceful structure. Four thousand square feet, he guessed—too large to be practical for anything but what it had been, a hotel.

He climbed the stone steps a pace ahead of Grace and held open the battered side door that led onto the screened porch. The dog met them, and Zac immediately crouched down to pet her, to examine her matted puppy fur and let her lick his face. He said, "What kind of dog are you anyhow?"

"A mutt," said Grace with a smile. "She's a nice dog. She slept in my room last night." Opening the door that led into the kitchen from the porch, she told Zac, "You can use the downstairs shower, and I'll find you a towel and something dry to put on."

"Thanks."

The answer was painfully casual. Grace remembered other morning runs and other showers. As she left him with the dog and went upstairs, she considered Zac's apathy and wondered if he was uncomfortable about what he'd told her at the hotel. That would be natural.

Up in her room, she found clothes for him. They were some of his that she'd taken when she'd moved out—a pair of cotton gym shorts and an Oxford sweatshirt.

Coming downstairs, she heard a sound she hadn't heard in the house for years. The piano. But Day had never played like that. Grace didn't recognize the piece, only that it was classical. And even though the instrument was out of tune, Zac made it sound like something from nature. A bird. A human voice.

She followed the music to the living room and found him sitting there playing, in wet clothes and wet hair, the skinny gray dog lying at his feet. When he stopped to check a sticky key, he saw Grace. His eyes froze on hers; then he stood up and closed the lid over the keys. The dog sat up, too, watching him.

Grace said, "I forgot you could do that." Sometimes after work he had played the piano at Jean-Michel's. Classical pieces. Blues. "Love Is Here to Stay."

Joining her now, he indicated the baby grand. "It's a good instrument."

Grace nodded toward the double doors to the Princess Room. "There's an old player piano in there." She handed him his clothes.

Zac recognized them. When he was evicted, he had noticed them missing and wondered if she'd taken them—or if he'd done something with them that he couldn't recall. Now he lifted the garments to his face, breathing in. He smiled at her. "They smell like you. Lemongrass."

Grace was eased by his smile. Maybe the Zac she'd seen the night before wasn't just something she'd dreamed up on heady Italian wine.

Once she'd gone upstairs, Zac did not go immediately to the shower. Instead, he went to the double doors. Princess Room. It must be the inn's dining room Grace had told him about. Carefully he released the bolts at the top and tried the doors. They opened.

Beyond lay a spacious room of almost a thousand square feet. It was cluttered with bicycles, a deflated raft, old tables and bed frames, rolls of tar paper and other sundry items. But Zac still noticed the big windows, which would admit the afternoon sunlight, and the French doors opening onto the screened porch and the patio. He could see where chandeliers or ceiling fans must have hung.

Making his way through the junk and around the player piano to the French doors, he looked out the dirty glass at the river. He could see the boiler from the riverboat, and he imagined the *Moab Princess* steaming down the Colorado, her paddle wheel turning.

Again it occurred to him that if he and Grace were to live together again, it couldn't be here. He needed to live where he could work. But how could he ask Grace to leave this place for him?

Of course, that wouldn't happen for a while. Reconciling with Grace had never promised to be easy. But now, new barriers had arisen between them. His sexier role in *Kah-Puh-Rats*. Her entrenchment in her father's business. And most of all, what had happened to him after she'd left.

He turned to leave the room and almost tripped over the dog. Sweet animal. Zac stooped to pet her. He'd grown up surrounded by dogs at Oakhurst, but he'd never seen one this starved—for food or companionship. As the dog looked up at him, waiting to see where he was going next, Zac reflected that he'd better find the owners soon—before he began to wish he couldn't.

Slipping out of the Princess Room with the puppy, he carefully secured the doors behind him, then started from the living room. His eyes caught the image over the mantel. Ophelia by the lily pond. Immediately he looked away. But as he headed for the downstairs bath Grace had said he could use, lines from *Hamlet* swarmed his brain:

"They say the owl was a baker's daughter. Lord, we know what we are but know not what we may be...."

Ophelia. Mad, mad Ophelia.

When Zac emerged from the bathroom ten minutes later, showered and dressed in dry clothes, he was greeted by the dog and a burst of aromas from the kitchen. Coffee. *Huevos rancheros.*

His wife was making breakfast.

Feeling as though he was finding his way home, Zac walked slowly to the kitchen and discovered Grace standing at the stove in a pair of blue jeans and a cropped, wine-colored cable-knit sweater that showed a glimpse of her slender waist. Her hair was twisted up from her long neck, and she seemed tall and sexy and... Graceful.

As the puppy lay down in its bed, Zac joined Grace at the counter.

She glanced up at him. His expression reminded her of what he'd said the day before about kitchens. Eyes playful, he said, "You're trying to seduce me again."

Remembering his recent remoteness, Grace chose not to be charmed. She indicated a basket of fruit on the counter. "Why don't you squeeze the oranges for juice?"

Grace heard him laughing and turned around. He was eyeing her breasts affectionately. "I'd rather fondle a couple of grapefruit."

Obviously he'd recovered from his hangover or whatever it was. Grace shoved her fist against the board of his stomach, and he grinned at her. Shaking her head, she said, "And to think I ever thought you had manners. At least pour the coffee."

Obediently Zac opened cabinets until he found the mugs. As he took down two and filled them, he asked, "Grace, would you mind if I looked at the upstairs today? I won't go in your room."

Grace knew his plans were to work on her house until the dog's appointment with the vet. *I won't go in your room.* Thinking of when they'd had no private zones, no rooms or beds of their own, she said, "That's fine. You can go anywhere. You're ... welcome." *You're my husband.*

AFTER SHE GOT into the Suburban and left for Rapid Riggers in the rain, Zac cleaned the kitchen, then toured the house and grounds, accompanied by the dog. Though he kept his word and didn't step foot in Grace's upstairs bedroom, he stood in the open doorway for a long time and looked at everything.

He found out what had happened to the things she'd had in their East Village apartment. She kept most of the items close to her, all but their quilt, which covered a bed downstairs. The heart crystal that had hung in their window now cast its rainbows from the French doors in Grace's room. A tapestry he'd given her of Echo and Narcissus hung beside her mirror, and an aluminum pagoda wind chime they'd bought together in Chinatown dangled from a hook near the window. Her pink jewelry box sat on top of the Victorian armoire, the music box he'd sent her beside it; and on the bulletin board over a small writing desk, he saw a snapshot of himself.

The discovery was unsettling. Comforting. Strange. Grace had been thinking about him. She had cared about him.

She had left.

Finally turning away from her room, Zac continued exploring the upstairs. The hardwood floors and plaster walls showed old water damage, probably from roof leaks. Nonetheless, the house was wonderful—close to five thousand square feet, including wide verandas with elegantly molded balustrades, and spacious rooms with individual hearths and private baths.

His inspection concluded, Zac went out to the porch. Casually he explored the junk collected there. He recognized a few small metal tables from photos he'd seen inside, showing the house when it was an inn. A broken ceiling fan lay beneath several damaged oars. But there were other things that could be salvaged.

Wondering what else was about, he ventured out into the rain and climbed the grassy slope to the stone carriage house, the dog padding behind him. The road to the building was choked with weeds, and Zac could barely distinguish two ruts made by tire tracks years before. The carriage house had been remodeled into a four-car garage, but now the glass in the windows was cracked, and the roof needed repair.

He entered by a heavy wooden door at the side of the building, and as his eyes adjusted to the shadows, he saw the boat. It sat on a trailer against the far wall, a two-headed beast covered by a tarp. Both bow and stern were high and pointed, the gunwales arcing downward to the center of each side. Dodging spiderwebs, Zac waded around stacks of boxes and paint cans and life vests and oars to reach the boat. Even before he untied two of the lines and raised the dusty tarp, he knew it was Grace's dory.

It was painted royal blue, with a yellow stripe against the gunwales, and the name was lettered on the prow he had uncovered. *Persephone.*

As he covered the boat again, he found himself thinking of the morning more than a year earlier when Day had called them in New York. Deliberately he bypassed what had been going on before the phone call—great sex. Instead, he recalled Grace's determination to return to Utah and run her father's business. Zac had admired her readiness to help her father. But not at the price of leaving her spouse.

While rain pattered on the roof, he stared at her boat in the shadows, remembering the argument—and his fateful mention of the green card.

She'd reacted instantaneously, interrogating him. And when he hadn't denied her accusations but simply told her that he loved her, everything had fallen apart. *I knew there was something wrong with this picture. I thought it was just that you couldn't handle emotion. But the fact is, you're just a bad actor....*

He'd cooled toward her then—till late that night in bed. Then, those emotions she said he couldn't handle had come out. He'd begged her to stay. She'd told him not to touch her.

In the morning he'd helped her pack.

It had been very ugly. And the recollection made him wonder what he was doing here now.

DISASTER AWAITED Grace at the office.

"This is my last season at Rapid Riggers."

Grace and Day stood in the reception area, staring at Nick Colter, listening to the incredible words that were like the sound of money flowing away from their father's river outfit.

Belatedly Grace remembered Day's forecast, that Nick would quit someday. She'd never dreamed someday would arrive so soon. Judging from her sister's expression, Day hadn't, either.

Well aware of what they were losing—one of the best guides in town, who was also an emergency medical technician trained in river rescue—Grace stared into Nick's dark brown eyes, searching for some clue that he wanted something he wasn't getting. More money?

Then she remembered the rest of what Day had projected, and her bad feeling got worse. She asked Nick, "What are you going to do?"

He looked slightly embarrassed, and she knew what was coming. "Start an outfit. A guy in Green River is selling permits for Deso and Labyrinth."

Desolation and Labyrinth canyons on the Green River. Permits were the backbone of any river outfit; it was illegal to carry passengers for hire without them. There was only a limited number of permits in existence, controlled by government agencies, and new ones were rarely issued, so anyone hoping to start a river outfit had to buy permits from another outfitter.

Grace's heart felt like concrete. Nick might start with a few permits, but in time he would rise to be a formidable competitor. He was a popular guide. Without trying, he might take a lot of Rapid Riggers' business.

She said sincerely if coolly, "I wish you luck."

Day lit a cigarette and leaned back against the reception counter in her red-and-white checkered straight skirt and white cashmere sweater. "I don't." Grace and Nick both looked at her, and she said, "Well, good grief. Why be gracious?" She glared at Nick in disgust. "You rat fink."

Grace began laughing, and a minute later Nick was teasing Day, and the tension was broken. But as they went into the kitchen and she studied the logbook to see how many trips were out, she couldn't stop thinking about the reality of losing Nick and what it would mean to Rapid Riggers. She and Day could manage of course, but . . .

She put her arms on the counter and her head in her hands.

Day might end up managing alone.

Zac had come to claim her, and the path he'd charted for them to follow was a walk to the stars, chasing his dreams.

It was a place Grace wasn't sure she wanted to go. Because what if he left her along the way?

What if he didn't love her enough?

CHAPTER SIX

IT WAS STILL RAINING when Zac drove into the Rapid Riggers lot later that morning. He needed to return to his hotel to call his agent and clean up before reporting to the production office, but he wanted to see Grace first.

As he ducked under the dripping porch eaves and dried his feet on the mat, he peered through the front window and saw her talking on the phone at the reception counter. When he pushed open the door, she was saying, "Unfortunately, Nort, there are no dams upstream from here, and we can't control the water level."

Nort Stills, Zac thought. He glanced through the streaming windows at the river. Today the Colorado was living up to the name the Spaniards had given it, the water an unearthly red. It was flowing fast, eating up the banks. Would high water present a problem for filming the movie?

Catching Zac's gaze, Grace said into the phone, "That's a novel idea. I never thought of diverting the water to run down the other side of the Rockies. But unfortunately that's totally out of our hands. We're in the state of Utah."

Zac was embarrassed. Who but someone from Hollywood would conceive of such a scheme? Nort's suggestion was absurd, and he felt ridiculous by association.

Hanging up the phone minutes later, Grace came around the counter to greet him. "You're a nice surprise. Where's the dog?"

"Back home on your porch, enjoying a treat from the vet. I thought if you had a minute, you could show me the rock art you said was across the street."

"Sure. Let me tell Day."

When she returned to the reception area moments later, Grace took a jacket from the coatrack and pulled the hood over her head. As they stepped out onto the porch, where the pouring rain made a deafening drumbeat on the awning and metal gutters, she asked, "What did the vet say? Anything interesting?"

"Yes. The dog's a Siberian husky. Probably five months old."

"Purebred?" Starting down the porch steps to the soaking mix of gravel and red mud in the lot, Grace said, "I'd think she'd have more fur."

"Malnourished. But when you pet her, you can feel that downy undercoat. Her leg is just sprained. By the way, the vet agreed with your theory—lost on vacation. So I put an ad in the paper. In a town this size, the owners should turn up soon. If they're about."

Grace was sure they weren't. And she suspected Zac would like to keep the husky.

Changing the subject, she told him about her morning. "Nick's quitting at the end of the season." As she and Zac climbed the embankment to cross the highway, she said, "It's bad for us. He's our best guide, but he's more than that. He trains new boatmen and takes care of equipment. And he's leaving to start an outfit of his own."

Zac's conscience pricked him. Grace was trying to run her father's business, and she needed help—not someone trying to lure her away from it. If she left, Day would be abandoned. Zachary considered another option. He'd helped his parents with the hotel at Oakhurst, and he doubted there was anything he couldn't learn about the river business, given time.

But he wouldn't do it. Couldn't. He was an actor.

Grace said, "I knew we'd lose Nick someday. River guiding is great if you're young and single and don't want to be tied down. But Nick has a lot of drive—and some money."

Zac asked, "What does a river outfit go for?"

"Rapid Riggers? Maybe half a million dollars. Maybe more, the way tourism is hitting Moab. But Nick won't be starting that big." Grace nodded at a slickrock outcropping rising to a mesa on the far side of the road. "The pictograph panel is up there."

As they crossed the highway and hiked up a trail into the rocks, Zac noticed the geology. Some of the exposed layers were as old as the dinosaurs; in the rain it was easy to see how, over the millennia, the wind and water and minerals and the shifting of the earth had formed a landscape of such riotous colors and shapes.

Grace paused to point to the slope beside them. The ground was covered with a knobby black crust. "That's cryptogamic soil. It helps prevent erosion. It's held together by microscopic plant life, and it takes hundreds of thousands of years to form, so you shouldn't step on it."

Zac studied the cryptogam. The dark layer was composed of what looked like hundreds of tiny sand castles, some only half an inch high. He said, "It's beautiful." Hearing a low rumble behind them, he turned to see a sliver of lightning split the smoke-colored sky above the Moab Rim.

"It's far away," Grace said over the rain. "But we're pretty exposed up here. Let's hurry."

The path was steep, muddy sand and loose rock alternating with patches of sandstone as slick as its name. When they reached the base of a sheer vertical wall, Grace said, "There," and pointed at the panels. Zac saw them— russet figures as big as people, painted on pale beige stone.

Thunder boomed again, growing closer, and Grace peered through the downpour at the lightning, but it was still far off. She told Zac, "These pictographs were done by the Fremont Indians maybe a thousand years ago. They used pigments made from mineral deposits." The sky strobed gray-white, and a great crack made them both jump. Grace said, "That's our cue to go back." Cold mud and rain spattered their legs as they hurried down the trail, past sodden clusters of sagebrush.

As they crossed the highway and began their return to Rapid Riggers, Zac asked, "Grace, do you ever think about being a chef again?"

She shrugged. "My mom was a cook, you know. She was from New Orleans. She did all the cooking at the inn."

Zac hadn't known. Thinking of the Princess Room, the tables stacked against one wall, he said, "Perhaps your talent is inherited."

Grace gave him a smile like sunshine, reminding him that she'd never really known her mom.

Avoiding thoughts of his own mother, Zac focused on the inn. "That place has real possibilities." *Possibilities for what?* But he knew. Moab was a visitor town. Had Grace never considered—

As they walked, she tugged her hood more securely over her head. The rain was falling harder now. "It's still zoned commercial."

She *had* considered it.

"But bringing the building up to code would be expensive. Also labor intensive. Really... impossible," she murmured as they reached the Rapid Riggers lot.

Zac was glad she perceived it that way. To him, restoring the inn on the Colorado to what it used to be—and more—didn't seem impossible at all.

He followed Grace up the porch steps but grabbed her arm before she could go inside.

She turned under the dripping awning. "What?"

Zachary eased her back against the siding near the door, out of view of the window. His mouth bent down toward hers. "I didn't *really* stop by to see the rock art...."

THE RAIN STOPPED after lunch, and Grace drove out to the production office to present her proposed menu for the Cataract Canyon trip to Hal Markley. After much thought, she had suggested a week's worth of meals, with three different entrées per night, including dishes for the many vegetarians among the cast and crew. The producers had offered to fly in fresh ingredients daily from as far away as California. And with the studio's generators, Grace could actually run some restaurant equipment. A blender, for instance. She should be able to prepare almost any meal that she could at home.

Visiting the production office would serve a dual purpose. Perhaps she could get a look at the actress who would play Seneca Howland's wife—and lover.

Grace found the Uratomic Building busy, with people in the corridors and talking on phones in the various rooms. The door to Hal Markley's office was shut, so she continued down the hall. In a large meeting room on the right, Martin Place and Kip Hetherington, who would play George Y. Bradley, Powell's second in command, were rehearsing a scene under Meshach Stoker's direction. Carrie Dorchester stood at one side of the room watching. Grace considered giving the coproducer the menu, but instead, she kept wandering, peeping in other open doors. Where was Zac?

Snatches of conversation came to her as she made her way toward the front door, but Grace paid little attention until she heard voices from a room on her left. A man and a woman. One of them sounded like—

Grace stopped at the door and looked in. Zac was leaning against a counter at the far end of the room talking to a pretty blonde in a black schoolgirl-style jumper and white blouse. They were the only people in the room, and their scripts lay on a folding table nearby.

It took little to start that warm longing in Grace's stomach. Just seeing the naturally sexy posture of his tall body. And the way his long hair swept back from his eyes, then forward at the ends, begging to be touched.

He saw her, and his face brightened. His smile was for her alone. "Grace. Come in. There's someone I want you to meet."

Grace crossed the room, trying not to feel anything about Zac's companion. The girl looked maybe eighteen. She was only five foot four or five, and her figure was lithe and elegant. Prettily she exclaimed, "Ah! Zachary's wife?" Beaming at Grace, she held out her hand. "I am Ingrid. I'm very pleased to meet you." She had a Scandinavian accent.

Taking Ingrid's hand, Grace felt as though she was reaching into a black widow's nest.

Ingrid said, "Your husband—he is so kind to me." She gave Zac a look of affection and asked Grace, "You and I will be friends?"

Grace wondered how she could think so but said, "It's nice to meet you."

Ingrid smiled again, then looked at the clock. Gathering up her script from the table, she told Zac, "Ten minutes till we show Meshach how good we are. I'll see you later, Grace." She waved and left the room.

Grace said, "I'm glad you're kind to her, Zac."

Zachary lifted his eyebrows mildly, and Grace regretted the sarcasm. She sounded jealous. And she was.

Zac knew. Obviously the notion of the bedroom scene bothered her. But it was going to happen. "Grace, I'm accepting Hal's offer."

Grace held herself straight, tried to be as indifferent as the river. "I know that." At least, she'd guessed, which wasn't the same as hearing him say it. She restrained her emotions, composing herself. She couldn't control Zac. She couldn't make him do what she wanted. She had to trust him.

Grace glanced down at the menu, then toward the door. "I'd better go."

Zac knew she was angry. In a perverse way, it made him respect her. It also gave him hope. She cared what he did. He said, "I want to see you tonight. I should be done by eight. Is there a good movie in town?"

"Just the usual Hollywood pabulum."

It was a phrase of his own, from the days when he'd turned up his nose at feature films. And Zac knew the dig extended to *Kah-Puh-Rats*. "All right. What else is going on? When does Day's musical open?"

"Next Thursday."

"What about the canyonlands slide show?"

"It's playing tonight." Grace could hardly see straight. "So what position are you going to use?"

Zac expelled a breath and went to the door and shut it. Then he returned to where she stood by the table. He said coldly, "As the scene reads, I'm going to be sitting against the headboard of the bed, and she's going to straddle me and—"

Grace didn't know she was moving. She only felt the hard, slapping contact of her palm against his face.

"*Grace*." He grabbed her wrist—then both wrists.

Grace's eyes were burning. She could see the red mark on his face, the hurt in his eyes, and she was ashamed of herself, but she couldn't stop. "You know why you're doing this? Because you want to. You're an exhibition-ist." She tried to jerk her hands from his grasp.

He held her, and she felt the roughness of his skin, a roughness that came from working with his hands on her house. Those hands made her wild. Those hands should touch only her.

Zac was angry now. "Don't say things you'll regret, and don't provoke me to say things I'll regret."

Grace knew he spoke wisely. She said, "They can put together a love scene without making money from your naked body."

That was true enough to sting. Zac believed any competent actor should be able to handle nudity with professionalism and without a blush, but he also knew his anatomy was what the producers of *Kah-Puh-Rats* wanted. What Grace said struck so hard, at such a core place, that for a moment he hated her for saying it. She'd called him cheap.

He felt cheap.

He thought of how desperate he'd become to make up for what had happened in New York. Desperate to succeed. But he also thought of who he was and what he'd chosen to do with his life and the obvious fact that the woman he'd married hated it.

Enough to hit him.

Releasing her hands, he turned and collected his script, a sheaf of white and blue pages, from the table. He spoke sharply. "Grace, if you're remotely interested in saving our marriage, I suggest you get one thing through your head. You married an actor. And that isn't going to change."

Grace felt like crying—not because he was an actor but because she had revealed how she felt about it and because a patch of red still stained the honey skin of his left cheekbone. Her gaze swept over him. The hair she had stroked as they lay in bed at night. His face. His rangy limbs.

He had been hers. She couldn't stand the thought of another woman's legs around him.

Quietly, as though they had not argued or exchanged some of the harshest words of their marriage, as though his wife had not struck him, Zac said, "I think the slide show starts at nine. I'll pick you up at eight-thirty."

Grace nodded. He did not touch her again, nor she him, and as they left the room together, she felt they were worlds apart.

SHE DIDN'T RETURN to Rapid Riggers immediately. Instead, she drove up the river road to a beach near the mouth of Negro Bill Canyon. Walking down a sand footpath to the river, Grace found that a mountain biker had claimed the spot for a camp site; so she followed the silty shoreline around the bend until she was alone.

On a low flat rock beside the river, she sat in the sun and watched the water. She had hit Zac. It was the ugliest thing she'd ever done, the ugliest thing that had ever passed between them. Even furious about the green card, she had not descended to that.

She was ashamed. Zac was an actor. What he was going to do wasn't adultery. She'd read a half-dozen times that filming love scenes was not remotely erotic for the actors.

But it made Grace crazy with fear. What if he became attracted to Ingrid?

Any temptation I feel is the result of sleeping alone for a year.

I can't sleep with him, Grace thought. *He hurt me too badly. He's hurting me now.*

But when she considered Zac taking off his clothes and pretending to make love with that beautiful girl, with her sitting on top and in front of him, where he would see her breasts and feel... And then going back to his hotel room, the same hotel where that actress was staying...

There was only one thing to do.

She had to get him back under her roof.

WHEN SHE RETURNED to Rapid Riggers, Grace put on her bikini and some cutoffs and went outdoors to repair a D-ring on a raft. She wanted to avoid Day. Grace had told her about Zac's role in the movie, but she wasn't ready to hear what her sister would say about the love scene.

Day had been around for the past fourteen months. And Grace couldn't break Zac's confidence and explain why he hadn't been. Naturally her sister was suspicious of him.

While she was working, Nick returned from rowing the Daily and came to see how the repair was progressing. Crouching beside her in the sand near the overturned raft, he said, "So, how are things going with your husband? Fast Susan said you went out with him last night."

News traveled fast at Rapid Riggers. Susan must have seen her with Zac. Grace longed to confide in Nick—ask him if *he* could lie in a movie-set bed with Ingrid Dolk without getting a hard-on. But what was between her and Zac was too personal to discuss with anyone.

When she didn't answer, Nick said, "I didn't mean to pry. I've just got a bug in my brain I can't shake. I wondered if you might be moving away from Moab with him."

Grace felt a little start go through her. She knew what Nick was working around to, and it felt threatening. "Day and I aren't selling this outfit, Nick."

As soon as she spoke, she wished she'd said it differently. Nick was more than an employee. She'd known him since he was fourteen and living a wild Huck Finn existence in caves along the river. No one knew where he'd come from or much about him, and her dad had looked after him as much as Nick would allow, just to keep social services away from the boy who was too much animal to sleep indoors, to answer to the orders of strict foster parents who didn't understand him.

It made her heart twist in a funny way to know that while he was thinking of starting an outfit of his own, he really wanted Rapid Riggers.

He couldn't have it.

Now he said, "Just checking." Smiling good-naturedly, he stood up and stretched. "I'd better go de-rig and carry out the trash for Her Royal Highness."

Grace squinted up at him. "We'll miss you."

Nick looked around the boat yard at the equipment—the buses, the Jeeps, the trailers, the rafts, all of which Grace knew he had somehow made his own through the work of his hands. He said, "I'll miss this place, too."

As he went inside, Grace thought of Zac and her marriage and what she'd told Nick. *Day and I aren't selling this outfit.*

What if they must?

What if she had to choose between her husband—a man who loved his career more than anything—and the business her father had built from scratch, one of the oldest river outfits in Moab, Utah?

Who am I kidding?

That was exactly the choice she faced.

SHE WANTED HIM home. She knew how much when she reached the house that evening, saw the work he'd done on the screens, saw the stray he'd taken in. The puppy was waiting for her on the porch, her coat clean and fluffy. Grace found the dog brush on a table near the kitchen door, with a box of dog biscuits. Zac had left the kitchen immaculate, and there was a vase of wildflowers on the maple trestle table.

Seeing a note beside the vase, Grace snapped on the overhead, went to the table and found two pieces of paper from a Paris hotel. The words on the top sheet were written in French, but she grasped what they were—a recipe from a chef named Claude Renault at the Maison de Something-or-other. On the second page, Zac had translated the recipe for a cream sauce.

He had thought of her this past year. Gifts. The music box. The recipe.

The phone rang, and Grace jumped. Turning from the table, she lifted the receiver from the old-fashioned wall unit. "Hello?"

In the transportation office at the Uratomic Building, Zac tried to relax. Their earlier battle had been a draw and the war was still on; but he would make peace however he could. Unfortunately what he had to say now wouldn't help. Glancing over his shoulder as a production assistant wandered in, he said into the phone, "It's me."

Zac heard her little intake of breath. Was she still angry, too?

She didn't sound like it as she answered, "Hi, Zachary."

It was only his name, but the way she said it made him feel as if he'd had the wind knocked out of him. The production assistant left the room, and Zac was glad. He had the transportation office to himself.

Grace said, "I'm sorry I hit you."

Zac was sorry he'd incited it. He had things to tell her, things he'd been thinking about, but he wasn't going to say them on the phone. Gently he replied, "Don't worry. I'll get my licks in sometime when we're alone."

Grace knew he wasn't talking about hitting. Heat seeped through her. And relief. He wasn't angry. He didn't think less of her. He was saying tender things on the telephone. She hugged herself.

Eyeing the flowers he'd left on the table, she said, "Thanks for the recipe. How did you get it?"

"It wasn't easy." Not wanting to think of the months he'd been without her or his habit of buying gifts for her, as though she was still his, he came to the reason for his call. "Grace, I can't make our date. It's going to be a late night here."

"Oh." Grace was crushed. She'd been looking forward to the date, to mending their rift. To making him forget how she felt about his job—and that she'd hit him.

This conversation was all she had. She asked, "Zac, would you like to stay here, instead of at the hotel? I could make up a room for you."

Zac clenched the phone receiver, his emotions seesawing. He didn't ask if she was sure. He didn't want her to change her mind. "Thank you. I'd like that."

Grace's heart eased. Shaky-hot inside, she said, "Since you'll be late, I'll leave the kitchen door unlocked. Your room is the one off the parlor. You shouldn't have trouble finding it. It's the only one with a bed."

"I know which it is." He'd seen it that morning—the butter-colored walls and French doors, the antique writing desk and the rocking chair, the full-size bed with captain's drawers beneath. The mattress was covered with the purple satin-and-velvet quilt he and Grace had used in New York.

Needless to say, it was not Grace's room.

He said, "I want to sleep with you."

Grace trembled, visualizing him climbing into her bed late that night as he used to when he came home from the theater. She checked the fantasy. "First let's make sure we're not going to hurt each other again."

Zac couldn't argue. Hardly realizing he was holding one arm hard against his stomach, straining to hold in his feelings, he said, "I'll be there about one. And I'll look forward to seeing you in the morning. We'll run again, all right?"

Hanging up the phone moments later, Grace impulsively embraced the dog. Zac was coming home. As the husky licked her nose, Grace remembered their old routine in New York, things she'd done for Zac when she knew he'd be late after rehearsal or a performance.

While the puppy dozed in its box bed, Grace set a bread dough to rise. Next she sliced onions and leeks to sauté, peeled and chopped yams and carrots, and grated ginger and lemon and lime peels for a sweet-potato-and-carrot soup. While the ingredients simmered in the stock, she sliced nuts for a brandy walnut tart. The occupation was satisfying. This was not Rapid Riggers. This was not Jean-Michel's. She had someone coming home. Zac was coming home.

Between tasks in the kitchen, she cleaned the downstairs bathroom and changed the sheets on the bed in her father's old room. She and Day had cleaned out the room after his death, and Nick had taken his bed to the carriage house and brought down another from upstairs. The room received afternoon sunlight through French doors on the west wall, and often when she came home from work Grace had lain reading on the bed, on the quilt that had been hers and Zac's.

Now she felt bittersweet anticipation because he would be sleeping in this room. While she emptied the bureau drawers and lined them, she avoided thoughts of their long separation and strange tales of madness she couldn't comprehend. Nor did she ponder the distant future—Hollywood looming on the horizon, a lifetime of tabloids and sexy love scenes. She thought only of the present, of the man she loved coming into her house that night, eating food she'd prepared, sleeping between sheets she'd washed.

Sleeping apart. It was for the best. She wouldn't allow it to dampen her spirits.

When the soup and bread were done, Grace wrote Zac a note and then went through the house closing up for the night. Leaving the kitchen door unlocked, the soup warming and the light burning over the stove, she climbed the stairs to her bedroom with the husky behind her.

But after she'd gotten ready for bed, she didn't immediately turn down the covers. Instead, she went to her mother's armoire. Beside Zac's music box sat the pink jewelry case her father had given her when she was seven.

Opening the lid, Grace removed trays loaded with baubles and reached into the bottom. The band of gold and that small hoop earring with the diamond and heart winked at her seductively in the glow from her lamp, but she touched neither. Instead, she pulled out a handmade card with a picture Zac had sketched of himself in his waiter's clothing. He'd written the words "Love is..." There was another picture inside the card. On the right, her in a chef's hat. On the left, Zac the waiter brought her a heart on a platter. Or, rather, three removable heart coupons secured to the card through a slot in the paper. The words inside concluded the message on the front: "...you and me."

Love is you and me. Yours truly, Zachary.

The card would never lose its power for her. Whenever she looked at it, she believed he had loved her. She believed until she put it away and could think, instead of only feel.

She pulled out the three coupons. Penned across the topmost heart was the inscription, "This coupon is good for 1 Romeo and Juliet Bed."

A handmade bed, like the one in Franco Zeffirelli's version of the Shakespearean tragedy. She and Zachary had watched the movie on video, and she had said, *What a great bed.* They'd rewound the film several times to look at it. Zac had said, *I could make a bed like that.*

Grace knew he could. He was a good carpenter, a good craftsman. He'd made them a cherry coffee table once, a replica of one they'd seen at the Metropolitan Museum of Art.

He'd cut a hole through the wall of their apartment.

Grace couldn't imagine it. The image seemed unreal, and swiftly she replaced it with thoughts of the romantic gift Zac had given her on Valentine's Day. A promise to build a bed for them.

She couldn't use the coupon now, so she slid it behind the others and examined the next heart, which read, "This coupon is good for Anything." And the third: "This coupon is good for Doing the Income Tax."

Angel, Grace thought. Almost any man who would offer to do the income tax was a keeper in her book.

But what Zac had done to her was so grave, so unforgivable...

Grace peered out the French doors at the water moving through the moon's reflection on the surface of the river. The sight reminded her of Br'er Rabbit tricking his friends into retrieving the moon from the millpond. Grace knew how Br'er Fox and the others must have felt when they discovered the treachery. It was how she'd felt learning Zac had married her for a green card.

Their love was the moon fallen in the water, suddenly within reach. It was only illusion, though. Couldn't be anything else. But Zac had made her believe it was real.

Then stolen it away.

WHEN HE PARKED the Austin-Healey under the cottonwoods, the only light Zac saw was a small glow from the kitchen, and he knew Grace had gone to bed. In the dark he carried his suitcase and garment bag across the muddy yard to the house. Leaving his shoes on the porch, he opened the kitchen door and let himself in.

At once the smell of food filled his nostrils. Zac spotted the bread cooling on a rack in the oven and the soup pot simmering on the stove, but before he could investigate, the husky pressed against his legs. She rubbed the sides of his jeans, then sat in front of him, looking up ex-

pectantly. Zac set down his luggage, then spent some time
with the dog, rubbing the fluffy fur he'd brushed that
morning. The husky licked his face, showing more energy than she had the day before. Knowing he and the dog
were alone, Zac murmured ridiculous endearments to her,
petted her and generally made much of her before he
stood and went to the stove.

Under the light he admired the loaves Grace had baked
and lifted the lid on the pot, inhaling. On the table was a
note tucked beneath the edge of a pie pan holding a walnut tart—his favorite.

Leaning over the table, Zac read what she'd written.

You can cut the bread and the tart and help yourself
to some soup. When you're finished, please put everything away. Also, there are tea leaves in the pot—
no caffeine. Sweet dreams.

                                             —Grace

Zac braced his hands on the table and stood there quietly for a long time. Then, picking up the pen she'd left
lying on the table, he wrote at the base of the note,
"Thank you, my sweet chef." He scrawled an X and an O
and signed his name, then filled the kettle and put it on the
stove and took out the cutting board to slice the bread.

Perhaps it was because of exhaustion after twelve hours
at the production office, but as he worked under her stove
light Zac couldn't control his thoughts, couldn't stop the
unproductive ones. Unwillingly he remembered month
after month of coming home at night to an empty apartment that was like a shell and fixing quick solitary meals
that always left him hungry. For Grace.

Now he was in her home. She'd made him a wonderful
meal. They were coming back together.

But it felt neither complete nor secure. This glimpse of
the heaven that had once been his was only his now by a

tenuous thread. He wanted to keep it. He wanted more. Things he'd once taken for granted that now he might never possess. Grace. A family.

The teakettle began to spurt steam. Lifting the whistle before it could scream and bother Grace upstairs, Zac held the kettle until it really boiled, then turned off the burner and fixed some tea. Half an hour later, after he'd eaten, put away the food and straightened the kitchen, he collected his suitcase and garment bag and took them through the parlor into the room where Grace had told him to sleep.

The husky padded after him, and Zac smiled at the dog, liking her pointed ears and different-colored eyes. The vet had predicted the dog's adult coat would be black with white markings, and Zac could see the white mask already delineated on her face. Trying to forget that he'd always wanted a husky and trying to remember that this one could not be his, Zac asked, "Spending the night with me?"

The puppy collapsed on the braided rug.

Grace had left on a small tiffany lamp that stood on the Victorian bureau. In its mellow light, Zac walked about the room, examining everything. A rocking chair in the corner that looked a hundred years old. A wedding portrait on the chest—Grace's parents. On the wall, faded photographs of the inn in its heyday.

Zac studied the pictures with interest. The random-width planks on the floor of the screened porch were buffed to a high polish, and the painted pillars were truly white. Seeing a photo of Grace's father and mother standing on the porch, arms about each other, Zac wondered how the owner of such a showplace could have let it go to ruin.

But then his eyes caught those of Grace's mother, and though the photo was black and white, he knew they were brown eyes. Brown eyes with arched black eyebrows.

He saw the way Sam Sutter was looking at his wife, and Zachary knew exactly how the house had fallen apart.

The man had fallen first, when he lost the woman he loved.

CHAPTER SEVEN

AT SIX-FIFTEEN, as Grace filled the French press with coffee grounds in the dawn light from the eastern window, she heard the alarm clock beep in her father's old room, then water running in the bathroom. The husky wandered into the kitchen, and Grace said, "Hello, there." A few minutes later, Zac whistled from the front porch, and the puppy trotted off through the dining room, answering the call to breakfast.

Soon after, Zac joined Grace in the kitchen. He was wearing threadbare gray sweatpants and looked sleepy and unshaven, like the person she used to wake up with every morning. Like her husband.

Grace had found the note he'd written beneath hers and had taken it upstairs to keep. Now, however, she thought of what had happened at the film office. It was the last time she'd seen him, and she still felt embarrassed over her loss of control.

Zachary ended her anxiety. Meeting her at the counter, he reached for her shoulders and hauled her to his bare chest, and Grace felt his heart knocking through her T-shirt as he hugged her close. As she held him, too.

"Good morning." His jaw scraped her silky skin, and his nose burrowed into her neck, feeding on her scent. Stepping back, he lifted her face with his hands, tipping her chin up. Touching. "Grace. Yesterday—" She opened her mouth, and he shook his head. "Let me talk. Obviously the idea of my filming a love scene distresses you."

He remembered the shocking contact of her hand with his face. "I think you're overreacting. But I would never hurt you intentionally. If you don't want me to accept the expanded role, I won't." The words almost made him choke, but there was no alternative. When she'd struck him, he'd seen the pain he was causing. Self-assured Grace—hitting. He was sorry it had come to that.

Grace stared up at him, feeling both the tightness in his body and the tenderness of his hands on her face. She knew what he was sacrificing. Zac had worked long for this chance. *Kah-Puh-Rats* wasn't great cinema, but it might mean a step to better roles. And it was a matter of timing that the producers wanted to expand Zac's part. He was this season's hot male model. Someone else might be hotter next month.

Grace felt the gift he'd offered—choice.

She gave it back to him. She'd been without him, and now, like a miracle, he was in her arms. "It's okay. I want you to do what you think is best for your career."

Zac's heart pressed closer to hers. She had handed him her trust. She wouldn't be sorry. "Thank you."

He was crushing her fiercely, and Grace adored it. But it reminded her how deep things had been, how far down they'd gone, exploring together till they ran out of air. Then—there—where they'd needed each other, they'd separated. And Zac, her love... Suppressing panic, Grace said, "Let's go running. Then I'll make buttermilk, wild-rice, pecan pancakes for breakfast."

Zac didn't let go. He hid his face in her hair, trammeling his thoughts, but they broke loose and filled his mind. Recollections of empty nights and solitary mornings, of strange days and nights in New York, of the bleak world he'd seen around him as he took out a saw and began cutting through the wall of their fourth-floor walk-up, looking for hidden wires, wires to explain the voices he was hearing. Warding off those images and others—the frightening days he'd spent among library stacks in New York and California, trying to learn what had happened to him—he thought of the photo on the wall of the room where he'd just awakened, the picture of Grace's father and the woman with the brown eyes.

His heart whispered the words he knew his mouth wouldn't say again, not after he'd said them and been ignored.

Gracie, don't ever leave me. Don't go....

HE HAD REHEARSAL all day. Grace came home for lunch, but Zac wasn't there, and she ate alone with the dog for company. Nor was he home when she returned that evening. He'd been there, however. Grace saw he'd made more progress on the porch, and she found a note on the kitchen table saying he hoped to be back by nine—but not to fix a meal because he wasn't sure.

During the evening, three people called in answer to his ad in the paper—"Found: Husky puppy. Call..." As she and Zac had agreed, Grace asked each caller the sex of the lost pet, color, and so on. None of the owners belonged to the animal sitting at her feet.

It was ten when the Austin-Healey bumped down the sand road that night. As Zac climbed out of the convertible, script in hand, the husky pushed open the screen door and came down the steps to greet him. Zac petted the dog, then went up to the house, and Grace met him on the porch.

Barefoot, wearing a pair of old gym shorts and a man's sleeveless undershirt, she looked voluptuous and sexy and womanly. Familiar. His. He grabbed her and held on.

Hugging back, she said, "There's soup on the stove." White bean and mushroom. "Also some *perciatelli* and *biscotti.*"

Homecoming. The feeling was so powerful Zac couldn't answer. He listened to leaves rustling and insects humming and the river kissing the shore. He felt the woman in his arms. The Anasazi Palace had nothing on the River Inn. The River Inn had Grace.

She finally pulled away. "Hey, Zac, don't knock yourself out fixing the house. You're working long days on the film."

Staring through a torn screen at the moonlight on the river, Zac wondered if she thought he was going to crack again, the way he had in New York. He didn't answer. He would refinish the floors upstairs and repair the walls, but it was wasted labor. His time in Grace's house by the Colorado was short. He had to return to California—or if not there, New York.

Nonetheless, he liked the work. He always had, even at Oakhurst, when he knew he was putting love and sweat into what would never be his.

The two situations seemed similar.

Grace said, "Come inside and eat."

Zac eyed her with pleasure and whistled a familiar melody as he followed her inside. "Love Is Here to Stay."

Grace glanced over her shoulder at him and smiled.

She'd laid a single place at the table. As the dog settled in its bed and Grace went to the stove to heat water for tea, Zac said, "You're not eating?"

"I ate earlier." Setting a bowl of soup at his place, she eyed the script in his hand and asked, "Why are some of the pages white and some blue and some pink?"

"Changes. The original is white. The first changes were blue. And I got the pink pages before I left tonight."

Wondering if the love scene was pink, Grace started to go back to the stove to get him more food. But Zac grabbed her hand.

"Don't wait on me, Grace. I can help myself."

She looked at him, at his tall body and the way his paisley flannel shirt clung loosely to his broad shoulders.

Aware of his hand holding her fingers, touching her palm, she said, "I want to."

And he wanted to take her to bed. "Leave the dishes. I'll wash up."

"Okay."

Zac sat down and watched her return to the stove to get him a plate of pasta. When she set it in front of him, he said, "Do you have a calendar, Grace? Let's make some plans."

It sounded good to her. Turning away, she took a hardware-store calendar off the wall by the phone. Then she pulled out a chair beside him. When the calendar lay before them, Zac held her hand under the table and let their linked fingers rest on top of his thigh as he scanned her schedule. Production on the film would begin a week from Saturday. On the calendar, Grace had noted certain days with names of places. Desolation Canyon. Labyrinth Canyon. Cataract Canyon.

She told Zac, "That's when you'll be filming on the river."

Zac pointed to the week after the start of production. "I'm going to New York on Tuesday. I have an interview on 'JoAnn.'"

"The JoAnn Carroll Show"? Grace thought. "JoAnn" was big, one of the most popular of the afternoon talk shows.

"I'll be back late Thursday. They're filming around me."

Grace reached across the table for a pen and handed it to him so that he could write on the calendar. Still holding her hand beneath the table, he smiled at her and marked the dates, and Grace felt the intimacy of coordinating schedules, of planning together. Of sitting in her house at ten at night holding hands with him. Of his hard thigh, warm beneath denim... He pressed her hand to his leg and moved his own so that he could eat. After a moment, Grace withdrew. She felt melting hot. Aroused.

Between bites of soup and *perciatelli* and *biscotti,* Zac asked, "Would you like to come to New York?"

Grace's heart rushed, and she stared at the calendar, trying to think if she could.

"I won't have much free time," Zac said. "But we can be together at night. Go out for dinner. Do some things." His eyes suggested what things.

"I'd like that a lot."

"So would I." Zac returned his attention to his food, but Grace saw he was still thinking about plans, and at last he asked, "Did you talk to your lawyer about the money?"

"They faxed me something this afternoon. You can pay them." She should drop the divorce suit now. They were really working things out.

But it had been only a few days.

Zac didn't seem interested in pursuing the topic. He said, "I want to give you some money for groceries and household expenses."

Grace felt strange feelings stirring inside her. He *had* been a good husband. Always. Until she'd left him and things had gotten so bad for him that he couldn't face her until he made his own life right again....

After a few minutes—after they'd set a date to see the musical and another for a picnic in Arches National Park—Grace got up from the table and hung up the calendar. While he sat at the table reading his script, she went upstairs and dressed for bed, putting on a long, white cotton nightgown that Zac used to like. Slipping a thick French terry robe over it, she went back downstairs. He had finished eating and cleaned up, and now he was in the bathroom with the water running. Remembering nights they'd shared a cup of tea before bed, Grace put the kettle on the stove. She was just filling the pot when Zac came into the kitchen.

He wore the faded jeans he'd had on earlier, and his flannel shirt was unbuttoned, as though he was ready to slide everything off and get into bed. Seeing that he could barely keep his eyes open, she set down the kettle and said, "Go to bed."

He smiled drowsily. "Not without a snack." He stood looking at her like a kid contemplating which end of a cookie to bite first. Grace stared back at him, studying all the bones in his face, his handsome features, the lips made for kissing her.

At last Zac took her face in his hands. She trembled, feeling the rough pads of his fingers brushing hair from her brow. Grace knew he saw her shaking. There was a tenderness in his expression that meant he was aware of her vulnerability. Eyes smiling down into hers, he moved half a step closer, saying, "It's all right, Gracie. It doesn't have to end in bed."

Her breath felt dry as the desert, and her voice sounded like tissue paper. "I know."

Zac's mouth came closer, and then it was on hers. Her knees threatened to fold against his. He was untying her robe, and she pulled her head away and choked out, "No."

He didn't pause. He slid his hands inside, wrapped his arms around her between her nightgown and robe. "This is all right, isn't it?" It was all right with him. It was making him hard.

It was heaven. Grace nodded, and then they were kissing again, and she was touching his chest. The words came out although she didn't intend them. "I love you."

Afraid of what he might say, Zac covered her lips before either of them could talk anymore. Some things were easier to communicate without words. And some things shouldn't be said.

Don't leave....

THE NEXT MORNING Zac was up before she was. When Grace went downstairs, the French doors in the parlor were open, and she looked through the screen to see him crouched in the grass beyond the stone patio, studying the ground. He was shirtless, his hair mussed as though he'd just awakened, and the dog hovered near him, wagging its tail. New behavior.

Smiling, Grace pushed open the screen door and went out.

The sky was foggy gray, the air damp, and right away she noticed the mosquitoes were out. She slapped one on her arm as Zac crossed to meet her on the stone steps.

Grace remembered their long kiss the night before, his tongue in her mouth, his hands holding her head and then her shoulders. And she remembered how she had felt when they'd said good-night and he had gone through the house locking up. He was just one person, but suddenly her home was full.

And this morning he was still here.

Zac glanced at the weeds behind him. He wanted to share his idea—a croquet pitch. But he was just dreaming, just having fun imagining...the inn. This was Grace's home, a place dear to her. He shouldn't make her hope they could stay. So all he asked was "Did anyone answer my ad last night?"

Grace nodded. "But not the owners." She told him about the calls.

Zac smiled at the dog, reminding himself not to become attached. "If no one claims her first, we'll have to do something with her when we go to New York. And down the river, of course."

"I'll ask Day if she'll watch her." As Zac threw a stick and the dog bounded after it, Grace said, "She's a nice dog, isn't she? We should call her something."

"She's not ours to name," Zac answered, telling himself as much as Grace.

"Hungry?" she asked after a moment.

"Yes." Zac came up the last two steps and put his arms around her. She wasn't wearing a bra, and the worn cotton of her shirt was little shield between her breasts and his skin. He thought of sex and of food. She sharpened all his appetites. For a man who'd grown up on meals prepared by servants more efficient than friendly, in a world that had been perilously uncertain in the most primal way, Grace's strength and talents were aphrodisiac and nourishment. He would never get enough of her. He said, "I'm always hungry. Tell me where to find a gym, though. I miss my weight machine."

Grace smiled. Zac was lean and rangy and possessed of a bottomless stomach. Putting weight on him was a lifetime task.

And they could have a lifetime....

IT WAS DIFFICULT to explain to Day.

"He's *living* with you?" Day looked at her watch. She looked at the calendar on her desk. She looked at Grace.

Grace knew what she was thinking. Zac had shown up only days ago. Four days. She said, a little defensively, "Well, he has his own room."

Day burst out laughing. "We know how long *that's* going to last."

Grace shut the office door and dropped a life vest on the couch to protect herself from the springs popping through. Sitting down, she faced the sister who had been with her through the hardest times, who'd seen her missing Zac while he'd ignored her existence—while he'd ignored her father's death. Now Day was sitting in her stenographer's chair, the computer humming and a cigarette burning in the ashtray beside her, waiting to know how he'd earned forgiveness.

Grace said, "Day, he had a good reason why he wasn't in touch with me, but it's nothing I can share." She added, "We're working things out."

Day's face betrayed a mix of reactions. Skepticism. Reflection. Acceptance. At last she said, "All right, if you like him, I can like him. Zac has his good points. Looks. Brains. Money. Sexy voice."

Kind to animals. Fixes things, thought Grace. Day would be less complimentary if she knew about the love scene Zac was going to do. Omitting that detail, Grace told her Zachary's movie role had been expanded and she was going to New York with him.

"Zac's going to be on 'JoAnn'?" Day exclaimed. "Is it because of those Ben Rogan ads?"

"I think so."

Day grinned. "You'll probably get to stay at some fabulous hotel and go to Twenty-One." Reaching for her cigarette with a mischievous expression, she asked, "Did you find out how much money he makes? Those Ben Rogan models rake it in. Some of those guys make three thousand dollars an hour."

Grace was stunned. No wonder he could afford to pay her legal bills.

No wonder he wasn't worried about the INS.

Day asked, "Are you bringing the movie star to the musical?"

"Opening night." Thursday, two days before shooting began. And on some unknown date after that, her husband would get into bed naked with Ingrid Dolk.

ON THURSDAY NIGHT Grace was home before Zac. The musical would start at eight, and he had promised he'd be finished with rehearsal by seven-thirty.

At six-thirty, Grace hurried downstairs in her bathrobe, wet-haired from a shower, to throw in a load of laundry. Remembering she'd told Zac she would wash some of his clothes, she went into his room to collect them. The puppy followed her.

She felt strange entering the room. It was Zac's space. It even had a masculine smell that was exclusively his. And all Grace's senses responded to the sight of clothes and books in one corner on the floor and of his shirts hanging in the closet. Once their clothes had been bunched together on the same rod.

Over the past week, they'd established a routine. After they took a morning run with the dog, Zac played the piano while Grace made breakfast. Then he left for the production office and she for Rapid Riggers, sometimes taking the husky along. If Zac had breaks during the day, he went home and worked on her house. And every night they spent a long time kissing... caressing. The night before, his hand had slid inside her gown, to her breasts. It had been hard to part and go to separate rooms. Separate beds. Grace had tossed restlessly, remembering what they'd had in New York.

But nothing would ever be that simple again.

Three times during the week she had found reasons to visit the production office. Meshach Stoker, the director, wanted the actors to practice rowing the Powell dories under the guidance of Rapid Riggers boatmen, so Grace had gone down to the film office to set up a time. On another occasion she'd given Cute Nick and Dirty Bob a ride to the Uratomic Building; they would be doing whitewater stunts for the film and needed to be seen by wardrobe and makeup. And a third time Grace had gone to take another look at the dories. *Talk about a lame excuse....*

She'd watched Zac rehearse with Ingrid. Grace didn't think he was attracted to the actress—though he could make anyone believe it when he was acting. But Grace couldn't help wondering if he'd prefer to be married to someone who shared his work. A man who looked like Zac could have his pick of women. What if he became bored with her and picked someone else?

Grace hid her worry. She never again wanted to reveal the insecurity that had made her hit him. That had made her leave him.

As she stood in his bedroom, she thought of her doubts and wondered if she'd ever be sure. The green card...well, she'd never forget it. But at some point she would have to choose whether to divorce Zac or trust him.

Grace looked at his neatly made bed, and the decision was easy. *I'll tell him tonight.*

They would make love and sleep in each other's arms. Feeling light, both nervous and excited, Grace went to the corner of the room and gathered up a pair of Ben Rogan jeans, a polka-dot shirt, socks and the shorts he wore running. His Oxford sweatshirt was on the bottom, and she picked that up, too, and smelled it. Clean.

As she moved to set it back down, her eyes fell on the books and papers lying against the baseboard. The papers were articles about huskies photocopied from the periodicals on CD-ROM at the Moab library. Zac hadn't been able to find a book about the breed, and he'd said most of the available articles were about sled-dog racing.

Crouching with Zac's laundry in her arms, Grace picked up one of those articles and read a few paragraphs. Though sprint races were popular in the early 1900s, the first long-distance races were run in the seventies. In recent years, the latter had lost much of their sponsorship and been condemned by animal-protection groups because of the number of dogs who died, usually from heart failure. But even the race conditions sounded harsh. Temperatures sometimes fifty degrees below zero, surprise blizzards, the dogs' paws bleeding through their booties.... Nonetheless, huskies were born for that climate. Instinctively they dug holes in the snow for warmth at night. And the mushers used only voice commands to direct their dogs, no whips or reins.

Glancing down at the puppy Zac had found, Grace reflected that once dog sleds had been the only cross-tundra transport. That was the heritage of the Siberian husky. Now the dog at her feet was living in the desert.

But where was her home? Would her owners ever turn up?

Grace set down the article and straightened, then scanned the titles of Zachary's books. A battered paperback collection of Tennessee Williams plays. A novel by Julio Cortázar. And *An Actor's Handbook* by Constantin Stanislavski. Beneath that lay a large paperback volume with a crimson cover. Grace couldn't see the front, so she glanced at the binding.

DSM-IV. Strange name. Probably another book about acting. As she dropped Zac's sweatshirt on the books, Grace heard the kitchen door, and the puppy raced out of the room. Zac was home. Still holding the dirty clothes, Grace went out to meet him.

He was greeting the dog, rubbing her head and scratching her ears. He had a treat in his hand, and when he saw Grace, he told the puppy, "Sit. Sit. Good girl." He gave her the dog biscuit, then carried the laundry to the utility room for Grace. As he lifted the lid on the washing machine, he looked down at the clothes and froze.

He'd thrown them in the corner of his room.

On top of the books.

Heart pounding, he stuffed the laundry into the machine and hurried back into the kitchen, his eyes immediately searching Grace's. She smiled at him.

She didn't see it.

He fought down the tense, panicky feeling binding his chest. It wasn't as though he needed to hide the book from her. After all, he'd told her the facts.

But he couldn't lose Grace again. She was his stability. In the world of acting, anything could and did change without notice. The script was five different colors now, and new decisions faced him daily. An invitation to model for his own calendar. Offers for interviews. His life was hurtling forward faster than he could control it.

Coming home to the River Inn at night, waking up there in the morning to the dog licking his hand, eating the meals Grace made, running, hammering nails...made him feel strong, like a different person than he'd been for the past year, when he was alone, haunted by what had happened in New York.

Here, he slept without nightmares.

Grace was still smiling at him. She was in her bathrobe, not yet dressed for the play, and Zac briefly placed his hands on her shoulders. "Wait here," he said. "Don't move."

He hurried down the hall and through the parlor to his room, where he went to the closet and dragged out his suitcase. He found the shopping bag and took out the dress. It was a Ben Rogan design, a glove-soft leather sheath in four colors—red, yellow, blue and black. He'd bought it on Rodeo Drive for Grace, when he wasn't sure if he'd ever see her wear it.

Leaving his suitcase, Zac turned to go back out to the kitchen, but his eyes caught his sweatshirt in the corner of the room.

Pulse tripping, he went over and picked it up, looking beneath. Tennessee Williams, Stanislavski and *Hopscotch* on top. Breathing hard, he grabbed the book under them and looked around the room for a place to put it. The shopping bag caught his eye. Battling guilt, he wrapped *DSM-IV* in the bag and closed it in his empty suitcase.

Then he went out to Grace.

THEY REACHED the Moab Community Theater at twenty to eight and found places in the fifth row with a crowd of boatmen from Rapid Riggers. Zac sat between Grace and Fast Susan, a six-foot thirty-eight-year-old guide with a blond mohawk. Susan had just returned from a Cataract Canyon trip. While the accompanist played songs from *Oklahoma!* on the piano and while they waited for the lights to dim, Susan talked about the river. To Zac it was a foreign language, but he got her gist. The river was high; the rapids were big; Cataract Canyon was scary.

"A Current Adventures guide hit a lateral and flipped a mini J-rig in Mile Long Rapid. One of the passengers got Maytagged in a keeper for a *long* time...."

Zac glanced over at Grace. She looked beautiful in the Ben Rogan dress. She'd exclaimed over it—then, with Graceful candor, asked him how much money he made. Now he could see that her mind was on the river.

Turning to Zac in the seat beside her, she asked, "You're going to row in the movie, aren't you?" She couldn't imagine he wouldn't. Zac had won his blue—the equivalent of earning a letter—in crew at Oxford and rowed in the Oxford-Cambridge Boat Race. When he nodded she said, "You need to put in some time at the oars. Why weren't you at the white-water clinics we set up for the actors?"

He'd had to rehearse. The producers had said, *You'll be fine. Don't worry about rowing.* He hadn't—simply because he'd had bigger worries. But his daily training at the Moab Athletic Club was no substitute for practice in white water. He asked Grace, "Will you take me out in your boat? I have tomorrow afternoon free."

Grace knew how rare that was. "I'd love to. We'll have a picnic." As the lights dimmed in the theater, she looked over at his profile in the dark and remembered the decision she'd made about their marriage. Her hand smoothed the exquisite soft leather of her dress. It was a lovely gift. But what mattered was that he'd thought about her when they were apart. Enough to wangle a recipe from a French chef. Enough to buy a Ben Rogan dress in her size. Enough to order a custom-made music box to remind her of the sweet early days of their courtship.

Enough. More than enough.

THE MUSICAL was delightful, and the pleasure of the audience was tangible. In a town as small as Moab, the opportunity to see a play came only a few times a year, and Zac could see that the community appreciated its actors.

At intermission, while he studied the program, Grace told him about the players. "Conrad owns the ice-cream parlor. He's always in the musicals. Great dancer. And I think Bart is going to be in *Suddenly Last Summer.* He was really great when they did *One Flew over the Cuckoo's Nest.*"

Listening to her, Zac envied the actors in the show—and in future Moab productions. Good plays. No twelve-hour days. No incessant script changes.

No money.

Zac knew he was lucky to be able to earn a living doing what he loved. He shouldn't think about how much more he loved the stage. But what attracted him about the theater had less to do with scripts or working conditions than with the interchange between actor and audience that occurred with a play. He missed it.

However, inevitably, watching the musical reminded him of the last time he'd been on stage and of the performance he hadn't finished.

Leaving Hong Kong.

As the lights dropped again and the curtain rose, he slid his hand into Grace's and held on, thinking of solitary nightmares and private things he'd never shared, even with her. And of New York.

He was still brooding when he became aware of Grace rustling in the seat beside him. She was making a note on her program. A note to herself, Zac thought.

But she passed it to him, and as the piano tinkled out the introduction to "Surrey with the Fringe on Top," Zachary peered down and read her writing in the dark.

COUPON. 1 Lifetime Married to You.

Zac felt a loose heat inside him at the top of his chest. He pressed back in the theater seat, his breath shallow. Eyes sliding over to hers, he placed the program back in her lap, and his hand closed on her bare thigh.

She looked at him with big dark eyes.

Moving his hand, Zac put his arm around her and pulled her against him. His head beside hers, his mouth touching her ear, he whispered, "I'll cash that right now."

CHAPTER EIGHT

ZAC WAS HARD for the rest of the play, thinking of sex, of getting home and removing Grace's clothes. After the final curtain call, he felt barely present as they congratulated Day and he gave her the flowers he'd bought.

Helping Grace into the Austin-Healey, he bent to kiss her, his tongue promising every conjugal pleasure. He wanted to be inside her, but he wanted other things, too. To hold her in his arms, her bottom nestled against his groin and his thigh, her back warming his chest as he drifted off to sleep. To awaken in the dark . . . with her.

They drove home with her hand over his on the stick shift, enough contact to call up the past, the way it had always been. The heat and affection and deep closeness. Impossible to take it slow.

When they reached the River Inn, Zac kept his arm around her and felt hers around him as they went inside. And when he turned to lock the door, Grace put her hands on the back of his jeans, feeling him. He ducked into his room to get condoms from his suitcase. Then, followed by the husky, he and Grace walked upstairs together.

On the way he unzipped her dress, and once they were in her room, standing in the moonlight coming through the French doors, she turned to him and began trying to unbutton his black paisley silk shirt.

The buttons were tight in the holes. Feeling his hands on her back where he'd opened her dress, Grace grew frustrated. "Take off your shirt, Zac." From the floor the puppy observed them curiously for a moment, then let her eyes flutter shut, as though content that all was well.

Zac kept his eyes on Grace's as he unbuttoned his shirt. She watched.

"Take off your dress, Gracie."

Her face felt hot. Loosening the leather sheath, she pulled it down. Off her shoulders. Over her breasts.

Zac stood looking at her underwear, the white cotton panties and bra with apples on them. They were his favorites, and Grace knew it. He said, "I think you planned this."

Grace met his eyes. "Yeah. The first time I saw you."

In the moonlight, Zac gazed at her long, strong limbs, her mix of tan lines from working outdoors in different clothes. Her high, beautiful breasts. She was the sexiest, most interesting woman he'd ever known. He wanted her hand on him, and he put it there, on his fly.

Grace's heartbeat quickened. Patience expired. She opened the buttons on his jeans. He unhooked her bra and drew it off. Greedy and eager, they came together, her nipples against his chest, all hands below deck. Sliding her panties down...

Grace felt old emotions shivering through her. She remembered this. Long subway rides, get home, rip off clothes. Make love for a long time. All night.

She jerked back from him, holding his arms lightly, savoring the feel of him as she said, "Wait." Naked she turned toward the armoire.

Immediately Zac noticed the music box. He stepped up behind her, slid his arms around her and began to sing softly, his mouth pausing to caress her jaw. Trembling, loving it, Grace opened her pink jewelry chest.

Zac knew what she was doing, and the song died on his lips. *Our love,* he thought. Here to stay.

Grace turned in his arms. In the dark Zac couldn't see the objects she held, but he knew what they were. He lifted his palm beneath her hand, between their bodies.

The cool metal fell against his skin, and his fingers closed on the two tiny trinkets. He looked into her eyes, then reached up and smoothed her hair behind her right ear. He carefully placed the hoop in the little hole in her lobe, then secured the back. Touching the heart and the diamond that dangled from the hoop, he put his mouth on the underside of her jaw, drinking her skin. As he kissed her, he groped for her left hand, pausing to stroke the wet place between her legs. Her right hand closed around his erection, applying pressure, and her other hand spread on his chest. In the midst of that marital intimacy, he put her wedding ring back on her finger.

They were in bed in a second. Zac lay on his back and gazed up at her as she moved over him, her long hair sweeping his face. He pressed up against her, unable to help it, and slid his hands beneath her, touching her while she touched him. While they looked into each other's eyes in the moon's glow.

She moved against him, made him feel her wetness, and his head went back. He said, "Grace, wait." Birth control. No babies now.

He shuttered up dark thoughts. New York...

Grace, knowing why he'd stopped her, was tearing open a packet, touching him, her eyes on his. Banishing worry, Zac concentrated on her, stroking her the way she liked. He was so hard.... She slid down on him, taking him inside.

"Gracie." Pressing deeper inside her, he grabbed her and pulled her tight against him.

She was already shuddering over him, saying his name, lying down on him, her heart on his. It was a ritual they'd performed countless times, as many ways as they knew, and now she was moaning, calling to him. And as she ran the waves, as they jarred her, shook through her, she heard Zachary answering in the same language, with inarticulate cries that were the most articulate words of love.

It seemed to last a long time, and then she lay against him, her body nerveless, her face against his skin. His arms enveloped her. His kisses covered her face. Tender emotion and whispered words. "I love you." Rolling onto his side with her, Zac tucked the covers around her. Moving her hair, he kissed her mouth again, touching his tongue to hers. Grace watched his face in the night. The face beside her on the pillow. Her best friend. Her husband. She would never leave him again. She would follow him to the ends of the earth.

Or somewhere darker and deeper.

Thoughts came to her. They pecked their way out of the dark corners of her mind. She imagined things she didn't want to imagine. Things that seemed unimaginable.

Zachary, standing naked on a fire escape. Zachary, sawing a hole in a wall. Zachary, her lover, her *husband,* sleeping in condemned buildings with homeless people.

Zachary.

Mad.

Rejecting the word as soon as it came to her, she brought her face to his chest, to his heart, smelling him, feeling the life in him. The strength. *He's all right now,* she thought. *He's all right.*

THE ALARM CHIRPED at six, and Zac felt Grace moving beside him, leaning across him to shut it off. As he rolled over and silenced the noise himself, the dog licked his hand. Grace relaxed against him, snuggling up to his back, her slim arm stretching around him, and Zac remembered the night before. Promises and love. Like it used to be but more. He found her hand, and his fingers wove into a knot with hers.

Grace felt the cords of muscles in his stomach as they held hands so tightly. After a while, he sat up sleepily and looked down at her from under sexy, bed-mussed hair. Her breasts were exposed above the sheet, and she saw him smiling at her body. He took her left hand and fingered her ring as he met her eyes, his own mossy green under a forest of black lashes. His five-o'clock shadow formed a rogue's mustache on his upper lip, a bandit's beard on his jaw, and Grace thought of the Ben Rogan ads. *If they photographed you like this, sales would really take off.*

He lay down beside her, the heavy weight of his arm falling across her, and drew her to him. Masculine insistence, powerful body, beckoning husband.

Grace moved closer. One of her legs slid between his, and their eyes met again, heads on the pillows. He was smiling, and she smiled, too.

He said, "Good morning, my wife."

They made love, coming hard enough to shake the floor, and afterward Grace begged off their run. While she showered, Zac went outside with the dog to stretch. Against the gray day, the Colorado had assumed a hue like rust, and mosquitoes and gnats, spawn of the water, whined around him. Part of the bank had disappeared overnight. There was a lot of water flowing by. A lot of river.

Zac was glad the inn was out of reach.

As he headed up the driveway with the husky, Zac tried to prolong the good feelings of the night. Grace was his again.

But it felt impermanent. What had happened before could happen again. She could leave. And even if she didn't . . . *She doesn't know how bad it was,* Zac thought. She couldn't know. Telling wasn't the same.

He distracted himself with plans. They'd stay in his apartment until they could find a new place in California, maybe in the hills or beside the ocean.

But what about the River Inn? Would Grace sell it? In his mind, Zac saw the faded photos in the room off the parlor. He imagined the floor of the screened porch polished and glossy, a ceiling fan turning lazily overhead, European tourists and cyclists in spandex sipping drinks at small tables while a couple of scrubbed and adorable children brought them appetizers from inside. *Family.* A dog, too. He eyed the homeless husky, running ahead of him. He thought of Grace in the kitchen kneading bread, chopping, stirring . . .

No, he thought. *I'm an actor. I'll always be an actor. And as for children . . .* His stomach wrenched. *We've got to talk about it,* he thought.

Soon.

When he returned to the inn, Grace was cooking breakfast. She didn't want help, so he went into the living room to play the piano. He should have it tuned—

We're not going to stay here.

His fingers touched the keys, and he lost himself in one of Chopin's polonaises, then a slow, somnolent nocturne. But he couldn't stop the thoughts that had come over him on his run. Kids.

Numbly he thought of his mother, and a memory shivered through him. The sound of sobbing behind the door. Voices. At least he hadn't inherited his mother's problems. But what was wrong with him?

Nothing.

His eyes slid to the mantel.

Dear maid, kind sister, sweet Ophelia!

He stopped playing, covered the keys, and got up and left the room, the dog scrambling to her feet to follow.

Despite the rain, Zac and Grace decided to take the afternoon raft trip they'd discussed at the play. Before leaving for the production office, Zac backed the Suburban up to the carriage house and hitched the boat trailer to the vehicle for Grace. She would take the dory to work, and he would meet her when he was finished with rehearsal.

That morning at the office, between chores for Rapid Riggers, Grace packed a picnic dinner for the river trip, then put together some things she wanted to give Zac. One was a watertight ammunition can. The cans were the catchall container of outfitters, good for keeping small personal items dry on the river. Each passenger was issued an ammo can at the beginning of a trip, and each boatman had his own.

Zac would be spending days on the river filming, so Grace searched out an old gray can in the upstairs loft. Locating some brown paint, she decorated it with primitive petroglyphlike figures and wrote his name on the lid. Then she collected a new Rapid Riggers plastic coffee cup and a black baseball cap with the outfit's crossed-oars logo on the front.

She was unearthing another item from the back of her desk drawer when Day came in. Turning to her sister, Grace held up the object. "Do you want this?"

Day shook her head. "No. Really, it doesn't mean anything to me."

"Can I give it away? I offered it to Nick when Dad died, but he has a much better one."

Day smiled, rolling her eyes a little. "Yeah. Nick always has the best toys. New kayak. New climbing harness." She sighed. "New river outfit."

Grace regarded the item in her hand. It wasn't a toy. But then, Day wasn't a river guide.

For the first time in her life, Grace found that worrisome. Granted, Day understood the river business—the permit system, taxes, marketing, dealing with tour operators and so on. And she participated in a wilderness medicine course every two years and kept her Red Cross certifications current.

But she was not a river guide. In fact, she was removed enough from the actual reality of what occurred on a river trip that she'd referred to a boatman's knife as a "toy."

Grace knew she had to think about it. She had promised herself to Zac, and that meant she would be leaving Rapid Riggers.

Could Day run the outfit alone?

Her sister distracted her from the question. Freshly lit cigarette in hand, she tossed something on Grace's desk. It was a new issue of a popular film magazine, and Day said, "I saw that in the grocery store today. Thought you might like to have it."

The cover showed a picture of a cartoon character from the latest Disney animated feature. But farther down were the words Sexy And Close To His Clothes: Is Zachary Key Close To Stardom, Too?

Day flipped open the magazine to the one-page article in the middle and the picture of Zac with his shirt open, tails out, plenty of five-o'clock shadow, sexy green eyes— too much like the way Grace had seen him in bed that morning when he was supposed to be just hers.

Grace pulled up her desk chair and sat down, staring at the photo. He was a sight to arouse any woman's fantasies, and she imagined there were already fans out there who felt too keenly the impact of that body, that face, that sun-singed long hair. Fans who might obsess over him. Who might even become dangerous.

Fame was no one's master. It had a life of its own.

Tearing her eyes from Zac's image, Grace read the interview while her sister leaned against the edge of the desk, smoking. She was shocked. The introductory paragraph described women gazing slack-jawed at a man on their television screens whose fingers were unbuttoning the fly of his Ben Rogan jeans. The ad was so popular that women taped it on their VCRs to replay whenever they liked. They bombarded networks and modeling agencies with letters—to Zachary Key.

Grace had never even seen the television ad. It was banned on all the stations out of Salt Lake City, and she didn't watch that much TV anyhow. Clearly she'd been missing a big part of the . . . well, picture.

According to the article, Zachary Key was the stuff of women's fantasies, and he was on his way up. The writer mentioned the voice with which he spoke "the Queen's English" and the fact that he wore loud shirts and had a smile that immediately made a woman think of bedrooms. And of course his role in *Kah-Puh-Rats*. She left the rest to the questions, and Zac's sense of humor and intelligence came through in spades. But the journalist's final question set the tone for the piece.

"Are you presently wearing underwear?"

His answer was "a sexy and inconclusive smile." Grace knew that smile.

Nowhere did the article say he was married.

Day grinned as she drew on her cigarette. "What do you think?"

Grace closed the magazine and shrugged, more shaken than she cared to admit. Before she could answer, Day's gasp drew her glance upward.

Her sister was staring at her left hand. "Your ring!"

Grace nodded. She'd called her attorney that morning. It was over.

And it had just begun.

Day asked, "Will you move to California?"

Grace stared at the glossy film magazine. "Yes."

She heard footsteps on the porch outside, and the bell on the door chimed. Grace glanced out the window and saw the Austin-Healey. Standing up, eyes blinking past Day's, she stepped over Zac's ammo can and hurried out the doorway to the reception area.

Zac was leaning his head and shoulders over the
swinging doors to the kitchen, looking for her. He wore
blue jeans and a polyester shirt in a black-and-white
checkerboard print—a Salvation Army special they'd
chosen together. The pattern would have looked gro-
tesque on another man. It epitomized Zac. *Don't change,*
she thought. *Don't let them change you.*

As she slipped behind the reception counter, Zac
turned. When she saw his face, Grace thought of the article and everything it meant. He moved toward her, and
Grace couldn't stop. She hurled herself against his body
and held on to him like a person trying to hold a planet
and keep it from its orbit.

She knew holding back Zachary would be just as impossible—and just as wrong.

THE RAIN HAD STOPPED, so they changed into bathing
suits, shorts and T-shirts for the river trip. Zac carried the
cooler and dry bags filled with extra clothing out to the
boat. Then he followed in the Austin-Healey as Grace
drove the Suburban hauling the boat trailer across the
bridge and left on the river road, heading upstream to the
Daily. They stopped at the takeout to leave Zac's car for
a shuttle vehicle; after that, he rode with Grace in the
Suburban to a little-used put-in just above Onion Creek
Rapid.

High water had submerged the boat ramp, but Zac got
the dory in the water while Grace kept both car and trailer
from being stuck in the silt. It took them twenty minutes
to finish rigging. Everything had to be tied down, so that
nothing would be lost if they flipped in a rapid. As they
worked Grace told Zac the most important safety rules for
the river.

When the boat was rigged, she locked the Suburban and
joined him at the water's edge. Nodding at the name on

the bow, Zac asked, "Why did you call her *Persephone?*"

"For Demeter's daughter in the Greek myth. You know. Each year when she comes up from the underworld to visit her mother, spring returns—river-running season."

Now the dory was riding high in the water, her blue paint immaculate, her form shapely. Grace hadn't used the boat since she'd returned from New York. She'd believed it would be a painful reminder of her father, but it was a good reminder, instead. And it would be a good boat for Zac to handle in his first white water.

Eyeing the water sweeping past the opposite bank, Grace shivered. The Daily should be a blast with this much water. But Cataract?

The morning clouds had disappeared and the sun was heating the beach, so she stripped down to her bikini and Zac pulled off his T-shirt. They were alone on the shore lined with tamarisk, isolated from eyes—rubbing sunscreen on each other's bodies became a lingering pleasure. As he massaged cream over her breastbone, his fingers sliding under the edges of her crocheted bikini top, Zac asked, "Are there any side canyons on this trip? Private beaches?"

Grace lowered her eyes, already wanting him. "Did you bring the condoms?"

"Of course. They're in my new ammo can. I'm glad we're going to make love, instead of war. At first I thought we needed ammo cans because you were expecting a shoot-out with a rival outfitter."

Grace laughed. Remembering the other thing she wanted to give him, she turned away, inviting caresses to her exposed backside as she bent over her own ammo can and found her father's river knife in its sheath. Sweeping up a life vest from the beach, she tossed it to Zac. "Here. Put this on."

He did, and Grace zipped the front and adjusted the straps. Then she showed him the river knife. "This was my dad's. You can have it now. There's a thumb release on the sheath. See?"

Touched, Zac took it from her. He tried the thumb release and pulled the blade from the sheath.

"I sharpened it this morning. You can put it on your life vest here—" Grace touched the loop "—and you'll have it if you ever get caught on a line or something. They're good for cutting out the floors of pinned rafts, too. But you won't be on a raft."

Zac ducked his head and kissed her mouth. Eyes on hers, he said, "Thank you. I'll treasure it."

Grace was sober. "Just remember you have it. The Daily's nothing, but Cataract Canyon can be scary. The river report today said it's running at seventy thousand cfs."

Cubic feet per second, Zac thought.

"The usual for this time of year is about twenty-five. And I think it'll go up some more before you film there."

Zac wasn't concerned. If Grace could handle it, so could he. Clipping the sheathed knife to the loop on his vest, he nodded at the other life jacket on the beach. As Grace scooped it up and put it on, he saw that her knife was already attached—and he was glad of it.

He asked, "Shall I shove off?"

"I will. You row."

Zac moved agilely from a flat rock on the shore and into the dory. Grace handed him her ammo can, and he tied it down for her. She untied the bowline and shoved the boat away from the shore, accepting his hand as she climbed aboard.

While she settled herself against the cooler and dry bags, and Zac rowed them out into the river, Grace said, "Ship the oars and let us drift. The river's moving fast.

We'll hit Onion Creek Rapid in a minute. Listen. You can hear it.''

The low, roaring sound of the white water grew louder, and as Grace located a bail bucket just in case, she told Zac about rafting techniques and reading the river.

After listening to a long stream of suggestions, Zac grinned at her, adding, ''And I should stay out of holes.''

''Well,'' said Grace, ''some holes you can actually run. You have to look at the shape of them, what the water's doing. If the surface current kicks outward and the hole looks like a smile as you approach it, then you can run it. The frowning holes, where the current flows inward, are the keepers.''

As the sound of the water became almost deafening, Zac looked downstream and saw the churning foam. Grace stood up and stepped over one oar to get behind him. Taking a seat, she peered around him at the rapid. Onion Creek was not the bed of ripples she remembered, and the route of choice was no longer the way she'd described it to Zac.

But he found the tongue amidst the swirling white and dug in with the oars, guiding the dory down the smooth V at the top of the rapid. Grace could barely tear her eyes from his body to watch the river.

There was a hole on the left, formed by a rock that in most years was above water. Zac slid past it, seeming to know instinctively when to let the river make the choices. As the first in a row of six-foot standing waves washed over the bow, dousing them with cold water, Grace began bailing.

When they were through the rapid, Zac pulled up the oars and helped her. Grace said, ''You're a good boatman. Want a job?''

Zac knew she was joking. But it hit him the same way it had when she'd given him her father's river knife. She had a life here, and he almost wished he could be part of it, rather than insisting she follow him. But he was an actor, and they needed the money.

In case . . .

He turned to her. She'd braided her hair and put on a wide-brimmed leather Indiana Jones hat that looked as though it had seen a hundred rivers. Finding her mouth beneath the dripping brim, Zac kissed her and said, "I love you."

In Professor Creek Rapid, they met a wave that swamped the boat. Spotting new rapids ahead, they eddied out and stopped at a beach on river right to empty the water. They'd started late in the day, and now theirs was the only boat on that stretch of the river. After Zac had tied the bowline around a bush growing beside the shore, he collected what he wanted from his ammo can and took Grace's hand.

Beyond the beach was an inviting side canyon. Holding hands, they followed a narrow path through scrub oak and over and around large red and black boulders, tall rock walls squeezing them from each side. Only because the sun was still high did patches of light reach the canyon floor, and the shape of the cliff walls hinted that they'd held walls of ice on cold winter days, year after year, for centuries.

As they walked he dropped her hand and slid his arm around her. They'd left life jackets and sun hats with the dory. Feeling his skin, Grace thought, *This is real. We love each other, and it has nothing to do with sexy ads or love scenes or fans who write him letters. . . .* But the other side of Zachary was real, too. She asked him, "When are you going to film that scene?"

Zac bent his head so that he could see her face. Her lush black eyebrows were drawn together almost imperceptibly. Wondering what she was thinking, he answered, "I don't know. I'll find out the day before we film it. By the way, it's scene twenty-five.''

And it would be nothing like what he did with Grace. He would not be making love to Ingrid. He would not, he hoped, get an erection. It would all be... acting.

Grace, on the other hand...

They made love at the end of the box canyon, where water falling from the clifftop had created a deep pool, a sinkhole in the rock and sand. They sat on a warm boulder, kissing and undressing each other, and then he slid down to stand on a ledge below. From there, he could press his lips to the insides of her thighs and caress her in the most loving and private way he knew. Grace lay against the warm rock, shuddering from the feel of his mouth. Trembling, she clung to him as he lifted her down onto the ledge.

Zac unfastened her hands from him. Gently turning her, he placed her palms on the hot sandstone, and Grace let her breasts and her thighs touch the sun-warmed boulder. It felt dryer and more healing than a sauna or a bath. She'd spent much of her life lying on such rocks, never wanting to move. Now the hot sandstone kissed her on one side as Zac hugged her on the other. He was cradling her, protecting her, holding her tight, shielding her with his body.

His words poured in her ears, rained down on her neck as he pulled her closer, pressed deeper into her, made her ache with love. There was a crying sound coming from her throat, and his hands reached in front of her to rub the heart spot above her breasts, to touch her breasts themselves, to keep her close. His face against her hair, he whispered soothing words that made her forget everything but the healing warmth of the sun and Zachary, guiding her through a maelstrom of feeling to a sea of love.

Afterward they sat down on the rock ledge together, nuzzling, kissing, touching. They were closed away from the world, away from all eyes but those of a golden eagle soaring on thermals overhead, and Grace felt Zac's love for her as much as her own for him. She wanted him to know the promises she'd made him were true. As Zac settled against the boulder, she laid her head in his lap and asked, "Where are we going to live in California?"

Fingers stroking her hair, Zac closed his eyes and put his head back, letting the sun warm his face. "I have an apartment in Santa Monica. I thought we'd find something else." He wanted a place that was theirs, a permanent place. Like Oakhurst.

Or the River Inn.

"I spend a lot of time in hotels. Will you hate that?"

Her eyes fluttered open. "'Wherever you go, I will go. Wherever you lodge, I will lodge, your people shall be my people, and your God my God.'"

Zac smiled. "You know who said that, don't you?"

Her eyes were closed again. "No."

"Ruth—to her mother-in-law. They were leaving Moab."

Grace laughed, and he felt her moving her head, brushing her lips against his stomach. The part of him he'd thought she'd sated began to stir. Her tongue licked sweat off his skin.

"Grace, remember that coupon you threw in the hearth?"

Her lips teased him, began to take him. "When have I ever made you use a coupon?"

CHAPTER NINE

FOUR DAYS LATER they left for New York for Zac's appearance on "The JoAnn Carroll Show."

Before they left they took the husky's bowls and food and brush over to Day's house and delivered the dog to Rapid Riggers. Zac hated to leave the puppy, but at least she'd spent enough time at the river outfit to know Day. She shouldn't be too unhappy.

Sitting on the dirty office couch in a powder blue linen suit, stockings and heels, Day petted the dog as she asked, "Does she have a name?"

Grace looked at Zac, but he was staring at the husky. He scraped his teeth lightly over his bottom lip. At last he said, "Ninochka."

After he'd said an extended goodbye to the puppy and he and Grace were in the Austin-Healey headed ten miles north to the airfield, she said, "Ninochka."

Zac's eyes remained on the road as he drove past the entrance to Arches National Park. "Between you and me she'll have plenty of attention."

Grace smothered a smile.

"We'll have her spayed when we get back." The vet had suggested it be done before the dog was six months old. Shots, too. Collar. Tags. Again Zac wondered where he and Grace would live when they returned to California. The husky would need room to run, as she had at the River Inn.

Grace asked, "Why Ninochka?"

He shrugged. "It's a Russian name. I heard it when I was young, and I've always liked it. It means 'girl.'" The husky had been Ninochka in his mind for a week, but he'd kept it to himself, never calling the dog anything. But now, like Grace, he doubted the original owners would return to find her. She'd been abandoned.

And she was his.

HE AND GRACE took a small propeller plane to Salt Lake City and flew first class to New York. Zac had no appointments till the following morning, when he would appear on "JoAnn," so they would have the evening to themselves in the city where they'd met and fallen in love.

On the plane they ordered Courvoisier and worked crossword puzzles and talked. As they flew over the Rockies Grace said, "This is kind of like a honeymoon."

They'd never had one. *Leaving Hong Kong* hadn't allowed it. Thinking of who he'd been when he married her—of why he'd married her—Zac looked down at Grace, in her denim bustier and jacket, jeans skirt and cowboy boots. He remembered her question that first night he'd come to the River Inn. Would he have married her if he hadn't needed a green card? He still didn't know. From the first their relationship had been like...white water. Faster and stronger than either of them.

Love that had made him lose his mind when she left.

Zac borrowed her pen and scrawled on a cocktail napkin, "Coupon good for one honeymoon." Handing it to her, he said, "This trip won't be a honeymoon. But we'll have one." And in the meantime he'd give her everything he could. He wanted to remind her of what they'd been together, what they'd had. But he knew that nothing could restore the innocence of the early days of their marriage.

Grace's leaving had changed him. Before, always, things had come easily to him. Scholastically. Athletically. Socially. At Eton, he'd been Keeper of the Oppidan Wall, captain of his team for the traditional Wall Game, a rare honor in context. Rowing in the Oxford-Cambridge Boat Race, the same. Acting was as natural to him as other skills—carpentry, music. Women liked him. There'd been little he'd wanted that he hadn't been able to get, by wit or finesse or tenacity. Until he'd met the INS. And when he'd had to choose between his honor and what he wanted, a green card, he'd chosen the latter. He did love Grace. But he'd never counted on loving her so much. Or on her leaving. And what happened afterward had shown him he was as vulnerable as anyone.

He thought of the book he'd left at home in one of the bureau drawers. Nothing in the *DSM-IV* had pointed conclusively to a genetic problem. Nonetheless, as soon as he had a chance, another break in filming, he would make himself see a doctor—for Grace and their future. No need to worry her till he had some answers.

God. What those might be.

A LIMO TOOK THEM from the airport to one of the finest hotels in the city. Their room was on the top floor and furnished in elegant dark woods with an old feel. Sheer curtains played over the windows, and there was just one king-size bed. They tried it out first thing.

Grace went into the bathroom to put on the red leather teddy Day had given her for a wedding gift so long ago. When she came out, Zac's smile was tender and affectionate. As they slid between the sheets together, he gathered her against him like treasure.

Later, when the scrap of red lay in the far corner of the room where he'd tossed it, he leaned back against the fluffy white pillows with Grace in his arms. The red teddy had made him think of Day, and Day made him think of Rapid Riggers—and taking Grace to California. He asked, "What are you going to do about that river out-fit?"

Grace knew what he meant. "How much time do I have?"

He shrugged, sliding down on the bed beside her. Grace saw honey-brown skin, broad shoulders over her, muscular arms reaching around her, mink-colored hair in her face. "You don't have to sell. But I've wondered—why don't you and Day swap? Your half of the river outfit for her half of the house. Or whatever's fair."

Grace barely breathed. "Are you thinking we could keep the house?"

"It's your family place. The old boiler from the steamboat. The spring and the still nearby." *Our children should have those things....* He killed the thought. But Day didn't want the River Inn; she called it a white elephant. In his eye, the place was a lady, a lady with her shoes off, lounging on the banks of a red river in one of those rare spots of wild country that might remain so for decades to come, because it was too hard for it to be anything else. He told Grace, "I'd love it to be our home. I don't know how much time we can spend there, but..." His eyes met hers.

Grace was thrilled. They couldn't reopen the inn, but at least they could keep it. She said, "I'll ask Day when we get back to Moab."

Grace had brought a suit to wear to sit in the audience of "The JoAnn Carroll Show," but Zac wanted to take her shopping for something new, so they ordered dinner from room service from the fine restaurant downstairs and showered while they waited for it. Forty-five minutes later, they rode the elevator down to the lobby to get a cab.

As the taxi carried them through the glittering streets, Grace looked out the windows. Recalling their old haunts—Jean-Michel's and their funky East Village walk-up—she felt no wistfulness. All she could think of was the day she'd left Zac there. And what had happened to him. Watching the passing lights play over his profile, Grace wondered if he was remembering, too. She put her hand in his and said, "We have a different New York now."

He read her thoughts, his own black. "Yes."

They went to a Madison Avenue boutique that was open late and found a three-piece Ben Rogan ensemble that suited Grace's figure and style faultlessly. Yellow bouclé jacket over a nautical black-and-white tee and black wide-legged pants. No alterations needed. While two saleswomen spent another half hour helping Grace choose accessories, Zac browsed the racks. Before they left, he asked Grace to try on a taffeta slip-dress with a full skirt and bustier top. It fit, too, and she liked it, and he had clothes, shoes and accessories sent back to the hotel. After that, they took a cab to a club called the Black-and-White Diner, where a jazz band was playing.

They'd been dancing for half an hour when the first strains of "Love Is Here to Stay" filled the club. Eyeing Zac suspiciously, Grace asked, "Did you plan this?" He'd been checking the newspapers before they left the hotel.

He smiled. "The first time I saw you."

As the saxophone wailed, serenading them, Grace felt the solidity of his body against her, heard him singing softly in her ear, noticed his arousal. Her lover. When the song ended, she looked up into his eyes and he said, "Let's get out of here."

They were leaving the dance floor when the band leader gave Zac a telling wink. Yes, thought Grace, he'd planned it.

Moments later Zac pushed open the door of the club and they stepped outside into the familiar smell of a Manhattan night. While Zachary searched the busy street for a cab, Grace watched some pedestrians approaching on the sidewalk. A group of women in evening black parted to pass a lone homeless man shuffling along the pavement. Suddenly disquieted, Grace stared at the figure.

As a cab pulled to the curb, Zac turned to help her inside, but Grace didn't move, except to open her purse.

"What are you doing?" he asked.

She slipped around him, holding out a twenty-dollar bill.

Then Zac, too, saw the man. Time stood still.

Meandering past them, his voluminous army surplus padding his body, the vagrant muttered, "Thick as thieves. The sinners don't know. Sinners are angels. Angels of repose." He stared at Grace, but didn't take her money, only walked on.

He reeked, and the smell seeped into Zachary's nostrils, an abysmal whiff of the past. Swallowing, he saw the man's red face, the cracks in his alligator-thick skin. Impressions bombarded him. Smells. Icy-cold feeling. Druglike haze. People who looked like animated clay figures. Like dough.

As the homeless man shambled on, Zac unwillingly recalled something he'd read in a book from the Santa Monica library. *Future generations will perceive the deplorable neglect of deinstitutionalized mental patients in the twentieth century as a horror worthy of the Dark Ages....*

"Zac?"

He started.

Grace had returned the twenty to her purse and was in the cab. Peering up at his face, half-illuminated by the lights from the restaurant, she saw the haunted look in his eyes. *I took up association with homeless people of unhappily like mind....* It was because of what Zac had told her that she had tried to give the man money. When she'd seen the vagrant, her mind had made an easy leap. It could have been Zachary.

With a last glance at the man, Zac joined Grace in the cab. As he closed the door and settled beside her, Grace noticed the taut muscles in his throat. She watched him swallow. She saw that his heart was racing.

He didn't meet her eyes but simply stared out the window with one of the bleakest expressions she'd ever seen in her life.

BACK AT THE HOTEL, they watched *Breakfast at Tiffany's,* from the hotel's offering of video classics and ordered frozen chocolate-mousse truffles and baked brie with garlic from room service. As they sat in bed sipping glasses of cognac from the room's bar and watching the last of the movie credits roll past, Grace thought about "The JoAnn Carroll Show." Setting her glass on the nightstand, she asked, "Are you nervous about tomorrow, Zac?"

Preoccupied, he interpreted her question in the broader sense. Tomorrow. The future. *Thick as thieves. The sinners don't know....* Again he saw the transient shuffling along the sidewalk.

Thinking of "JoAnn," he replied, "Somewhat." Zac wasn't keen on talk shows, but the exposure was good. He reached for the remote to flick off the set, but instead, he hit the button for the television.

Grace was looking right at the screen, and she saw his abdominal muscles, his fingers on the buttons of the jeans.

Zac saw, as well, and hit another button, which did nothing. He heard the music playing, sensed the strobe effect. The Ben Rogan ad.

Grace said, "My gosh."

He hit the power button.

"Zachary! I wanted to see it. They don't show it in Utah."

"Good." He set the remote on the nightstand nearest him, out of her reach.

Watching the play of muscles in his back as he moved, Grace said, "Why don't you want me to see it?"

Zac turned out the light and the room was cast into blackness. Grace felt his arms folding around her in the dark, and as she slid along the length of his body, he said nothing, just covered her mouth with his.

When she could she asked, "Are you embarrassed?"

"No. It's a job." But he didn't like the way the ads affected people. Strangers. Fame was a two-edged prospect. He feared it. And he wanted it. As he both feared and wanted Grace.

He put his hands on her, his mouth on her, taking her.

HE WAS PERFORMING on stage. Acting. He wasn't good; he could feel it, and when he looked out at the audience, people were leaving the theater. Desperation overcame him, and he began calling, "Don't go! Sit down!" As his panic rose, he looked back at his costar. It was Grace, and she was walking away, too, leaving stage right.

Anxiety welled in him. He went to the room backstage to stop her, but it wasn't a dressing room. It was a bedroom. A closed Tudor-style door. Silence behind it. Terrifying silence. He listened outside. He tried the handle, and it was locked. He shook it, calling . . .

He kicked it in.

The short cry awakened Grace. It was something between a moan and a scream. Opening her eyes, she knew where she was and turned to Zac, but he was already awake, his eyes wide in the dark. She knew he had cried out, that he must have had a nightmare.

Instinctively she reached for him, but at the first touch she realized his skin was cool—damp with sweat.

Feeling her hand, Zac said, "Sorry. It happens sometimes."

"To everybody." Grace stroked his body and his hair, and for a moment Zac closed his eyes, submitting. "What was it about?"

"Doesn't matter." He didn't want to talk about it. But this time, he hadn't awakened alone. He turned to Grace.

As they began to make love, Grace felt his tenderness, his automatic focus on her, his total presence. She returned the focus, the absorption, loving the sound of his voice as he said things that excited her.

But afterward, while he drowsed against her, drifting to sleep with the trust of a sated lover, the ghouls of three a.m. visited Grace. They'd been stirred by the nocturnal taxi ride through the city of her past and Zac's, and by the homeless man outside the Black-and-White Diner. They'd come alive with Zachary's cry in the night.

Now they paraded through her mind. They were her doubts. *What happened to you, Zac? Was it just a breakdown? Or something worse?*

THE NEXT MORNING Grace sat in the audience of "The JoAnn Carroll Show" and watched the famous blond talk-show host question Zac about *Kah-Puh-Rats,* then modeling, then his background. Skillfully, he steered the conversation away from his personal life and onto public ground—acting. His fame as a model had earned him this spot, but within two minutes everyone in the audience knew his mind was as fine as his body.

His understated British wit kept the audience in stitches. Grace laughed, too, but she was always aware that a camera might be trained on her face. JoAnn's guest was her own husband, and ten minutes into the show Grace was still trying to get over the wild reaction of the mostly female audience when he'd come out on stage. A coed directly behind her had stood up on her chair and yelled, "I want to have your baby!" And a large tattooed woman two seats down from Grace was wearing a tank top that read, "HIT THE SACK WITH ME, ZACHARY."

Now, on stage, JoAnn was leaning toward Zac with a curious smile, saying, "Would you mind— Oh, I hate to ask." She looked at her audience conspiratorially, winked at them, then turned back to her guest. "Would you mind taking off your shirt?"

Women stood up, screaming and whistling. Grace was afraid she was the only one still sitting. She was sure the camera was on her and didn't know what expression she was wearing.

Zachary said, "No, not at all."

The wildly enthusiastic crowd response made Grace want to cover her ears. Zac stood up to unbutton his blue silk shirt. His good-humored amusement and boy-next-door charm had everyone eating out of his hand. But Grace remembered how he'd turned off the Ben Rogan ad the night before. She knew he loved being in front of an audience. And he was too good an actor to show if he felt that doing this was even remotely demeaning. But how *did* he feel?

When his shirt was off, JoAnn walked around him with her microphone, taking a good look and exchanging glances with her audience. After a pregnant pause she said, "Now, would you mind taking off—"

"Yes, I would."

The audience laughed.

JoAnn winked at the crowd. "Let's break for a word from our sponsors, and then we'll take your questions for Zachary."

After the break Grace sat impassively as strangers plied Zac with questions that would have done credit to the INS. Sexual fantasies. Birth control. Underwear. Nothing was off-limits. He didn't always answer, but when the last inquisitor of the day asked him to describe his ideal woman, Zac said without hesitation, "My wife."

Grace smiled in case the camera was watching. But her thoughts flashed to a celebrity interview she'd read the year before, in which a popular actor had been asked the same thing and replied the same way.

A month later he'd left his wife of six years for an actress.

THE REST OF THE TIME in New York flew. Thursday evening Grace and Zac were back in Moab, and the next morning when he stopped at the production office to pick up his call sheet Zac saw that the infamous scene twenty-five would be shot that night. Meshach caught him in the hall as he was reading the sheet and said, "You and Ingrid will get it in a couple of takes, and then it'll be behind you."

Zac understood what he hadn't said—that if it wasn't effective, they would submit the script for more changes, trim his part again.

He was to report to makeup at four o'clock at the base camp near the Dewey Bridge, thirty miles up the river road from Moab. That afternoon they would film Powell coming to meet with Seneca and his brother, Captain O. G. Howland, to ask them to join the expedition. The meeting would take place at O.G.'s house, and then Seneca would return home to his wife, Melody, and tell her the news. The first scene would be shot at an old farmhouse along the river road, the next in another house ten miles north. Zac knew the schedule was tight, and he had to give strong and effective performances.

At midmorning he left the production office and drove to Rapid Riggers. The day was sunny and dry, the forecast clear, and weather shouldn't interfere with filming. When he reached the river outfit, Grace and Day were on the porch talking. Ninochka was at Grace's feet, but she immediately trotted down to greet Zac. As he got out of the car, both women waved, then Day went inside, and Grace came to meet him.

Zac hugged her. "Come home with me. I have to be at work at four, and it's going to go all night."

Grace said, "Let me tell Day."

Minutes later she was closing her eyes in the passenger seat of the convertible. The husky climbed on her lap as Zac drove down the River Inn Road. Over the wind he said, "They're going to shoot scene twenty-five tonight. Do you want to come?"

The love scene. It was here. Her view of him blocked by Ninochka's fluffy tail, she said, "Whatever you want."

Zac kept his eyes on the snaking yellow line on the blacktop. "How about bringing a book and waiting in my trailer?"

Grace knew he wanted her close so that he could see her before and after. This love scene was a first for him as an actor, too. She put her hand over his on the stick shift. "I'd like that."

At the house Grace made an asparagus-mushroom quiche for lunch while he worked on an upstairs floor, correcting warps. Later, while they were eating at an iron patio table on the screened porch, a blue heron swept past, its rhythm as slow and even as the flow of the Colorado. Zac knew visitors would love the setting. He could imagine the inn as a retreat, like the finest hotels. A weight room in the downstairs northwest corner. A turndown service at night. Twenty-four-hour room service. He'd already seen where the croquet pitch could go, and he had a place in mind for a shuffleboard court. They could build a replica of the *Moab Princess*. Grace had the river permits....

Calling him back to this world, Grace said, "I asked Day about swapping the property. She was game."

"Great." But he sounded preoccupied. As they finished eating he said, "We have a couple of hours. Shall we go to the bookstore and find you something to read tonight?"

To take her mind off what he'd be doing.

Grace nodded, trying not to feel the threat to what was hers, trying to forget both Ingrid Dolk and the women in the audience of "The JoAnn Carroll Show." For all the love she and Zachary shared, one thing had never changed. He'd married her so he could do this job. Act.

He loved her.

But he loved his work most of all.

CHAPTER TEN

AT ELEVEN THAT NIGHT the stage was lit, and everyone was dismissed but the skeleton crew who would be filming the scene. In the dim light, Zac tried to tune out the other people, all but Ingrid, naked on the white sheets of the nineteenth-century high-post spool bed. He was too much a man not to admire her delicate shoulders and collarbone, her slim waist and her breasts, as perfect in their way as Grace's. She was a small, very beautiful woman.

She was not Grace.

As he came toward the bed, he felt the character of Seneca Howland sliding over him like a cloak. But he was also aware of himself. Of everything. Not just the scene they'd only talked through, not just this role, but how Ingrid was feeling. And how her character, Seneca's wife, Melody, was feeling.

Zac lay down with her, met her blue eyes and felt her warm skin and unfamiliar body brush his; a powerful uneasiness swept over him. He was aware of the camera's red light, of eyes watching, and he knew he was in no danger of arousal. But as he bent his head over Melody's—he was Seneca now—he knew he had never in his life walked so close to the line between right and wrong. He knew this was a place where any man could fall, and many had.

He touched Ingrid's cool lips with his, and he thought of Grace and of what he was trying to accomplish in the scene. He felt how strongly Seneca loved his wife, and he looked down at Melody and remembered that he was leaving on a dangerous expedition, that he might not return, that this woman needed him....

He began acting, playing it as it came, and so did Ingrid. And when he looked into her eyes, he saw Melody, a woman who didn't want to lose her husband. Ingrid was clinging to his shoulders, but he knew she was thinking what he was. *Let's get it in one take....*

CRICKETS WERE CHIRPING outside the trailer, but Grace didn't hear them. That afternoon Zac had bought her a new mystery novel by one of her favorite authors and she was swept up and lost, lying on the bed shivery-scared. When she heard the click of the door, she started, more in the book's world than in reality.

Zac stepped up into the trailer, and when he saw her he smiled, then closed the door and walked to the bed. He lay down beside her in his blue jeans and Oxford sweatshirt, his weight sinking the mattress. Seeing how far she'd plowed through the book, he said, "I bet you wish I'd go away so you can finish it."

That was true enough to make her laugh, but she laid aside the book and hugged him, remembering where he'd been. It was over. What she'd feared for so long hadn't been much worse than waiting for him at the dentist's office.

Zac saw her eyes and felt a purity inside him he hadn't known was there. He wanted to tell her how much he loved her, how sacred were the bonds between them, but he couldn't think of words to express the preternatural tingling of his body, the relief.

Because he knew that even the confidence he felt was dangerous, and that many married men had said, *It won't happen to me.* He was lucky. That was all.

Now he should renew his bond with Grace. If he continued to be lucky he would not be haunted by the feel and memory of a woman not his wife.

He said, "Let me shower, and we'll go home."

HE HAD ANOTHER BAD DREAM that night. Grace heard his scream, and in her own dreams she thought it was a child crying for its mother. When she opened her eyes, she saw Zac with his hand against his head. A gesture of apology. Ninochka had awakened, too. Front paws on the bed, she regarded Zachary with a worried expression.

Absently petting the husky, accepting her kisses, Zac looked at Grace in the moonlight shining through the French doors. "I'm sorry."

Recalling his nightmare in the hotel in New York, Grace said, "It's all right." She moved closer to him and found his skin and the sheets damp, as before. "That must be some dream." The last time Grace had woken up in a sweat, she'd had chicken pox. She asked, "Do you feel okay?"

"Sure. Down, Ninochka. That's a good girl. I'm fine."

His heart was racing. Grace asked, "Was it the same dream?"

"No." But close enough.

She watched him in the half-dark, waiting.

Zac sighed. "I...sometimes...dream about people I love killing themselves."

"That's awful," said Grace. "Did— Has that ever happened?"

"No."

Grace wondered if it was a reaction to what had happened to him in New York. She thought of the homeless man they'd seen when they were leaving the club. Zachary's response had been tangible. And he'd awakened with a scream that night. Grace's heart began beating as hard and fast as his, her mind locked in memory. *Don't leave, Grace....*

But she *had* left, and now Zac dreamed nightmares of the cruelest form of desertion.

The bed shook.

Zac said, "Ninochka—settle down. Nina."

As the fluffy dog insinuated herself between them, turning and squirming until she was comfortable and her people were not, Grace laughed. But she understood the husky's instincts. Something was troubling Zac.

Zachary coaxed the dog to the foot of the bed, and then he and Grace maneuvered around her until they lay skin to skin, holding each other close. Every fire of love sprang up between them, and the first kisses licked away the dark fears of the night. Soon, whispered sounds of lovemaking filled the air.

"Shh. *Gracie...*"

"Zac... I love you."

The puppy settled on the covers on the lower corner of the mattress and went to sleep.

THE NEXT DAY Grace was busy at Rapid Riggers. Though the Cataract Canyon launch date was still more than a week away, food had to be ordered, deliveries arranged. And river filming would begin in Desolation Canyon in just two days. Though a caterer would provide meals there, Grace needed to help Nick and the other boatmen ready the rafts, jetboats and other equipment.

At about five-thirty Day came outside to the boatyard where Grace was working with Nick. "Zac's on the phone."

Pushing her hair off her forehead, Grace followed Day inside to take the call. She paused on the enclosed back porch to pet Ninochka, who was dozing on an old sleeping bag, then elbowed through the kitchen doors and picked up the phone on the reception counter.

Zachary said, "Hi. It's me."

Grace's heart pounded. "Hi, Zac." She was glad to hear his voice. What he'd said about his nightmares had unnerved her. It had haunted her all day.

"How's Ninochka?" Zac had left her at the vet early that morning to be spayed. Grace had picked her up.

"She's fine. Day said she'll watch her again while we're on the river." Grace paused. "When will you be home? What do you want for dinner?"

The timbre of the conversation became sexual. His answer had nothing to do with food, and Grace felt Day watching her from the door of the inner office. As she hung up the phone, she noticed her sister's odd expression.

"What is it?"

Day shook her head with a bittersweet smile. Then, suddenly, her face seemed to fall apart, and she said, "Dammit, you're really leaving. I'm going to miss you."

Grace went to her and hugged her, remembering an afternoon just weeks before when Day had embraced her, comforted her because she was divorcing Zachary. Now Day was crying and dabbing at her mascara, and she said, "Well, I've figured out how to get our commodore to stick around."

Nick. Day must have realized she would have trouble running Rapid Riggers alone.

Day said, "I think he'll stay if you sell him your half of the outfit. Then you can buy me out of the house."

Before Grace could respond, the swinging kitchen doors banged open, and the man in question looked in. Staring in astonishment at Day's tears, Nick said, "Day! You miss me already. That's why you're crying, right?"

Day rolled her red-rimmed eyes. "Why don't you go swim Cataract without a life jacket?"

Nick came over and hugged her.

Grace watched her sister submit for all of one second before she shook him off and said, "Leave me alone, deserter. I need a cigarette.'' But her eyes spoke to Grace, saying again that selling to Nick was the solution.

Two days later the Rapid Riggers boatmen and a fleet of rafts, mini J-rigs, jetboats, dories, and sport boats were assembled at the Green River put-in to Desolation Canyon at seven in the morning. The film crew arrived shortly afterward, and rigging took until nine. There was equipment to load and protect, dry bags to pack and label, and a wealth of coolers packed by the caterers to see the cast and crew through the day's shoot.

The morning was sunny and cloudless. The BLM ranger arrived and began checking boatmen's licenses and equipment. He would accompany the film crew on the river, making sure regulations were followed, protecting the natural resource. A park-service ranger would do the same when they filmed in Cataract Canyon.

There were several commercial trips launching that morning, and Grace noticed that the actors stayed out of sight in their trailers at the base camp near the put-in. A few of the cast, including Ingrid Dolk, had finished filming and returned to California.

Before launching, Nick and Grace and the other boatmen gave the film crew and actors an extensive safety lecture, including such topics as the health hazards of drinking river water and how to swim a rapid. Some of the points they would repeat over the next few days, and Grace knew the river guides' conversation on the water would be littered with anecdotes more sobering than any warnings.

When Zac finished with makeup, he came over to where Grace was rigging her raft, tying in two coolers with the help of one of the caterers. She made sure the lines were snug, then straightened and turned to Zac.

Dressed as Seneca Howland in a blue shirt, gray trousers, suspenders and knee-high boots, he looked like a time-traveler. There were too many people nearby for them to be alone, but they stole up the beach to exchange a few words, and Zac kissed her before they parted. When they put in soon afterward, Grace saw him rowing one of the dories, his stroke as strong and sure as that of any boatman on the river.

The day dragged, progress on the river slow. After lunch, they tried to film a scene in which George Bradley fell out of the boat. But Martin Place, rowing with one arm as Major Powell, took a big standing wave abreast and capsized the dory, cameraman and all. The actors were soaked and had to be taken back to base camp by jetboat to go to wardrobe and makeup.

While he waited for the others to return, Meshach set up cameras A, B and C on the shoreline and filmed Zac's crew running the rapid in the dory called *No Name*. Sitting with Nick on a rock ledge overlooking the river, Grace watched Zachary choose the perfect route.

Nick remarked, "He's a good boatman. Your dad would have liked it that you married someone who could do that."

Nick had been present at her father's graveside when Zachary was not. Grace was glad the guide had something good to say about Zac, but his comment evoked complicated feelings. She changed the topic. She had something to discuss with Nick, something she'd been putting off for two days.

"Nick, a while ago I told you Day and I weren't going to sell Rapid Riggers. But it turns out I need to sell my half."

The boatman glanced toward the river and Zac, then back at Grace. He grinned, perhaps in understanding of the ways of love. Or maybe because he'd heard her offer. "What do you want for it?"

She told him.

Meeting her eyes, Nick held out his hand.

As they shook on the promise, Grace felt as though she'd just sold her child. But she'd given Zac her vow. *Wherever you go, I will go. Wherever you lodge, I will lodge....*

FOR THREE DAYS they filmed on that stretch of the Green River. Then they moved downstream to Labyrinth Canyon and spent a day filming there. Afterward the crew moved back to Moab. Day and night they filmed. Zac's hours were erratic, but whenever he was done he went to Rapid Riggers to collect Ninochka, then returned to the house by the river, where he refinished floors and repaired the walls in the upstairs hallway. The dog followed him everywhere. She was the most loyal animal Zac had ever known—and the sweetest. They both forgot she'd ever been anyone else's.

Grace and Day and Nick began the paperwork to sell Day's half of the River Inn and Grace's half of Rapid Riggers. When both deals had closed, Grace would have money for renovations on the inn.

Though, of course, it would not be an inn.

At the end of the week they launched for Cataract Canyon. Because of the canyon's distance from civilization, cast and crew had agreed to camp on the river. A chopper would visit the set daily, bringing supplies, script changes and fresh ingredients for the meals Grace and her crew would prepare. Wine, seafood, fowl, meat, eggs, dairy products and fresh vegetables—far more variety than could be stowed in coolers on an average river trip.

The night before the launch, the Rapid Riggers crew transported their boats to the put-in at Mineral Bottom. From there they would start down the Green River through Stillwater Canyon to the confluence with the Colorado and onward to the white water of Cataract Canyon.

Zachary camped at the put-in with Grace. Once filming resumed, they wouln't get to see much of each other, and both wanted the time together.

It was a precious night. The Rapid Riggers boatmen had the beach to themselves. After a casual meal around the camp fire, when the beach lay in darkness, Nick and Fast Susan set up an old survey tent to make a sauna. Grace and Zac collected the rocks for the sweat in a metal bucket, and they sat together by the fire while the stones heated in the flames.

Zac reclined in a low camping chair. With a beer in hand, Grace sat in the sand and leaned back against his shoulder and his chest. Listening to the sparks in the fire, the music of the river and the quiet sounds of insects in the air, she savored the smell of wood and tried not to wonder when she'd see the Green River again. She tried not to think of favorite campsites. Of rapids. Of friends she'd be leaving behind when she went away with Zac.

Dirty Bob's voice floated across the beach in the darkness. "Didn't somebody die in the Big Drop in '87?"

Fast Susan said, "Wrong year, wrong rapid. You're thinking of..."

Zac tuned in to the distant conversation. The white water stories were incessant, and he was beginning to wonder how much credence to give them. How much to fear the river. Certainly, this section of the Green was calm. But miles downstream, it joined the Colorado, increasing that river's volume. And then, the river descended more quickly.... A cataract.

Dropping his head back, he stared at the stars, more than he'd ever seen at one time, so many it was hard to find the bars of Orion.

Grace sat up. "The rocks are ready."

Zac stirred, started to slide into his shoes.

"Shake 'em out," Grace warned. "Scorpions."

"Saw one as big as your hand once at Spanish Bottom," contributed Nick, joining them. "Those rocks done?"

The river stories continued as the boatmen squeezed together in the sauna. Fast Susan poured water onto the rocks from an old coffeepot. As they sizzled and the dome filled with steam, Dirty Bob told Zac, "Bet Grace never told you about the time she flipped in Stillwater."

"Oh, shut up," Grace said, laughing.

"She didn't tie anything down—"

"There's no white water!"

"Which made that flip all the more *amazing*, Grace...."

Laughter. More ribbing. Zac heard the comradeship among them. The heat in the tent increased with the sound of the rocks hissing as someone poured on more water.

It was some time later, when they were all splashing in the shallows at the edge of the river, cooling off, that Dirty Bob turned to Zac and said, "I guess there's no white water in Los Angeles, huh?"

"No." Zac stole a look at Grace, who was bathing in river mud in the moonlight. Her face coated with silt, she seemed to have become part of the earth and the river itself. Her eyes met his, then darted away. But not before Zac saw what it was costing her to leave.

When they had rinsed off a last time and were toweling each other on the beach, some distance away from the others, he mentioned it, and she looked at him in surprise and threw her arms around him.

"Oh, Zac, the happiest time of my life was in New York. With you. California will be like that."

But she sounded as though she was trying to convince herself.

They both knew nothing would be like that ever again.

THE MOVIE CREW and the park service escort arrived before seven, and the whole party put in. That afternoon, they stopped in Stillwater Canyon, where the size of their party forced them to camp on three different beaches. They set up one large kitchen, where everyone congregated for dinner, but snacks had to be provided for each of the three camps. There were peanut-butter-and-pretzel log cabins to build for appetizers, Cornish game hens to bone, morel mushrooms to clean, spinach miso soup to cook and purée. Every boatman worked on food preparation, and when Grace glanced up in a frazzle from adjusting the fire beneath a dutch oven she saw Zachary just feet away slicing artichoke hearts for risotto.

Joining him, Grace said, "You don't have to do that, Zac."

He hooked a finger in the waistband of her cut-offs and cast his eyes over her breasts in her cotton crop-top. His hand closed on her bare waist. "And leave you alone in the camp kitchen with Cute Nick and Dirty Bob?"

Grace whispered, "I love you."

His eyes echoed her words.

By dinner time, the Rapid Riggers crew had created twenty-one separate courses. Over a slice of frozen almond cappuccino dacquoise for dessert, Nort Stills remarked, "This is really something, you know? Chez River."

Hal Markley, spending a token night on the set, had understanding in his eyes as he told Grace, "You're a remarkable woman."

From the camping chair where he sat, Zac winked at her with pride, and Grace longed to move closer to him and take advantage of the brief opportunity to talk together. But Hal was showing her his cellular phone, demonstrating that, indeed, it did not work on the river. And later, Grace was busy with clean-up, while Zachary had a night shoot that lasted until four in the morning. When he finally joined her in the ridiculously large tent the studio had provided, it was only to pull off his clothes and drop against her, his arm thrown over her, and fall instantly asleep. Barely an hour later, Grace left the tent to start breakfast and prep for lunch.

By day, Grace's raft carried much of the lighting gear, plus five members of the lighting crew. She enjoyed chatting with the technicians while she rowed. And during breaks, while the crew was filming on shore, she kneaded rising bread dough for dinner and mentally rehearsed lunch plans.

Overall, the film crew seemed cheerful, and Grace attributed that to their surroundings, good attitudes, good food and the Rapid Riggers guides. She saw Fast Susan drawing a hearty laugh from Martin Place, while Dirty Bob enthralled his passengers with river stories Grace knew were alternately hilarious and terrifying.

But when they reached the Confluence and the Green spilled into the Colorado, Grace's stomach began to draw into knots, and she knew the other boatmen were feeling the same thing. Everywhere they looked was an altered shoreline, with familiar landmarks submerged by high water. And there was no denying the sheer volume, the force of the water carrying them downstream.

What would Cataract be like?

FILMING IN the interim had been limited to a few calm-water and hiking scenes, and now excitement was high. Zac glimpsed the white water from his seat at the oars of the *No Name* and he remembered Grace's instructions to him at their last stop, *Whatever you do, don't miss Spanish Bottom.*

He eddied out at the beach, and one by one the other boats did the same. The sound of the water was warning enough. *Hear me. Fear me.* And there was no missing the cautionary sign on the river just before the beach:

STOP
CATARACT CANYON
HAZARDOUS RAPIDS
200 YARDS AHEAD

At sunset Grace left her guides to serve steamed mussels and grilled quail to a crew who had already dined on appetizers—artichoke heart and asparagus salad and honey walnut bread—and she joined the park-service ranger, Meshach, Zac and Nick on a traverse over the boulders to scout Brown Betty Rapid.

Zac was two steps behind Grace, and he paused when she did, to stare down at the rushing mass of foam below, much bigger than he had imagined. His mouth went dry, and his legs felt like rubber.

Under the sound of the torrent, he heard Nick Colter, behind him, say, "I think I'm going to throw up."

Apparently, fear didn't fade with experience.

But as the director surveyed the rapid from above, his primary concern was the placing of cameras on the shore, and he plied Nick and Grace with questions about which route the boats would have to take—and whether a boat could take a different course to film the dories from another angle.

Together, Grace, Nick and the ranger fielded Meshach's questions and cautioned him with facts about the river. The biggest rapids were at the end of the canyon in the Big Drop, where the river fell thirty feet in less than a mile. The river was running at 80,000 cfs, and in 1983, when the number was 100,000, two dozen J-rigs, pontoon boats and dories had been stopped by the Big Drop. They'd huddled in eddies and eventually signaled for helicopters to carry their passengers to where they could be ferried back to Moab and Green River by jetboat. This was very big white water.

Brown Betty was neither the most nor least difficult rapid in the canyon. But now the waves looked larger than Grace had ever seen them. She knew she would sleep badly.

Zac was silent as they walked back to camp. The fading sunlight cast bright shades of orange and brown and black on the riffles in the river and the rocks and sand on both banks, and Grace caught his eyes following a bluish Colorado River toad as it hopped near the shore. Glancing up at his profile, she said, "Zac, don't you want to use a stuntman?"

"No." His smile made Grace think of what Nick had said about her father. He was right. Sam Sutter would have liked it that she'd married a man who could row.

Others were less enthusiastic about the white water. During dinner and on into the evening, as Meshach gathered with Nort Stills and the crew, rumors flooded the camp. Which actors wanted to row, which didn't. Martin Place and Zac were the only ones interested in guiding dories, so Rapid Riggers boatmen were sized by wardrobe and told to report to makeup in the morning. Because there would be more boats than guides, and to facilitate additional takes, a chopper specially equipped with filters to protect it from the sand would meet them downstream at Cross Canyon and lift them back to Spanish Bottom to take more boats down the rapids.

That night, Grace and Zac climbed back to the scouting place, and she told him everything she could remember about the rapids ahead. Zachary listened attentively and asked the right questions, and later in their tent, they made silent, shaking love. And even when he was inside her, Zac could still hear the roar of the white water, could still in his mind see the white foam.

THE MORNING DAWNED GRAY against the ceaseless sound of rushing rapids. As she served breakfast, Grace heard

Nort Stills grumble, "Could hardly sleep with that noise. It could make you go mad."

The river.

After breakfast Grace put on her wet suit in anticipation of the rapids. Rigging her boat, she was glad for the protection of the neoprene against the chill air.

Her only passenger would be the still photographer, who hoped to snap shots of the cameramen and actors in the dories. Anyone else not immediately involved with filming would remain behind at Spanish Bottom. There, her guides would serve lunch to the bulk of the crew, while Grace fed the others on one of the beaches downstream.

As Meshach hiked down from the rocks where he'd been helping to place a camera, Grace looked across the beach at Zac. The specially designed life vest he wore beneath the costume of Seneca Howland gave him only a little extra bulk, and Grace didn't trust it. Zac was all muscle and bone—highly sinkable. What if the vest didn't provide enough buoyancy?

At last she crossed the beach and joined him. His eyes held a private look, a reminder of the night before, as he said, "Meet you in our tent at Cross Canyon."

She didn't answer, just patted his shirt, feeling the place where she'd used dental floss to sew the sheath holding his river knife to his vest. Zac's lips grazed her neck and her mouth and for a moment his hands locked around hers. A long look passed between him and Grace, private communication. *I love you.*

I love you, too.

Ten minutes later they launched.

Grace was in the second raft, with the *Emma Dean,* the dory named for Powell's wife, following. Nick rowed *Kitty Clyde's Sister,* and behind him was Zac at the oars of the *No Name.* The last crafts were the park-service boat and a J-rig carrying Meshach, a script supervisor and some other crew members. Rapid Riggers guides filled in for a few of the actors in the dories. Dirty Bob was with Zac in the *No Name*.

The whole fleet ran the first two rapids without incident and eddied out for a short break. As the boats gathered along the shore and crew members ran from boat to boat checking things, Grace could see exhilaration and triumph all around. Meshach's smile was the broadest. Noting the excitement in his eyes, Grace knew the director was thinking that the hardship of transporting the crew down the river had been worth it.

But the biggest rapids were ahead. While the camera loaders worked busily, actors and boatmen walked down the shore to scout. The third rapid had virtually washed out at the higher water level, and the next wasn't yet in sight. Everyone set out again, moving downstream. Soon Grace heard the white water and searched for a place to pull over and view the rapid. But when she glanced back upstream, she saw Meshach standing in the J-rig, waving everyone on like a general ordering his troops to charge.

Grace looked at Nick in *Kitty Clyde's Sister,* and he shrugged at her. These rapids shouldn't be that bad. They rowed on.

Larry, the photographer, suggested to Grace, "See if you can get over on the right so I can snap photos of the *Emma Dean.*"

Grace did as he requested, but as the first dory went by, Meshach hailed her from the J-rig and waved her down the river. While Larry snapped photos of the two dories following, Grace rowed toward the foam.

She saw at once that she'd made a mistake. The high water had changed the river, and the usual route was now a mass of standing waves. Clearer passage was over to the left, and she rowed hard to make it, but the rapid already owned the raft. Dead ahead was a frowning hole like the Mariana Trench. It had *keeper* written all over it.

Feet planted against a cooler, Grace pulled on the oars, but the raft still hurtled forward and poured down over the fall into the liquid chasm.

It was the worst white-water trouble Grace had seen in her life, and she rowed straight at the wave, determined to escape the hole before it caught the boat. But the wave was much bigger than the raft, and as the brown water rose up in front of her and the gray-and-yellow tube of her raft tried to climb it, Grace knew what was going to happen, and it did.

The raft flipped, and a wall of water slammed her, crushing her against coolers and ammo cans. Grace tried to get her bearings, but the raft was moving too fast, plunging, and she was caught on it, carried with it. She felt air and saw sunlight and gasped water, and then the boat jerked, moved up and flipped again. She felt her body bouncing like a puppet, felt her weight dangling from the strap on the back of her life vest as it buoyed her up under the overturned raft in a world where there was no air, only water pressing her against the sharp edges of the gear tied in the boat. Upside down, she felt the raft rise again, felt her body and neck twist awkwardly in an involuntary somersault.

God help me, she thought, throwing her arms over her head, preparing for the next impact. It was like one of those amusement-park rides when a person couldn't tell which way was up. But there was no safety code here. The wave slammed the raft down, and she was beneath it in a no-air world of brown. The boat dragged her.

Grace tried to fight her way up around the tube, anywhere to air, but the force of the river was too strong, and she could feel a line wrapped around her body. *Knife.* As she slid the blade from its sheath, the raft slammed an obstacle, a rock, and her body jerked. Her knife stabbed one of the tubes and slipped from her hand. The raft spun.

Air. Air. Grace tried to find the surface, tried to unzip her vest to free herself. *Got to breathe. Going to drown.*

In her mind she saw Zachary's eyes. *Lover,* she thought. She couldn't die. She couldn't die when she had so much to live for.

Her mind cried out for him.

CHAPTER ELEVEN

ZAC WATCHED the wave lift the boat a third time and smack it down. He was less horrified by the size of the hole than by the sight of Grace dangling against the raft, tossed in the waves like a dummy. She was trapped by a line threaded through rings on the tubes, and if the keeper kept pummeling the boat she would break her neck. As the raft rose up again, he saw it jerking her, saw her back twist.

Behind him Dirty Bob said, "She's caught on the chicken line."

Looking past the cameraman in the bow of the dory, Zac saw the route the *Emma Dean* had taken. He needed to go the same way—away from the keeper that held Grace's boat. He was rowing. There were other lives at stake.

His wife was dying.

Grace's raft plunged out of the hole and onto the tongue upside down, and Zac knew she was beneath it. He said, "Bob, take the oars. I'm going."

Dirty Bob said, "Do it." Rough, brown river-guide hands crowded Zachary's on the oars.

The dory was nearing the raft, and Zac stood up and jumped into the white water beside the rapid. He didn't feel the cold, only the pull of the river as it tried to suck him away from the gray-and-yellow raft. There were D-rings on the upturned bottom of the boat, and he grabbed one of them and held on.

She was there, beneath the tube, twisting to try to reach the top.

Bracing himself against the raft as it bounded through foam, Zac unsheathed the knife she'd given him, her father's knife, and reached out a long arm for her. He sliced the white line stretched taut around her and severed the strap on her life vest. Immediately she bounced away from him like a corpse, disappearing under the boat.

Zac didn't see the wave, only felt the water pressing down on his head, tearing him from the boat, making everything gray-brown. When he came up there was only white water, cold around him. Then he saw the edge of the boat, the slick tube. A line swirled near him in the water, and he grabbed it and pulled himself to the raft. Crawling up on the underside as the boat hurled toward the next rapid, he looked all around the seething waves. No Grace. He slid back into the water and tried to go under the boat, but the river changed, became a mass of swirling, and there was nothing he could do but let it carry him.

In the chaos of tossing water, his mind went sick, and he saw things that had nothing to do with Grace. He saw nightmare images—the Tudor door, the shape on the bed—and he felt empty inside as the mighty river swept him along.

MESHACH TOSSED a throw bag from the J-rig, and Grace saw the white line spiraling through the air. She caught it and held it. As Fast Susan steered for an eddy, Grace let the pontoon boat carry her through the water until she felt silt beneath her feet.

Clinging to the line, she slogged through the mud, battered and ready to drop in her tracks. Suddenly she remembered the photographer who'd been in her boat. Still gasping, she called out to Susan, "Where's Larry?"

Susan pointed to the far shore, where the photographer was dumping water out of one of his wet-suit booties. Through the dripping tangle of her hair, Grace stared downstream after the dories, looking for the *No Name*. Zac would be worried.

Susan yelled, "Get on! We've got to go get Zac!"

Zachary! Grace's stomach plunged. Had Zac fallen out in the white water? He wasn't even wearing a wet suit. Hypothermia could set in fast, especially for someone as lean as Zac.

She scrambled toward the J-rig, and Meshach and one of the crew reached down to haul her aboard. As she settled on one of the pontoons, she gazed downstream. She saw the *No Name,* but Zachary was nowhere in sight.

Susan yelled as she gunned the outboard. "He jumped in to grab the raft. He must have cut you free, and then he went under..."

Grace felt sick. He had saved her life and she had never known he was there.

Zac, she thought, *where are you?*

ZACHARY HIKED up the shore as far as he could, climbing the rocks. Then he saw the dories coming toward the eddy, and he looked for Grace, but she wasn't there. She'd never come up.

The sun emerged from the clouds, but it didn't warm him. Shivering, he peered at the raft on the beach. He'd turned it over himself to make sure she really wasn't underneath. One tube was punctured, slashed by a knife. His knife had found its way back into its sheath, but Zac couldn't remember when.

In the sun he leaned against a rock wall behind him, hardly noticing the red dust smearing to mud on his clothes and face and body. He remembered how Grace had looked under the raft and that maybe she'd already been dead. All he wanted was to find her body, and he made himself keep climbing as he stared down on the white water and the J-rig.

They were all yelling at him, and he squinted and thought he saw Grace, but it didn't seem real.

NICK, IN HIS ROLE as Emergency Medical Technician, insisted Grace sit down and be checked out before going after Zac. "Dirty Bob will get him."

Grace submitted to Nick's questions, then said, "I'm fine," and got up. She'd seen Zac standing over the river, and she'd known he was looking for her. Back aching from her pummeling in the keeper, she crossed the beach and started up the rocks. She wanted nothing but to touch her husband and let him see she was fine.

As she climbed the trail, she saw the two men coming down. Zac looked wet and wild. Unshaven. Dark. Like Heathcliff roaming the moors, only this was the Utah desert.

They met on the path, and he stared at her, then said, "Hi."

Grace reached for him and they held each other for a long time.

She needed to patch her boat, and Meshach was eager to get on with shooting. The flipped raft had spoiled the scene, and he wanted another take. He told Zac, "You can talk to your wife for a bit. Then we'll go down to Cross Canyon, meet the chopper, fly back up stream and run the whole thing again."

Kneeling in the sand examining her raft, Grace wished she could protest. But this was why they'd come. They would film until they got the shots they wanted or ran out of boats. The director was already walking away.

Zac crouched beside her in the sand. "Are you really all right? Your neck isn't hurt? You didn't hit your head?"

"I'm fine." She sat back on the shore in her wet suit and looked at him. He was filthy, covered with red desert earth. "What about you?"

"The same." He shook his hair, and Grace saw him trying to get water out of his ears.

She gazed down the beach at Meshach and company. "I think they're ready. You should go and get dry."

Zac nodded. Her voice seemed loud to him, and he shook his head again, trying to return his ears to their normal equilibrium. Staring into her brown eyes, he said, "Don't go down the next rapids till we get back."

"I won't." Grace glanced up the beach to where the photographer was reloading his camera and hunting in his dry bag for other equipment. "Meshach's leaving almost everyone here. I'm fine."

"Okay." Zac kissed her, the first kiss since their swim in the rapid. He was aware of the shape of her lips, of their temperature, of everything. Even the day seemed to have become more bright, so bright he didn't see how he would make it down the river without sunglasses. But he had to. He said, "I love you," and then he got up and walked back toward the others.

Unsettled, Grace watched him go. A warning bell, a nameless fear, was tolling inside her, and she didn't know why. It was probably the shock of what they'd both just survived.

Her eyes followed Zachary as he got into the dory, and she felt her heart reaching out to his, trying to keep him close.

THE TIME PASSED QUICKLY. Trying to ignore the physical effects of her battering in the keeper, Grace set up the lunch buffet she'd carried in her boat. Two kinds of chilled soup, two salads, sandwich makings, whole-wheat currant rolls, poppy seed cake, slightly mashed raspberry cheesecake and chocolate espresso cookies, with a wide array of beverages in a cooler nearby. She was boiling water for washing the dishes when she heard the heartbeat sound of the helicopter and saw its shadow pass overhead, going upstream.

After clean-up, she turned her attention to her boat. Because any permanent patch needed twenty-four hours to dry, Grace decided to mend the tube temporarily, so the raft could make it through the remaining rapids to Cross Canyon beach.

Larry photographed her mending the tear, then scrambled up the rocks to find a spot from which to shoot the dories when they came down again. The cameramen had already placed their tripods where Meshach had indicated, and now they, too, were waiting.

When she had repaired the raft and inflated the damaged tube, Grace checked the gear that had gone through the keeper, then took a paperback out of her ammo can. She put on some sunscreen, grabbed extra clothes, sunglasses and a water bottle, and hiked up the rocks above the rapid.

Sunbathing in her bikini, resting her sore, bruised body, Grace read three chapters of her mystery before she heard the helicopter returning, signaling the cameramen that the dories were coming. She put on her shorts and a red hooded sweatshirt and went to stand over the river to watch the boats.

The *No Name* was the second boat, following a J-rig, and Zac was rowing. From the bank, Grace admired his skill in the rapids. As he guided the dory toward the shore, she hurried down the loose rock trail to the beach. Reaching the boat, she grabbed the bowline and said, "Good run." Zac stared at her, then stood up indecisively.

Meshach, approaching on the J-rig, yelled into the hailer, "We're pulling over. Get out and stretch your legs."

Grace could see that the rest of the crew was now following from Spanish Bottom. The helicopter had flown downstream to the beach at Cross Canyon, where everyone would camp that night, and Grace knew it would make several trips back and forth, transporting actors and equipment. Not everyone in the crew was willing to face the white water, and Grace was sure news of her flip had made the rounds at Spanish Bottom.

Eventually Zac got out of the boat and stood on the shore. His new costume was soaked, as the first had been.

Grace said, "I love to watch you row."

Zac wanted to tell her not to talk so loudly, but he thought the problem was water in his ears. The thunder of the rapids was rock-concert volume. In fact, all his senses were heightened. The colors of the rocks seemed brighter, their shapes almost alive.

"Zac."

He blinked at Meshach.

The director clapped a hand on his shoulder. "Good job. You look good at those oars."

"Thank you." Why was everyone shouting?

He saw all the people coming down the rapids in boats, the crew calling out as the J-rigs plunged onward down the river, and it seemed more like a holiday than the making of a movie.

Meshach said, "Take a break, and then let's get those boats down to Cross Canyon. You're done for today, Zac. If you want to go with your wife, I think we can find someone to row that dory."

One of the J-rigs was pulling off into an eddy with an extra boatman aboard. Grace called to him, and Zac winced at the sound of her shout.

As Meshach moved away, Grace asked, "Are you okay, Zachary?"

He nodded, pounding his head as though to get water out of his ears.

Grace rerigged her boat and pumped more air into the damaged chamber using a hand pump. Eventually Zac nudged her aside and finished the job for her, but Grace was a little surprised at how long it had taken him to think of it. He must be tired.

When they set out in her raft, she offered him the oars and he took them with little reaction, but Grace saw he knew where to enter the white water. He had run this rapid earlier.

Zac's thoughts wandered. Why were they running the same sections of river again? After a moment he remembered about the film. That was why. He turned to Grace. She seemed familiar and yet a stranger in her river hat and life vest. As she smiled at him, he stared at her brown eyes, and a grounding sense of time and place washed over him.

She was his wife. Sometimes they lived together in the inn by the river, and she snuggled next to him under the covers while their gray dog slept at the foot of the bed and crickets chirped outside.

The motion of the boat reminded him of the rapid. Returning his gaze to the white water, he found the tongue and followed it. Reading the river was second nature to him, though he found the raft clumsy after the sleek dory. As a wave dashed over the bow, soaking him, he looked back at Grace. The sun glittered in wet droplets on her suntanned thighs. She was like Persephone. She had come up from the "underworld"—ha-ha—and now it was spring.

"Zac! The rapid. Watch what you're doing."

He turned his head. One oar stroke saved them from a hole.

In a minute they were at the shore, and Grace jumped out and grabbed the bowline. Zac got out, too, and watched her haul the heavy raft up onto the beach. He was amazed by how strong she was.

But her dark eyes looked strange—almost suspicious—as she asked, "Want to pitch the tent?"

He considered her question. Should they pitch the tent? Or should they sleep under the stars?

(*"Pitch the tent."*)

The thought startled Zac, it was so powerful. Almost more than a thought. More like . . . a voice.

A faint recollection came to him, a sense of something not good, something he should think about. His book, *DSM-IV* . . . Hearing voices. *Auditory hallucinations are by far the most common and characteristic—*

Grace said, "All right. I'll do it." She reached into the boat and began untying straps. A moment later Nick Colter came over and joined her, and Zac wondered why the river guide was helping.

Nick said, "How're you doing, Gracie?"

"Fine." She knew he was asking as EMT, as well as coworker. Her body did ache. Why was Zac just standing there? She could use his help.

Annoyed, she told herself he'd already put in a long day. It wasn't his fault that hers wasn't over. But it embarrassed her that Nick was helping now—and casting nasty looks at Zac. Nick respected people who did their share of work on the river and disparaged those who did not. Usually Zac was the first to help. But now he just stood watching. When at last he picked up the big sack containing the tent and trudged off toward an empty section of beach, Grace nearly sighed aloud.

Nick stared after him. "Are you two fighting?"

"Not that I know of." But Zac's strange behavior troubled her. As soon as she could, Grace took the dry bag containing sleeping bags and clothing over to the tent. He wasn't there. He must have gone to change out of his costume, remove his makeup.

In any case, she needed to start the evening meal. Guides were already setting up coolers and tables, and Grace began slicing fresh vegetables to grill. The dinner menu would include several Mexican courses, as well as barbecued chicken and cornmeal-crusted catfish served with snap peas and french-fried shoestring potatoes. Preparations were comparatively easy, but as darkness fell on the beach Grace grew increasingly anxious about Zac. Where was he? At the first opportunity, she made another search of the camp.

Nick came and found her. "Zac's missing?"

Grace nodded. She was outside her tent, pulling on her pile cardigan. As she picked up her headlamp she told Nick, "I'm going to walk up the canyon and look for him. Will you please keep searching camp?"

"I'll get some help. Don't go too far on your own."

"I won't." But Grace was worried. If Zac had decided to go for a hike in the dark, he might have gotten lost or fallen on the rocks and been injured.

The canyon wound through tamarisk and between rocky slots on a little-known path that eventually led to the top of the two-thousand-foot cliffs. Grace couldn't imagine Zac hiking that far without water, especially not in the boots he'd worn to play Seneca Howland.

The canyon was quiet but for the sound of insects in the brush and water dripping somewhere. Nonetheless, even as she walked farther from the camp, Grace could hear the river.

She jumped as twigs brushed her in the dark, but the path was made of soft sand and easy to follow and she used her headlamp only intermittently. "Zac?" She shivered in the cool May night. She was going to feel silly yelling for him up in this canyon if it turned out he was back at camp.

But when Grace shone her headlamp on the ground she saw a fresh boot track. She was sure it had come from the boots he'd been wearing.

A chill swept over her, and she thought irrationally of a mystery she'd read, a story of a madman hiding in a canyon and a woman who'd gone there and found—

Something rustled in the brush off to her left.

"Zachary?"

An enormous owl surged up in the darkness, wings flapping, and Grace gasped. But then it was gone, and she stood quaking in the brush, terrified. Voice tremulous, she cried, "Zac! Where are you?"

She trained her headlamp on the ground again, looking for more tracks. Eventually she found them. Using the light, she followed the footprints, but she was nervous, although she had no idea what was scaring her. This canyon was remote in the extreme. There could be no one up here but Zachary.

Where was he?

She flashed her headlamp through the brush lining the narrow, curved walls of the canyon. As the beam caught white cotton fabric and a human forearm, she started. *Zac.*

At once she was afraid.

He was crouched in a low alcove behind a cluster of scrub oak, peering at her from between the leaves. Just crouched there, in his Seneca Howland clothes. And it *was* Zachary, his long hair tangled from rowing the silty river. But for some reason he looked like a stranger, and Grace felt something awful in the pit of her stomach. An instinct told her to turn away, to go, to run back out of the canyon and get help, but she thought, *No, this is Zac. This is my husband, my love.*

She clutched her arms around herself, and he looked out at her. In the glow from her headlamp, which she trained not on him but near him, his eyes looked different than she'd ever seen them. She realized he was frightened.

What had scared him?

Grace glanced over her shoulder and up the canyon, then shone her headlamp along the path and against the nearby rock wall. Nothing. Turning off the light, she tried to see Zac in the dark. There were his eyes—two glistening things—and the slope of his nose.

She couldn't think why he'd be crouched there as though he was waiting for something. For a moment it seemed to her he was predator, rather than frightened prey, and then she thought how ridiculous both ideas were.

She said, "Zac, come out. I've been looking for you."

He didn't answer, and that sent another chill through her. Again she thought of leaving the canyon, going for Nick. Why did she feel this way? The man in the alcove was Zac, the person closest to her in the world...

But at the moment she felt almost as though she didn't know him.

I'm afraid of him, she realized. She took a step backward on the path, even afraid to let him know she was scared.

In the darkness Zac watched her. He thought it was Grace, but everyone looked so different, and he knew how good these people were with makeup. But why would they make someone look like Grace?

("What for?")

("I don't know, but if then, so what?")

Zac creased his forehead, trying to squeeze the voices away. They were soft, but he could hear them, and they annoyed him. He felt confused. Why was Grace frightened? Were they after her?

He whispered, "Grace, it's all right. Come here." Then it occurred to him again that maybe it wasn't Grace.

The light flicked on once more, and it was too bright. He decided to go out there, where she was. He folded his body out of the alcove and stood up between the rock and the brush. Branches rubbed his face and his shirt.

Grace said, "Zac, come out. I'm not going in there."

He paused, uneasy. Was it Grace?

("What for?")

("Beyond what?")

("And so on, then you can go, but don't sleep...")

He tried to listen to the conversation, but he couldn't follow it. And Grace had spoken too quickly.

Then, abruptly, came a crashing sound, like branches breaking, and a loud voice calling, "Grace? Grace!"

Zac crouched, hiding behind the shrubs.

In the dark Grace watched him. She was afraid to talk to him again, and she didn't know why. What was wrong with him? What was wrong with Zachary?

A shadow fell over her, and she jumped and turned. It was Nick, his long hair blue-black as a raven's wing in the night. He asked, "Did you find him?"

Grace said, "Uh, yeah." And then, because she knew intuitively that speaking to Zac wouldn't help, she gestured toward the shrubs.

She saw the alarm in Nick's eyes, and she knew he must think Zac was hurt—or worse. He shone his own headlamp into the bushes until it fell on Zac's frightened eyes, and then he instantly turned it off. He crouched on the trail and peered through the leaves at Zac. "How're you doing, Zac?"

Zac didn't answer. *Nick,* he thought. Could Nick be trusted?

("What for?")

He stood up and pushed aside the scratching bushes that seemed like live monsters. As he stepped out onto the trail, he saw Grace. She stood back from him, as though there was something wrong with him, a reaction that hurt at some point inside him beyond the voices.

("What for?")

("If so, then what?")

("Do not dream about such things in the black of night...")

Nick was watching him. "Zac, are you sure you didn't hit your head today? Do you have any bumps?"

Zac shook his head, trying to remember when he might have hit it.

"Dizzy?"

Zac considered. Was this "dizzy"? "No."

("What for?")

("Even though he said...")

"Think you can walk back to camp?"

What are they going to do to me? Zac thought. Standing on the trail in the grip of indecision, he looked at Grace. Beneath her messy braid, her beautiful arched eyebrows were drawn together. It was his job to protect her. Moving near her, he said in a low voice, "Let's go."

Grace glanced up at him uneasily. He wasn't looking toward camp. He was staring back into the canyon.

She thought of Nick's idea, that perhaps Zac had a head injury. That would explain his confusion. It might be an emergency. She looked up at him and shook her head. "You need to go back to camp. I think you hit your head. That's why you're feeling funny." And *acting* funny.

Zac glanced down at her. He was feeling funny. Maybe she was right. He said, "Okay."

IN THE TENT Grace shared with Zachary, Nick and the set medic, whose name was Colin, checked him over. They examined his head for lumps, shone a flashlight in his eyes, probed his neck, and asked questions.

"Who is the president?"

"Do you know where you are?"

Although Zac submitted, Grace could see him growing edgy. Every time the EMTs made an inquiry, his expression darkened and he grew more restless. He glanced frequently toward the tent flap, and he seemed to regard even her with suspicion. Grace wanted to talk to him, to ask what was wrong, but she knew she should let the EMTs complete their examination first. They asked him about his health and if he ever used drugs, and Nick asked if he'd picked up any Colorado River toads—the amphibians emitted a toxin through their skin.

Zac shook his head and regarded the EMTs with a look of profound distrust that Grace had never seen before. He seemed ... She couldn't put her finger on it. Paranoid, maybe.

A memory surged through her like an electric shock.

I entertained the most florid delusions imaginable of persecution...

She blinked.

No.

Zac wasn't running around naked. He wasn't talking about microscopic recording equipment in his clothing. He was hardly talking at all.

Grace looked at his face.

Something was wrong. She knew it. His pupils were even, but there was something about his expression, the way he was holding his face...

Grace asked, "Zac, do you feel at all like you did in New York?"

He stared at her for a moment, and then he seemed suddenly happier. "Yes," he said, and met her eyes. "But better. Immeasurably better. Everything's been better since—" He glanced at Nick and Colin and cut off the sentence. He told them, "I'm fine. I don't know why you're doing this."

Voice full of enthusiasm, he told Grace, "I want to go out and gaze at the stars with you. Let's go for a walk." He pulled on her hand.

Nick and Colin looked at each other, and Colin lifted his shoulders, as though to say *Why not?*

("*What for?*")

("*Therefore, he is not to go...*")

Zac frowned. "Does someone have a radio on?"

The other men and Grace listened, then shook their heads.

They left the tent, and outside Zac stared at the beach and the fires and the river and smelled the smoke in the air.

"How are you doing, Zac?" It was Meshach, pushing his glasses up on his nose. The director glanced at Colin. "Is he okay?"

The set medic smiled. "Seems to be."

Grace felt an uneasiness in her heart, and her eyes darted to Nick's. Did he think Zac was all right?

The boatman stuffed his hands in the pockets of his shorts. "It was kind of a hairy day. Swimming a rapid. Almost dying." He met Grace's eyes and shrugged.

Grace thought, *Maybe that's all. Stress.*

She looked up, wanting to touch Zac.

He was walking away, across the beach.

AS THE NIGHT WORE ON, Grace became convinced that something was wrong with him. He wouldn't change out of his costume. He seemed uninterested in having his smeared and dirty makeup removed. He didn't want to sleep. And Grace had only to talk to him for a few minutes to realize that he was at least disoriented and confused. At worst...

When they were alone, sitting on a rock by the shore, Grace questioned him. "Zac, remember what you told me about New York, after I left you?"

He stared at the water rushing by. He blinked.

("New York is gone.")

("Tell her to shut up.")

The voices pestered. They were sometimes querulous, sometimes simply annoying, always unpleasant. They made it difficult to think.

"Do you remember what you told me about *Leaving Hong Kong?*"

"I was Adrian. What are you talking about?" He frowned. "I don't want to talk."

Grace took his hand and sat silently beside him. After a bit she asked, "How are you feeling?"

"I feel wonderful." He looked at her. "Really, I feel touched by God. But sometimes it's hard to be chosen, because your senses are so acute. I'm special, because I'm an actor, but I need to rest now, not have people pestering me with questions."

("What for?")

"Shut up," he said.

Grace knew he wasn't talking to her.

Zac moved on the rock beside her and heaved a great sigh. "I'm going for a walk." He jumped down to the sand, faltering a little, as though something was affecting his normal agility.

Remembering how she'd found him in the canyon, Grace sprang down beside him, concerned. Nervously she glanced across the beach. Near one of the camp fires, Nick was in caucus with Colin, Meshach, Nort Stills and the park-service ranger. Grace wondered if they were talking about Zac or if they'd decided he was all right.

He definitely wasn't.

Worried as he started down the shore, Grace said, "Zac, I want some coffee. Will you come help me make it?"

He turned, frowning. "I wish you wouldn't talk so fast."

Grace looked across the beach, silently beckoning Nick. Miraculously the guide stood up and moved toward them. Zac saw him coming.

Panic swept over his face. His eyes grew wide, as though a group of terrorists with Uzis had suddenly emerged from behind the rocks. He ran. Fast. He headed downstream toward the base of the cliffs that walled the river gorge. Boulders were piled at its base, and in horror

Grace watched him scramble up them without care. She could see his coordination was off. If any of those rocks rolled even once...

Zac.

She ran after him across the beach. Pausing at the base of the boulders, she stared up. He was still climbing.

Footsteps pounded behind her in the dark, and then Nick was there, watching Zachary scale the cliff face. The full moon illuminated his journey, and Nick said, "Don't worry. He'll get rimrocked before he gets too high. There aren't any cracks or toeholds after a while."

Grace hugged herself, eyes on Zac. *Don't fall,* she thought. *Don't fall.* She wanted to go after him, but she sensed that he was afraid, that he thought he was being chased.

Was this what he'd been like in New York?

Nick's voice startled her out of her reverie. "So what's wrong with your husband, Amazing Grace?" His eyes drifted toward hers, then stared back up at the figure on the cliff. "Does Zac have some mental health problems we should know about?"

Mental health problems.

The words were a puzzle piece fitting into place. Standing on the beach in the moonlight, with white water roaring beside her, Grace wondered why that had never occurred to her before. She and Zac had just...swept it under the carpet. A breakdown.

Mad.

She looked at Nick. "I guess so."

THE BEACH WAS BUSY all night. News of Zac's condition had spread among the crew members, and Grace saw people standing by tents, talking. Several came over to peer up at the rocky ledge where Zac had stopped his ascent. But the two EMTs persuaded people to go away and leave him alone.

Nick told Grace, "At least if he stays up there, we know where he is."

Meshach eventually turned in, while Nort Stills and Grace and Colin and Nick sat in camping chairs on the beach some distance from the foot of the rocks. The moon had gone behind the walls of the river gorge, and the beach lay in darkness, but a lunar glow still illuminated the ledge where Zachary sat. There was a wall of Precambrian schist at his back, and the effect was absurdly like that of a stage, with a spotlight on the actor. Who was still in costume.

Zac sat back against the schist with his knees drawn up, arms resting negligently on them, and occasionally he spoke to Grace and the others keeping vigil.

It wasn't Shakespeare.

Once he said, "Hi." Another time, seeing them all looking at him, he said, "I don't feel like acting now." And once he began speaking very fast, too quickly to follow, saying things that made no sense, and Grace realized he wasn't talking to them at all but to someone else. Someone who wasn't there. The realization was frightening, and she couldn't help thinking of the things he'd told her that night in the Anasazi Palace, of sleeping in condemned buildings with homeless people. Remembering the filthy man they'd seen on their trip to New York, walking down the street muttering to himself, Grace couldn't help but picture Zac in a similar condition. Alone and confused, because there was no one who cared about him.

She hadn't been there. . . .

But she was here now. Watching him from below as he sat brooding beside the wall of rock that was as old as the earth, she thought of the past weeks, of the sun he had shone on her life with his love for her. She thought, *I will never leave you.*

In the shadows on the beach, Nort Stills said, "This is gonna play havoc with production." He asked Nick and Colin, "Can't you give him something?"

They shook their heads.

Nick asked, "When's that chopper coming tomorrow?"

"Four o'clock," answered Nort.

Grace huddled in her jacket, her sleeping bag around her legs for warmth. She asked Nick, "Don't you think he might be better in the morning?"

Colin's expression was doubtful. Both he and Nick had now heard the story of Zac's breakdown in New York.

Nick said, "It's possible he'll be better. But we need a contingency plan if he's not."

Grace's mind resisted the obvious. She said, "I could use one of the J-rigs and take him back up the river."

Nick looked at her.

Stills said, "If you could just give him something...he could finish filming and take a couple of days off." He gestured at Colin. "Isn't there *something* you can give him?"

Irritated, Grace said, "Maybe they can give *you* something."

Stills looked dumbfounded.

Nick cleared his throat. "I say we wake everybody before light and get the tents down and the beach cleared."

Oh, God, Grace thought. *Oh, God.* In her mind, she saw the orange life vests laid in an X on the beach. She saw the signal mirror flashing. She saw the helicopter with the red cross hovering overhead, descending to the beach.

Coming to get the man she loved.

CHAPTER TWELVE

"ZACHARY, YOU NEED a doctor."

Zac didn't look at her. In the dark he stared down at the people on the beach, his handsome eyebrows drawn together. He seemed to be deep in thought. Grace had brought her sleeping bag up to the ledge, but he wouldn't use it, so she did. The air by the river was damp.

She told him, "We're going to call a helicopter with a medical team tomorrow."

"There's nothing wrong with me."

"You had a stressful day. Maybe something happened to you in the rapids. Or when you saved me. You saved my life, you know."

Zac's face looked off center. He seemed to be listening for something, and she wasn't sure he'd even heard her. There were times when he spoke almost normally, when she felt as though they were having a sane conversation. But then he'd say something strange, and it was like falling into ice water. She felt silly for listening to him. But she was also glad to listen, to be with him. Because he needed someone, and she was his wife, and she loved him.

But he had to be made to understand he was sick. She told him, "I'm worried about you. You're behaving strangely. Colin and Nick don't think you hit your head, but we should find out what's wrong. So we're going to signal a plane to send a helicopter."

Zac couldn't follow her. It was hard to understand anything because of all the talking.

("Never before done this way.")
("After the fact, but before the present.")
("What for?")

He looked at Grace, and he wondered if she could hear it, too.

But she was asking, "Would you like to come down and go to sleep with me?"

Zac blinked, the world clearing for a moment. Grace, her face against his chest, her fingers threaded with his. Drowsy warmth, drifting...

The vision clouded over. Gone.

Grace asked, "Did you understand what I said about tomorrow?"

Zac pondered her words. Tomorrow.

"Zachary, listen to me. Tomorrow, a helicopter will come with a medical team to fly you to the hospital in Grand Junction."

Hospital? thought Zac. He wasn't sick.

HE WASN'T SICK and he knew why they were sending a helicopter. To take him away. To deport him, except that wasn't what would happen. They had something worse in mind.

It wasn't light yet, and already the beach was crawling with people. He had to get away. He told Grace, "I'm going down."

Bad plan, Grace thought. In the past few hours she had climbed up and down the rocks several times, talking with Zac, reporting to Nick and Colin. Finally she'd asked the EMTs, "What if he won't get on the helicopter?"

The men had exchanged a look, and Colin, who'd spent years riding with an ambulance in Los Angeles, had said, "Oh, they'll get him on."

The words were ominous. In a straitjacket? she wondered.

Now Zac stood up, ready to go down to the beach. Although he'd been up all night, he seemed wide awake. Grace was weak with fatigue, her body battered by its ordeal in the keeper, her mind exhausted from trying to understand Zachary's.

Gathering up her sleeping bag, she handed it to Zac, thinking it might slow him, and they made their way down the rocks. As they descended, Grace scanned the beach under the lightening sky. With a feeling beyond gratitude, she saw that Fast Susan and Dirty Bob were already busy in the kitchen, starting breakfast. The other boatmen were moving dories to the far end of the beach and turning rafts upside down, stowing gear under them so it wouldn't be blown away by the propeller blades. Not all the tents were down. Five remained standing, and Grace saw Meshach beside one of them giving directions to a crew member.

Zac hadn't stopped the production, and Grace supposed that was good. Losing a day's filming would be expensive for the studio; as well, the shooting would draw attention away from Zachary. But although Meshach and Nort Stills made noises of concern, Grace sensed their underlying disesteem, as though Zac's worth in their eyes had lessened. The realization made Grace think of the homeless man on the street in New York. If Zachary was regarded this way, what happened to the people who had no one?

Grace knew she should at least check in at the kitchen. But how could she cook and keep an eye on Zac?

As they reached the foot of the cliff and jumped down onto the sand, she asked him, "How about some breakfast?"

He squinted at her. "I think I have a call. At seven. What time is it?"

Did he really think he could work?

Maybe he can, Grace thought. He would need to use one of the solar showers to bathe. And he was still in his costume from the day before. Did she dare leave him to the crew?

At last Nick came over and Grace said, "I should see if Susan and Bob need me."

The guide said, "Okay," and she knew he'd look after Zac.

Unencumbered, Grace hurried to help the guides make breakfast. As she worked through a haze of exhaustion, preparing blue cornmeal and sunflower pancakes, bacon, French toast, rice pudding and fruit salad, she thought, *Maybe Zac will be okay. Maybe he's getting better. Maybe working will help.*

But as the cast and crew filed by with plates, getting their food, she looked past them and saw two boatmen laying life vests on the beach in two perpendicular lines to form a giant X.

As she poured orange juice for one of the crew members, he asked, "Why do you have to signal a plane? Why not use radios? Or one of the cellulars?"

"They don't work in this section of the canyon." Grace nodded toward the walls of the river gorge. The sun wouldn't rise above them for hours. "Those cliffs are two thousand feet high, and we're miles from the nearest town."

All they could do was wait for a plane to pass—or the helicopter the studio had hired to arrive at four that evening. When breakfast had been served, Grace slipped away to see how Zac was doing and bring him some food.

Miraculously he had showered and was in a fresh costume. Hoping things were improving, Grace brought his plate into the tent where the makeup artist was working on him. He frowned at the food but said nothing as she found a place for it on the table.

Grace studied his eyes and his face. He wasn't himself, but the fact that he was cooperating, trying to do his job, seemed hopeful. Leaving him, she went out to where Nick, signal mirror in hand, was watching the sky for planes. The guide looked as exhausted as she was. Like her, he was still in the same clothes he'd worn the night before.

Grace indicated the life vests on the beach. "Do you think we're going overboard?"

He glanced toward the makeup tent and shrugged.

"Maybe it was just reaction to what happened yesterday," Grace said. "He's under control now. Maybe he's getting over it."

Just then she heard a sound behind her and turned to see the makeup artist emerge from the tent. The woman came right over to them. "Um . . ." Her eyes darted between Grace and Nick.

Both of them looked at the tent.

"He's gone."

HE'D PLANNED it while he gathered things for his shower, stuffing everything in Grace's day pack. Two bottles of water. Clothes. Running shoes. Sunscreen. His river knife.

While Nick waited outside the makeup tent, he had put the plan into action. He'd cut a slit in the back of the tent and gone out.

He knew where they'd expect him to go. Back into Cross Canyon, back to the trail he'd seen the night before, the trail that led up to above. But that would make it too easy. He'd seen the faint switchback winding along the cliff face. They could pick him off easily there.

No, there was only one way out of here. First back into canyon, bluffing, and then... His dog. They might try to get to him through Ninochka. He had to go to Moab and reach her before they did.

What about Grace? he thought as he ran. Was she part of this?

What if they hurt *her?*

("Lies will tell in sleepless days...")

("Don't let him go up there.")

("Why not?")

He stopped long enough to throw the boots in the shrubs and put on his running shoes. As he switched routes, climbing back along the rock wall to the beach, he tried to guard his thoughts. They might have thought-reading equipment. He wouldn't think about anything that mattered. He wouldn't think about his dog. Or about... her.

"HE HAS A PACK?" Grace asked when she'd heard the makeup artist's brief report. Her eyes scanned the beach. Zac must have gone back into the canyon. That was where he'd wanted to go the night before. Heart racing, she stared at the switchback zigzagging up the canyon wall, exposed for thousands of vertical feet. The trail was narrow as a brick in places. And Zachary's coordination was impaired.

Turning, Grace hurried to her tent, and Nick followed. After a quick glance inside she told him, "He's got my pack and the water bottles. And the knife of course. Who knows what else he took?" She looked at Nick, panic surging through her. "Do you have a pack?"

"You can't go after him, Grace. He's psychotic, and he has a knife."

Psychotic. That sounded a lot uglier than "mental health problems."

Grace said, "He's my husband. Believe me, he's less likely to hurt me than anyone else. Besides, he's a gentle person."

"He's not *himself.*"

She looked toward the canyon, where she knew Zac had gone. It was the only way to go, except the river.

The river.

She glanced first at the rafts overturned on the beach, then at the shore. *Zachary.* Disbelieving, she saw him pushing a dory away from the shore.

"Zac!" He wasn't even wearing a life jacket.

People on the beach stared at her as she ran. She heard Nick calling her, and she kept going, right to the river. Zac was watching her from the eddy as he fitted the oars in the oarlocks. Grace kept running—into the river, into the cold, turbulent water. The current sucked at her.

Tossing hair back from his eyes, Zac said, "I'm going."

She reached the side of the boat and grabbed the gunwale. "No, you're not."

"We can't wait! Get in!" His eyes, green irises in a field of white, roved the shore. Seeing Nick splashing into the shallows, Zachary pushed on the oars. "Goodbye, Grace. I'll find you again."

Grace clung to the gunwale, but the dory was twenty-one feet long and propelled by a strong man. Her feet dragged in the silt, then came out from under her as the dory swept out of the eddy into the current with her holding on, slipping down in the cold water, soaking her clothes.

From the shore, Nick yelled curses at them both. "Grace, you got shit for brains or what?"

Grace stared at the rapid ahead, then back at the shore. She'd already made her choice, and now she started hauling herself up over the gunwale as the water filled her tennis shoes, numbed her legs. Zac turned from the oars to help her into the boat. As his hands locked around her arms and Grace pulled a leg over the gunwale, Nick yelled, "Range Canyon! Got it? Range Canyon!"

Grace heard. The chopper could land in Range Canyon—which was well before the Big Drop. She yelled, "Ten-four, commodore!"

Zac steadied her as she scrambled into the dory, water streaming off her clothes onto the floor of the boat. In his face Grace saw confusion and illness, and her heart ached.

Oh, Zachary, she thought. *Come back.*

The white water roared near. Zac was at the oars, and it was too late to change places. Working to slow her pulse, Grace said, "Turn around and row, Zac."

Straddling the seat, he looked at her, then down at the space between them, the floor of the boat. His expression was terribly sad. But after a moment, he swung a long, muscular leg over the seat and took the oars.

Grace drew a breath. The dory was already tossing toward the white water. Like a good boatman, Zac rowed toward the V at the top.

We're going to be okay, Grace thought, feeling naked without a life vest. As she looked around and found a bail bucket, stowed beneath the seat, she began to plan. Range Canyon.

THERE WAS A STRETCH of calm water after the first set of rapids, but Zac kept rowing. "They'll come after us. They have other boats."

Grace hoped Nick would have the sense not to follow. He must know Zac was scared. She said, "Zachary, ship the oars. Just let us drift. I need to talk to you."

("Don't talk.)

("Liars in the alley. Don't drop the goose.")

Who was talking? Zac wondered. Letting the oars dangle in the water, he whispered, "Grace, can you hear them?"

Grace heard the fear in his voice, and she moved up to straddle the seat where Zac sat. She grabbed the left oar and pulled it into the boat. Her shorts and pile sweater were soaked, and she was chilled and eager to see the sun. Zachary's body heat would have to do in the meantime. Her thigh behind him, she reached her arm around him, under the backpack he wore, to try to grasp the other oar.

Zac pulled it in. She put both arms around him, pressed her face against his shoulder. "What are you hearing, Zac?"

"They talk to me."

He had said he'd heard voices in New York. Grace rubbed his back gently. *Stay calm,* she thought. If she could just keep him calm until Range Canyon. If she could just persuade him to stop there.

"I can't think when they talk."

Grace didn't know what doctors did for someone in Zachary's condition. Could they make him better? Could they make the voices stop? She hoped so. She held him tight.

Zac moved so that he could see her. Grace. He was glad to have her along. He smiled, satisfied that they were together.

She wasn't smiling. She said, "Zac, do you trust me?"

He thought about it, then nodded.

"I want to tell you something." Her brown eyes were earnest. "You're putting our lives in danger right now. You don't realize it, because something's wrong with you. You need to go to the hospital. I want you to go. I love you. I won't let anyone hurt you."

("Bargains at five!")

("That's a real dollar value.")

"We shouldn't be on the river, Zachary. There are very big rapids ahead, and we have no life vests."

Zac frowned. For a moment an image flashed through his mind. A raft rising vertically from the river, Grace dangling like a rag doll from a rope.

"Zac, remember the movie? Remember your work?"

His eyes grew fearful. He peered about the peaceful canyon. They were alone. Lowering his head to hers, he whispered urgently, "They're in this together. I don't know why."

Grace kept her eyes on his. "Zachary. What you're thinking is not real. What I'm telling you is real. Your mind isn't working right. You need a doctor."

Could she be right? *DSM-IV.* Was it published by the INS? Puzzling over it, Zac studied the river, the reflection of the orange walls on the water. The sun shone on the right side, reaching halfway down the cliff face.

He frowned and said, "Okay."

Grace thought, *Thank you, God.*

It was a brief reprieve.

Before the next rapid, Zac became agitated again. He nearly rowed them into a hole, and afterward, as Grace bailed, he resumed talk of escaping.

Knowing Range Canyon was approaching, Grace said, "Pull over at the beach on the right. Mile Long Rapid's ahead. We shouldn't run it without scouting." That was true, but Grace cringed at her chicanery.

Zac took her at her word.

He pushed for the beach, guided the dory into an eddy. Grace climbed up on the bow. The sunshine was hitting the shore, and it touched her skin as she leapt from the boat with the bowline.

Her heart pounded as she looked at Zac. She was going to have to be the actor now. "Pull up the oars." Glancing into the little box canyon, she said, "We'll need a big rock to put on the bowline."

Zac climbed out of the boat, stepping into the water. It swirled around his knees, and again Grace noticed his slight clumsiness. As he slogged toward her through the water, she pointed at a large rock some distance up the beach. "That one."

Zac nodded and started walking toward it.

Careful to let her feet splash the water as little as possible, Grace stepped into the cold river and began to move downstream, holding the gunwale of the boat. She could hardly breathe.

Past the eddy. Get out of the eddy.

The water on her legs felt like ice. She didn't look up. As she pulled the boat downstream, the current tugged at the dory. The stern swung out into the river.

Go, baby, go. Take it.

She grabbed the bow and shoved, and the dory swept out into the current, floating for Mile Long Rapid.

"WHAT ARE YOU DOING?"

His voice came from immediately behind her, and Grace jumped, shaking to her shoes. When she turned she saw Zac, inches away, eyes wide and intense, muscles quivering. "Why did you do that?" He was whispering now, his voice ragged. *"Why did you do that?"*

He was too close, too big, too out of control. As he stepped toward her, his eyes like a stranger's, Grace saw the muscles in his neck, in his shoulders and lean, sinewy arms.

"Zac—"

"You tricked me." His eyes narrowed.

Grace was afraid. She whispered, "Calm down."

"No! You lied to me! You're turning me in! *Why don't you love me?*"

Grace drew up, holding her ground, forcing herself to breathe. She tried to draw on a power inside her, something she knew must be there, the strength to confront any situation.

She stared at Zachary and saw the sun on his hair. She saw his smeared makeup, which had the effect of making him look more insane. But underneath she also saw the cleft chin, the jaw, the straight nose, the sensuous lips, the face she had kissed. The face that had kissed her in the most intimate ways. For a moment she remembered those times, the closeness, the love coming from him. The tenderness. This person in front of her was the same man.

Somewhere inside him, he was.

She forced herself to be calm, unafraid, even though his whole body was shaking, even though his face was so altered.

Even though he was psychotic.

She said, "I do love you."

Drawing a breath, she glanced at him one more time, then turned away and walked out of the frigid water, up the beach and into the sunshine. *Relax,* she told herself. *Relax, and he'll relax.*

She thought of the river knife and what Nick had said. Zachary probably shouldn't have it. Partway up the beach, she paused and looked back at him. He was staring at the boat tumbling through the froth, disappearing from sight. He seemed sad, but calm.

Grace knew it would upset him if she tried to take the knife.

She stood for a moment surveying the beach, which was bordered by rock and water. The box canyon was tiny, the walls vertical, impossible to scale without climbing aids.

She thought, *Good choice, Nick. Good choice.*

There was no way out of here.

Casting one last glance at Zachary standing beside the river, she collapsed on the silty shore, lay back and closed her eyes. And tried to stop shaking.

SHE DOZED, awakening only to the sound of the plane passing. It tipped its wings as it flew over, and she waved, knowing the pilot must have seen the signal on the other beach. The ranger had probably spoken to him by radio.

She sat up and looked around. Zac sat in the shade against the cliff wall, her day pack beside him. He'd taken off his clothes.

Grace closed her eyes and went back to sleep.

ZAC HEARD THE CHOPPER before she did, and he knew it was coming for him. As he stared up at the big white bird with the red cross on the side, emotion crawled up his throat. Rescue, he thought. The sight was comforting. *Take care of me,* he thought. *Someone take care of me.*

("Drink it up, Alice. Drink the last drop.")

The sound of the propellers beating was loud, and he saw Grace coming toward him across the beach. Grace, who had pushed the boat down the river. She stopped and picked up his pants—Seneca's pants—and Zac's running shoes.

The helicopter was louder than the voices. It drowned them out. As the aircraft descended, Zac felt his hair start to blow. His heartbeat quickened. What were they going to do to him?

Grace stood in front of him and yelled, "Want to put on your pants?"

Zac stared down at the clothes she held. He nodded and reached for them.

Grace was relieved. Maybe this wouldn't be so bad. She touched his back as he bent over, sliding the pants on, his hair hanging in his face. He needed suspenders, but they were gone.

Grace said, "They'll stay up! It's okay!"

Zac focused on her eyes, his own blinking. He felt like crying. Why was this happening?

The whirlybird came lower. Zac's hair whipped all around his face, and the earth seemed to shake. His heart was throbbing in time with the giant white bird. What was happening? Why did he have to get on the helicopter?

Grace put her arm around him, smelling the salty sweat on his body. There was sweat on his upper lip, too, under the five-o'clock shadow. Scared sweat. But he stood straight and tall, his green eyes staring intently at the chopper as it came down and alighted on the beach.

Thinking of everything she'd learned about helicopter rescues, Grace told Zac, "Just stay back here! We'll wait for them." She knew the exhaust from the chopper was hot enough to burn them to a crisp.

The doors opened.

As uniformed attendants in light blue shirts got out, Zac backed against the rock wall. Grace saw two people bringing out a folding gurney, while a tall blond man with a bushy mustache, dressed in blue jeans and a polo shirt, jogged across the sand toward her and Zachary.

Zac's eyes were on the gurney. Grace felt his muscles tighten, felt him trembling. He slipped free from her grasp, pushing hair out of his eyes, and stared at the helicopter. Moving backward, he edged along under the overhanging cliff ledge, his eyes big.

The blond man reached Grace and held out his hand. "Dr. Jake Caruthers. I'm with Air Rescue. What's going on?" He glanced at Zac, who was creeping away.

As concisely as possible, Grace told him everything, including what she knew about Zachary's problems in New York.

"Has he been violent?"

Grace hesitated, remembering when he'd yelled at her. "His moods swing. He's very scared."

"Has he taken any drugs? Is he on medication?

Grace shook her head. She turned to look at Zac. He'd disappeared.

The doctor said, "Don't worry. We'll find him. He doesn't have any weapons, does he?"

Grace remembered the knife. The pack was at her feet, and she picked it up, searched inside and found the river knife, the knife he'd used to save her. She drew a shaky breath. "No."

"Okay. We'll take care of him." The doctor gave her a reassuring look and strode back toward the helicopter to confer with the rest of the team. They peered up toward

the canyon, and when Grace went over to join them, one
of the men asked, "Do you know the terrain? Can he get
out of there?"

"He can't." Grace wished she'd thought to reacquaint
herself with the canyon earlier, but she knew it was small.
Barely a canyon at all.

The doctor said, "Okay, we'll make a line and spread
out. Find him, talk to him, see how he's doing, let him
know what's happening. Grace, why don't you stay here?
We'll probably have to take him down and give him some
medication, and it's better if there's nothing else for him
to worry about."

Take him down? Grace thought.

ZAC HUDDLED under an overhang at the base of the cliff
wall. Beneath him was wet sand, seeping up between his
toes; his head rubbed against silt from the rock. All
around him, he could smell the canyon. Wet desert smells.
Dry wet.

A group of strangers stood before him. The man in
street clothes had crouched down and was talking to him.

"Zac, I'm Dr. Caruthers, and your friends up the river
summoned the Air Rescue team because they thought you
needed someone to take you out of the canyon. Your wife
says you're not feeling well. Is that right?"

Zac felt his face quivering. "Don't touch me."

"No one's going to touch you right now. But we need
you to take control of yourself. Can you do that?"

"I'm in control. I'm in control. I'm in control."

("Echoing harshness, acting by night in light of day.")
He wished his body would stop shaking.

"Zac, see if you can calm down. We can walk out of
here. You can get on the gurney, we'll give you some
medication, and we can go to the hospital."

Zac shivered. He didn't want to go with them. He didn't know them. Why was he alone? Why did he have to be alone? What were they going to do to him?

Nearby a bush twitched, shivering in the wind, and he started. He stared into the leaves. Other canyon. Grace in her bikini. Kissing, taking off each other's clothes. That feeling when they held each other, when their skin touched, when he saw her eyes. Love.

"Zac?"

He jumped.

The blond man was looking at him. "Zac, let me tell you what we're going to do."

Zac couldn't follow the words. Why were they doing this to him? Why was Grace letting them? He had to get away.

("Forevermore and not until.")

("No, you may not use the WC.")

Watching them, he ducked out of the alcove and started to stand.

They sprang at him, grabbing his limbs, pushing him down on his face, holding him.

Zac yanked against them, but he was pinned hard. There was dirt in his face, in his eyes and nose and teeth, and his chest pounded. He'd never been held so tight in his life, and he didn't know why it seemed good, good that someone was in control. But it wasn't him, and he started screaming.

Someone was pulling at his clothes. He shrieked.

"Zac, buddy, you're gonna feel a little sting."

He realized he was laughing hysterically. They stabbed him, and he yelled, "Stop it! Leave me alone! Don't do this to me! Help! Someone help me!" Laughing, eyes watering, crying out, he tried to twist his head, tried to see, but all he could find was the sleeve of a blue shirt.

A stranger's voice said, "You're all right, Zac. You'll feel better soon."

They were going to stuff him like a deer that had been shot. He tried to get up, but they were all holding him so tight.

He heard them talking, but he couldn't follow any of it, and then they were rolling him, and there was something beneath him. The faces of strangers looked down at him. A man in a blue shirt said, "Zac, you're going to be all right. We're going to restrain you so you don't hurt yourself or anyone on the helicopter."

Wide straps were going around him. He moved his head, reaching out, trying to bite an arm. If he caught someone he would hang on like one of those Gila monsters, bite hard... But no one was close enough, so he tried to break the straps. "I'm going to slap a malpractice suit on you! This is against the law! This is against any law! I'm a legal alien! I have a green card! There's a British Embassy here! You won't get away with this! I'm an Old Etonian and an Oxford man, and my father's an earl!"

A woman above him was smiling, as though he was funny. Who were these people? "Settle down, Zac. No one's going to hurt you."

("What for?")

("Never forget this.")

They were still holding him. A man was near him, and Zac spit at him. He spit at them all. Then he saw the woman, and he was too embarrassed to spit at her. Somebody said, "We've got to calm him down. We can't take him up like this."

He heard Grace's voice, but he couldn't make sense of the words. Someone was asking her questions. Zac knew they were going to operate on him, and he tried to scream again, but he couldn't make himself.

"Don't thrash." It was the woman. She turned and told someone, "More..." Instead of saying anything, she made a pumping motion with her thumb and fingers. Another shot.

Zac screamed at her. He was screaming for a long time, and he was hardly aware that they were carrying him.

"Zac?"

The eyes looking down at him were familiar. Brown. Someone was stroking his hair. He felt a strange calm seeping over him, but he was still afraid. He watched Grace's mouth. One side moved more than the other, but he couldn't sort out which was which, only that it was her.

She said, "I love you."

"Don't let them . . ." But he was afraid to finish, to say it out loud, in case they hadn't thought of it. *Taxidermy.*

Grace stared down at his frightened face. She let her fingers slide through his hair, and she said again, "I really love you. Don't be afraid. I wouldn't let anyone hurt you, Zachary."

The feeling of calmness increased. It didn't feel natural, but it felt better. And it felt good to have Grace touching him. He couldn't follow her words, something about seeing him at the hospital, but he wasn't so afraid anymore.

CHAPTER THIRTEEN

FAST SUSAN SHOWED UP in the J-rig a few minutes after the chopper left. She'd been waiting farther up the river, and she told Grace the studio's helicopter would pick her up and take her back to Moab so she could be with Zac. The guides had known she couldn't ride with Air Rescue.

The studio helicopter arrived early, and by two o'clock, Grace was winging over the canyonlands, on her way to Zac. Day met her at the Moab air terminal to drive her the 120 miles to Grand Junction, Colorado. Thinking ahead, Day had gone to the house and packed clothes for Grace and Zac. As the Suburban carried them east through the desert on I-70, Grace told her sister what had happened on the river—and in New York.

She felt as though she was walking the brink of an emotional abyss. It was part exhaustion. Her muscles were stiff from rowing, her body sore from banging coolers and ammo cans, from twisting unnaturally in the keeper. It hurt to move, but it was the memory of Zac that kept her most on edge. She felt as though she'd been shivering for hours from listening to him, watching him, walking the convoluted paths of his mind. And her heart felt bruised, tender, because she realized how much she loved him, how much she wanted the real Zachary back. And how much she needed to hold on to the parts of him she could still touch. He was in there. He would be normal again....

She was so lonely without him.

Day said, "Gosh, Grace, some of those mental illnesses are pretty bad. I saw a special about it on a talk show once. People Zachary's age get sick and never get well."

Grace clutched herself.

Zac... like this forever?

Day glanced across the seat and said, "Oh, God, I'm sorry." She pulled the truck over two lanes and onto a ranch road and stopped. Reaching for her sister, holding her, she said, "I'm sorry, Gracie."

Grace just cried, saying things that felt true to the deepest places inside her. "I love him. I'm never going to leave him." But through the blur of her tears, she saw Day's face and imagined what her sister might have seen on the talk show. That sometimes people *had* to leave.

IT WAS DARK when they reached the hospital. Grace felt as dirty as she was drained. Although she'd put on a clean T-shirt and jeans in the airport bathroom, the silt of the Colorado lingered on her skin and hair. She would find a hotel nearby and shower and sleep—after she saw Zac.

As Day parked in the visitors' lot, Grace realized how hard it would be to go into the hospital. This was where her father had died. This was where Nick and Day had told her he was dead. Wanting to protect her sister from the memories, Grace asked, "Would you mind going and finding a hotel nearby for me?"

Day gave her a look and pushed open the driver's door. "Yes, I would."

They went in together.

A receptionist at admissions directed them to the emergency room. There, a nurse told Grace they'd taken Zac to the "locked ward." Grace listened to directions, then turned to Day. Her sister was pale, and Grace knew the trip to the hospital was affecting her.

As they headed down the hall, Grace said, "Look, I don't think they'll let you in this place. I'd really appreciate it if you'd check me into a hotel." She opened her wallet to give her a credit card, but Day waved it away.

"All right, I'll go, and then I'll meet you outside Zac's ward. You want me to find a place with a kitchenette? You might be here for a while."

"Thanks."

Day smiled. "Tell him his dog misses him." Then, looking as though she'd been tactless, she added, "She misses you, too, of course."

Grace didn't mind being an afterthought. Ninochka was Zac's dog. She responded to no one as she did to him. At the sight or sound of the Austin-Healey, she always dashed out of the house or river office. *Like me,* Grace thought. *In love.*

After her sister had left, she found her way to the appropriate wing of the hospital. At the desk outside sat an athletic-looking redhead in street clothes. Noting the big locked door she knew must lead into the unit, Grace said, "I'm Grace Key. I think my husband, Zachary, is here."

The redhead showed instant recognition—in a way that made Grace wonder what Zac had been doing. "I doubt they'll let you see him, but let me check." She got on the phone. Hanging up moments later, she said, "Dr. Holyoak is coming out to talk to you. Why don't you have a seat?"

Grace sat in the waiting area, and soon she heard the door unlocking and saw a man come out. He was in his forties, tall and bearded, with thick mahogany hair that needed a trim. His khaki chinos and blue oxford-cloth shirt were wrinkled, and Grace liked his face, which was craggy and comfortable.

As she stood up, he came toward her and held out his hand. "Mrs. Key? I'm Dr. Michael Holyoak." The psychiatrist's manner was comfortable and reassuring. "I know you want to see your husband, and we'll do what we can in that direction, but let me fill you in first. After you see him, we can sit down and have a longer chat."

Hungry to see Zac but trying to be patient, Grace listened as the doctor told her they didn't know why Zachary was exhibiting psychotic symptoms. Tests had been run to assure that neither an organic problem nor a brain injury was causing the problem. He was refusing medication, and the period of time during which the hospital could give it to him without his consent had elapsed. Now, drug treatment could not be resumed without the hospital's proving that Zac was a danger to himself or others. As attending physician, Dr. Holyoak planned to petition the court to have Zachary involuntarily medicated. If Grace preferred, she need not be involved at all.

Frowning, Grace asked, "Can't we see if he gets better on his own?"

"I think the sooner he receives treatment, the more quickly he'll recover." Before Grace could respond, the psychiatrist delivered the next blow. "He's in seclusion now, and we don't encourage visits to patients there. It tends to agitate them. But what I can do is let you look at him through a window."

Grace made an exclamation of dismay. She didn't want to see Zac through a window. She wanted to be in the same room with him. To touch him. "Why can't I talk to him? I'm his wife. I promised him I'd come."

"We're trying to calm him down. I know you'd like to talk to him, but our first obligation is to the patient. This is what's best for him. And he has been violent."

Grace wasn't surprised. Zac had been terrified when they took him out of Cataract. Now he was locked up by strangers. She said, "I think it would soothe him to see me. Maybe I could persuade him to take medication."

The doctor smiled a little. "It's pretty hard to persuade a psychotic person of anything." Without agreeing to her suggestion, he stood up. "Let's go take a look at him."

Dr. Holyoak led her to the door through which he'd come. He unlocked it, and they went through, and it shut behind them, locking automatically. Then he opened a second door. As that, too, bolted behind them, Grace was acutely aware of the place in which they'd put Zachary. Locked ward. She could go out. He could not.

She couldn't even talk to him.

The psychiatrist led her down a narrow hall. A man in street clothes walked past, and Grace wondered if he was a doctor. But as she and Dr. Holyoak reached the nurse's station, she realized none of the personnel in the wing were wearing hospital clothes. Probably uniforms upset the patients.

At the nurse's desk, a muscular black man sat writing. A voice was coming from a speaker somewhere nearby, and after a moment Grace realized it was Zac speaking, but she couldn't make out the words.

Off to her left were two rooms. As Dr. Holyoak led her toward one of them, the door opened and the tallest man Grace had ever seen came out. The door swung shut behind him with the snick of a lock.

The psychiatrist said, "How are we doing?"

The attendant smiled ruefully. "Ripping the place apart."

A phone rang at the nurse's station, and the call was for Dr. Holyoak. Before he left to take it, he said, "Leif, this is Mrs. Key. She'd like to look through the window at her husband."

Leif—*Lanky Leif,* Grace thought—smiled obligingly and led her to the door of the room he'd just left. He indicated the reinforced window and Grace peered through.

Zachary.

He was pacing the floor, wearing only pajama bottoms. Despite his condition—which was apparent in a glance—Grace was consoled to see him. Her husband. Behind her, she could still hear his voice from the speaker at the reception desk, and as she watched Zac through the glass he seemed to be talking to someone invisible, almost as though he was rehearsing. He looked wild. He looked what he was.

Mentally ill.

But Grace remembered his vulnerability in Range Canyon, how he'd fought to free himself from the restraints, his green eyes wildly frightened, then calming on hers as the medication began to take effect. She felt a love for him so intense and overwhelming it was hard to recognize as the same love that glued them together in marriage. But it was the same love. This was the first time she'd known its power. It was bigger than she was. It was all she could feel. He was her husband.

She wanted him back.

Hugging herself, Grace surveyed the small room through the glass. The only furnishings were a sink, a toilet and a bare mattress. The mattress had been thrown over the sink, undoubtedly by Zac. She looked up at Leif. "There's not much in there."

Leif winked at her. "Don't worry. He's not bored." Then, sobering, he said, "Actually we can't let them have much. They kill themselves."

God, thought Grace. In the room Zac nervously inspected his arms and chest and ran his hands over himself, as though he had hives.

"We go in every ten or fifteen minutes and tell him where he is and what's happened to him and that no one's going to hurt him." In a serious straightforward way, Leif told her, "We're taking care of him."

After Cataract Canyon, Grace knew she could not. Not as he was now.

But he wouldn't be like this forever. He couldn't be. From the speaker behind her, Zac's voice intruded on her thoughts. She heard him say, "You must be silent, for I cannot think in the hell of your words. There are no answers here...."

Staring through the window, watching him, Grace felt reality slamming home.

Zachary was mad.

DAY WAS WAITING when Grace emerged from the locked area. Grace had answered many questions for Dr. Holyoak, relating all she had told the Air Rescue team and more. He'd seemed interested in Zac's problems in New York but didn't share his thoughts except to say, "We'll have to see how he does."

Day drove her to the hotel, which was just a block from the hospital and had a room with a kitchenette. After her sister had left for Moab, Grace lay down on the bed and tried not to think.

She knew she should call Zac's parents, but she'd hardly ever spoken to them—and not since she'd left him. What if Zac's mother was having one of her spells of depression? Upset, Grace consulted the clock and was relieved to find it was the middle of the night in England.

Without bothering to change clothes, she kicked off her shoes, got into bed and tried to sleep. But she couldn't, and she turned on her side, wanting him so badly that soon she was gasping tears into the pillow. She had never been so terribly afraid.

When she slept, she dreamed of the keeper and knew she was drowning. At the threshold of death, she started awake, and it took a moment to come back to reality. Where she was. Why.

A blackness deeper than the nightmare gripped her. She felt utterly alone. Zac was gone, as though he'd become someone else. And she wanted him back so much.

Why aren't you here? she thought, knowing the question was irrational. *Why are you never here when I need you most?*

"IF YOU LAY A HAND on me, I'll take you and this so-called hospital for all you're worth!" exclaimed Zac, advancing toward the phony doctor and his cohort. The second man was seven feet tall. Everyone here was large.

The man with the beard, the quack, said, "No one's touching you."

It felt as though someone *was* touching him. Someone or something. Zac had felt bugs crawling on him ever since he'd gotten to this place. Lice. He was sure of it. This wasn't a hospital. It was a medieval asylum. At any moment, they'd take him away for cold showers and electric shock. A lobotomy. Zac drew his emotions in line. "You do not know who you're dealing with. My father belongs to the House of Lords. I am the Honourable Zachary Key, and I demand my release."

"Zac, no one here is going to hurt you. You're in Grand Mesa Hospital. I'm Dr. Michael Holyoak, and I'm a psychiatrist."

For one moment, Zac wondered if what they'd been telling him could be true. If he was really in a hospital. If they were really there to help him. If he was…psychotic.

DSM-IV. He saw the book in his mind.

("Drink it up, now.")

("Never too late.")

("How much?")

Dr. Holyoak said, "We want you to be in control. Someone has to be in control. It's going to be us or you, and we want it to be you."

Zac tried to grasp the words. In between each, the voices came.

("What for?")

("Have not said...")

He had to get out of here before they decided to operate. Brain implants. Lobotomy. Castration.

He eyed the seven-foot-tall man. Both he and the doctor were in front of the door.

Zac lunged toward them. The tall man shouted something, and the door flew open. More large people. Zac had met them before, and he sprang backward, yelling, "Back off! Keep your hands off me!"

They did.

They left, and he dove to catch the door before it closed. It wouldn't open, and he kicked it and pounded it with his fist and yelled, vaguely remembering another door that wouldn't open. He was trapped. And the bugs... He could feel their legs walking on his skin, everywhere, even on his genitals, and he cried, "Get them off me! Please get them off!" He tried to brush them away with his hands, but he couldn't even see them with his eyes, and he knew he was being tortured, and he prayed it would stop.

Someone make it stop!

GRACE DIDN'T GO to the hearing the next morning. She waited at the hospital, in the area beside the lockup, reading a new mystery. She'd picked it up in the gift shop on a glance, but now she regretted the choice.

The back-cover blurb read, "A dangerous psychotic is terrorizing the small Midwestern town of..."

A dangerous psychotic.

All her life, Grace had heard the word psychotic used only that way. Psycho. Norman Bates outside the shower curtain.

But Zac wasn't like that. He was afraid. Hearing voices...

No one would let her in to look at Zac without the doctor's okay, and the doctor had gone to the hearing. But at about eleven in the morning, Grace saw the psychiatrist coming down the hallway with a clipboard and several pieces of paper in hand. "Well, we got it." The court order. "We'll see how he does on some antipsychotic medication." Promising to come out and talk with her after he spoke to Zac—and of course wrote his orders—the doctor went into the locked ward. Soon three big men, nurses and technicians from other parts of the hospital, arrived and went inside, also.

Grace knew why they'd come. In her mind, she could still hear Zac's bloodcurdling screams filling Range Canyon, echoing off the walls, as the Air Rescue team restrained him. Now he was going through the same thing again, and Grace wished they would let her be there to tell him it was all right, to calm him afterward.

Almost an hour later, Dr. Holyoak emerged from the ward and joined her in the otherwise empty waiting area. Sitting down, he laid aside his clipboard and started to talk. They'd given Zac the medication and now it was a matter of waiting to see if it helped.

Grace asked, "Do you know what's wrong with him?"

He shook his head. "All I can tell you is that right now he's acutely psychotic. His CT scan was negative. This might just be a brief psychotic episode—a reaction to what happened on the river. But since you've said this has happened before, we need to look at other possibilities." He glanced at his notes. "Let me ask you a couple of questions."

They spoke for fifteen minutes, and finally he asked if she'd make an appointment at his office for the next day to tell him more about Zac.

238   THE KEEPER

Grace agreed, but before he could leave she asked, "Is there a book you could recommend about mental illness?" She wanted to understand what was happening to Zac.

The doctor looked hesitant. "Well . . . yes. But please realize, Grace, that mental illness is complicated. Making a diagnosis can be difficult, and when we do make it, it's sometimes not as precise as we'd like. What I wouldn't want is for you to read a lot of books and decide Zac is schizophrenic or bipolar or what have you. That said—" he took a pharmaceutical company notepad from his shirt pocket "—there's a very good and popular book for families of people with mental illnesses. It provides a sensitive picture of the kinds of things a psychotic person may feel. It also deals with situations that may affect you. Things like what went on today. He refused medication. We had to go to court."

Grace asked, "When can I see him again?"

He glanced toward the door. "Let me go see how he's doing. It takes a while for a shot to work."

Several minutes later, Lanky Leif came out and escorted her back into the seclusion area so she could look through the window at Zac. He was still shirtless, and he sat against the wall with his knees up, brooding.

Grace stared at him, willing him to glance up. He did not. Her powerlessness terrified her, and her heart cried out to him, pleading harder than he'd ever begged her. *Come back. Dammit, come back!*

GRACE RETURNED to her hotel. She'd already called Zac's agent and explained what was happening. She'd also called the production office and talked to Hal Markley. Though eager to have Zac back on the set, the producer was understanding. "We'll shoot around him," he said. "Let me know if there's anything we can do to help."

Grace knew there was one more phone call she should make, and she dreaded it. She still remembered her last experience trying to reach Lord and Lady Key. *His Lordship is traveling, and Her Ladyship is unavailable. Who? Mr. Zachary Key no longer lives here. No, I can't tell you any more.*

Sitting on the hotel bed, Grace dug her address book out of her purse. She glanced at the clock. It would be after ten at night in England, but she shouldn't wait any longer.

When the phone began to ring, she held her breath. Although Zac had called them several times while he'd been living with her in New York, Grace had talked with his parents only once. They'd asked her about herself and made small talk, and all the time she knew they were wondering why their son had married a woman he'd known such a short time. She doubted Zac had ever told them the truth.

"Key here."

Grace's heart pounded. The earl's accent was much more pronounced that Zachary's, and Grace remembered thinking when they spoke the last time that he was hard to understand.

Trying to speak clearly, she said, "Your Lordship, this is Grace. Your daughter-in-law." She felt as though she'd stepped off a cliff.

"Who? Who is that?"

"It's Grace. Zachary's wife. Calling from the United States."

"Grace?" He sounded alarmed, and Grace knew he was afraid something might have happened to his son.

Reassured by his concern, she said carefully, "Zachary is in the hospital here. He's having some...mental health problems." Suddenly she wondered if she should have called. She really didn't know much about Zac's relationship with his parents. His father the earl. His depressed mother. Zac's brother, Pip, was several years older than he was, but Grace knew they were good friends, went rowing together on the river near Oakhurst when Zac was in England. Now, of course, they were an ocean apart.

Lord Key said, "Grace, I'm so glad you called. Please tell me everything." A woman's voice murmured in the background, and the earl answered, "It's Grace, calling about Zachary. He's...having some difficulty."

Grace heard the astonished response. "Grace?"

Grace thought of how she'd left their son, her husband, in New York. She remembered the homeless man shuffling down the street....

As coherently as she could, she explained what had happened to Zac. His mother picked up the phone, too, and Grace thought again of what Zac had said about her depression. She sounded fine now. Grace's heart flooded with warmth as the Keys repeatedly thanked her for calling. They asked for several numbers. Hers, the hospital, Zac's doctor.

Then his mother asked, "Grace, are you...are you with him, then?"

In a flash Grace saw the whole history of her marriage, most of all the last few weeks. Nothing mattered anymore except the love she and Zac shared, the vows they'd made. *In sickness and in health.* The words really meant something now. That she would be there for him.

But she knew she would be there because she loved him.

"Yes. We've...worked things out. We're, um, very married."

Lord Key cleared his throat. "Good." He rushed on to say that they would talk again very soon, and Grace had never been so grateful for the English habit of avoiding awkward topics.

BECAUSE DAY HAD GOTTEN her a room with a kitchenette, she decided to make a dessert to take to Zac. She walked to a bookstore where she found the book the doctor had recommended and from there to a grocery store. It was blocks away, and she was tired when she returned to her room, but she set to work in the unfamiliar kitchenette, sipping a glass of wine as she used the limited utensils to make a lemon meringue pie.

As she made the meringue, she thought of Zac in that seclusion room. And the Zac she loved. Running. Laughing. Coupons. She pictured him working on her house. Playing the piano. Befriending strays. Making love.

He'll be that way again, she thought. *He has to be.*

While the pie was baking, she called the hospital. Leif said, "Yeah. He's a little better. We just gave him another shot."

Grace asked him if Zac could eat a pie if she brought it.

"Let me check with the doc, but I think it's fine."

After hanging up, Grace opened the book on mental illness. The first thing she learned was that at any one time an estimated twenty percent of the U.S. population suffered from mental health problems serious enough to warrant care. But the percentage of people who sought care was much smaller, in part because of the associated stigma. Grace was stunned by the statistics. Until Zac, she'd never known anyone who was mentally ill. At least she didn't think so. But perhaps people didn't talk about it.

The scope of mental disorders was vast. Substance-related, schizophrenia and psychotic disorders, mood disorders, depression....

Depression. When Zac had told her about his mom, she hadn't perceived the problem as illness. Everyone got depressed sometimes.

Interested, Grace continued reading, acquainting herself with life from the point of view of a psychotic person. The book confirmed what she had intuited—that Zac's mind was playing cruel tricks on him, creating a world whose demons ranged from the annoying to the terrifying.

She read about hallucinations of all kinds. Of sight and sound and touch. The voices heard by a psychotic person, she learned, weren't like thoughts. Rather, it truly seemed that someone—or several someones—was speaking. But auditory hallucinations could take a host of forms beyond voices. The sound of a beating heart, of rushing blood. Choirs singing. Meaningless babble. Nonsense sounds.

Zac must have been terrified to experience such bizarre phenomena without knowing the cause.

But how strange that he hadn't tried to find out. Zachary was a highly educated man. A man who knew the medical resources available to him, knew when it was appropriate to see a doctor. A man who used the library if he wanted to learn about something. A man who, had he looked into it, would have been alarmed by what he read about his symptoms.

Despite Dr. Holyoak's warnings, Grace grew worried as she read. With Zac's symptoms, he could have any of a number of awful things. And what Day had told her was true. A few of the illnesses mentioned came on when people were in their twenties—and stayed.

Oh, God, Grace thought. *What if he doesn't get well?*

ZAC LAY ON THE MATTRESS on the floor. Leif had just come in again to tell him where he was and what was going on and that no one was going to hurt him. Now he believed it. He didn't understand everything, but he'd been told that he was psychotic, that he'd refused medication, and that the hospital had received a court order to give him medication, anyhow.

He tried to piece it together. Cataract Canyon, the movie, Grace...*DSM-IV.* The thoughts filled him with panic, so he focused on the present. On what had happened since he'd come to the hospital.

He'd given people a lot of trouble, and the thought made him ashamed. Where was Grace? What did she think of him now?

Hearing a sound at the door, Zac looked up and saw a tall bearded man and the even taller Leif. He sat up sleepily, and the man with the beard said, "Hello, Zac. I'm Dr. Michael Holyoak. We've met, but I'm not sure you remember me."

Zac remembered. Embarrassed by his recent behavior, he said, "Hello."

"Do you know where you are and why you're here?"

Zac looked about the bare cell. He was caged like an animal. He knew it was because he'd behaved like one. Nodding, he said, "I'm in a hospital because I'm psychotic." But he felt only drowsy, and he wanted Grace. Where was she? Zac wished things were clearer.

The psychiatrist asked, "How are you feeling now?"

He couldn't think of anything to say. At last he shrugged.

"Hearing any voices?"

Zac stirred uneasily. How did Dr. Holyoak know about the voices? He shook his head. "I feel better."

"Good." The doctor nodded. "Would you like to see your wife?"

Zac peered past him toward the door. He couldn't see anyone through the window. "Yes."

"She brought you something to eat."

Eyes stinging, Zac buried his feelings. "Oh."

Michael Holyoak went to the door and Leif opened it, and Grace came in, wearing a pink cotton sweater and patched jeans and carrying a pie.

Grace's heartbeat picked up when she saw Zac. He looked groggy but much calmer than before. His long hair was uncombed, his beard rough, and Grace was embarrassed to discover she found him very sexy in hospital pajama bottoms.

But in his face, she saw illness. The drugs were just containing the symptoms. When he saw her he stood up.

Trying to ignore the others, Grace stepped toward him and hugged him with one arm. Warm skin and muscle under her hand. *Zachary.* He returned the caress—halfheartedly, she thought.

Zac felt as though they were on a date with chaperons. Did the men think he would hurt Grace? Hoping she didn't think so, he asked her, "Want to sit down?"

They both sat on the mattress, and she gave him the lemon meringue pie. She had two napkins and two plastic spoons. As they dug in, Zac felt his appetite returning. Soon Dr. Holyoak and Leif stepped out into the hall.

Immediately Zac set down the pie plate. Grace put both her arms around him, and they hugged tight, hard, the way they hadn't in front of the two men. She kissed him on the mouth, and he let himself kiss her back. But his eyes felt hot again and a little wet, so he stopped kissing her and just held her, his face in her hair.

Grace said, "I want you to get better so you can come home. I miss you." Remembering Day's message, she said, "So does Ninochka."

The dog. In his mind Zac felt her fur beneath his hands, saw her chasing her tail in the yard at the River Inn. The thoughts affected him like Grace's bringing the pie. He longed for home, for his life. Zac squeezed Grace tighter, not answering, and they were finding each other's mouths again when Dr. Holyoak came back in with a chair.

Sitting down, he explained that they would move Zac to a regular room in the same ward. Then he told Zac, "We'll start you on oral medication now. It should work as well as what we've given you. You'll probably still be taking it when you leave the hospital, and it's important that you do so methodically, even if your wife has to remind you."

Zac nodded. He hated taking even aspirin, but there was no choice. He didn't want to be psychotic. Remembering enough of his research to dread the answer, he nonetheless asked, "What are the side effects?"

The doctor said antipsychotic agents were among the safest drugs available in medicine. He named possible side effects—restlessness, diminished spontaneity, slurred speech, tremors of the hands and feet, impotence and tardive dyskinesia, a condition involving involuntary muscle movements. The last, he said, was generally a concern for people who were on antipsychotic drugs for a number of years; it was not a side effect at all of the drug Zac was taking.

When Grace looked at Zac, he had his head in his hands. She knew what he must be thinking. How could he be an actor with those kinds of problems?

Dr. Holyoak said, "I wouldn't think too much about side effects right now. From what you've said, Grace, when this happened before in New York it subsided on its own after a short time. Is that right?"

He was looking at Zac, and Zachary nodded.

"Do you know about how long?"

"Twenty-five days."

Grace drew in a breath. *Zachary,* she thought. *You worried alone.*

Dr. Holyoak studied him. "I'm going to ask you about that in more detail. Perhaps, when you're a little sharper, you could write it all down—or ask Grace to help. It might help us figure out what's happened to you."

Zac thought of his mother and everything he'd read in *DSM-IV.* He wasn't sure he wanted to figure out what had happened.

He wasn't sure he wanted to know.

CHAPTER FOURTEEN

DR. HOLYOAK'S OFFICE was in a clinic adjoining the hospital, and Grace met him there at one the next day. They sat in a comfortable room with easy chairs, a couch and a bookcase, and for an hour she answered his questions about Zac.

The doctor told her, "Whatever you say here is confidential. Feel free to tell me anything about Zachary you think will help us get to the bottom of this. We all have the same goal. His recovery."

Grace told the psychiatrist about meeting Zac. Marrying him. Leaving him. As she spoke, she again felt a twinge of resentment that Zac hadn't been there for her when she needed him. Of course, on the river he'd saved her life. But when her father died... Telling Dr. Holyoak about her strange phone conversation with Zac after her father's death, Grace commented, "He sounded so self-absorbed. I guess he was hallucinating or something."

"Very possibly." Her underlying feelings must have shown because the psychiatrist watched her intently for a moment, then said, "You know, Grace, what's happened to Zac is not within his control. He was reacting to the trauma of your accident on the river. We see the same thing in soldiers under enemy fire, people who've been through a flood or other disaster. The mind can handle only so much."

"I was the one who almost drowned." *I handled it,* she thought.

The doctor said, "Seeing that this has happened before, it's probably safe to say Zac has some kind of genetic predisposition to this kind of thing."

Grace understood. Zac was sick and couldn't help it. It wasn't a matter of emotional weakness. It wasn't his fault—or hers. *Genetic predisposition.* Worried, she asked, "Is he going to get better? I mean, I've been reading that book..."

He smiled a little. "I think this is just a brief psychotic episode. It could be something worse, but he says the last episode didn't last long and he's been fine since. Can you tell me more about that?"

Grace repeated the story Zac had told her at the Anasazi Palace. Then she told the psychiatrist about his nightmares—dreams of people he loved killing themselves. "I've wondered if it's because I left him. He never used to have bad dreams when we lived together."

The psychiatrist shrugged noncommittally. "It could say something about his anxiety level. Also, it sounds as though he hasn't been getting a lot of sleep lately. In some people, that can trigger things of this nature."

Dr. Holyoak questioned her about Zac's moods, habits, social life and background. Grace told him what she knew. Prep school, grammar school, Eton, Oxford. Oakhurst. She said, "His mother's depressed. I just read about depression in that book you recommended. This probably sounds incredibly ignorant, but I didn't know it was a mental illness."

"It's not always. But it sounds as though what you're talking about with Zac's mother is. Tell me what you know about that. Is she on medication?"

"I don't know." Grace repeated what Zachary had told her. Frowning, she asked, "Could it be related to what happened to Zac?"

"Yes—which isn't to say it's the same thing. There's a lot we don't know about how these things work. It seems as though both of Zac's psychotic episodes were triggered by stressful incidents, in each case involving loss—or the threat of loss. Which resonates in interesting ways with what you said about his dreams." He looked thoughtful. "Tell me about his work."

She did. She told him about before she knew Zac, when he'd performed off-off-off Broadway. In back alleys, on a stage made from plywood boards laid across the counter of an East Village bar. She explained about the banned jeans ads and about *Kah-Puh-Rats*. "He's such a good actor I used to wonder what was real and what wasn't. In our personal lives. I don't feel that way now, but I still don't understand his emotions."

Dr. Holyoak answered, "With that kind of background—boarding schools, et cetera—he may have trouble expressing emotion. In the scope of things, channeling his feelings into acting is a reasonable response."

He changed the subject. "I'm interested in knowing more about his mother. His parents did call, but I haven't gotten back to them. I think I'll do that as soon as I can. What's the time difference between here and England?"

Grace told him. As the meeting ended and she got up to leave the office, her eyes swept the bookcase. Something on the shelf triggered a reaction in her, and she did a double take.

Dr. Holyoak, who had another appointment, moved toward the doorway, and Grace knew she should go. But she couldn't tear her gaze from the shelf. Among the other volumes was a large crimson book with saffron lettering on the binding: *DSM-IV.* Stunned to see it there, she read the subtitle: *Diagnostic and Statistical Manual of Mental Disorders*.

Her heart thudded. *He knew.* Zac knew he was sick.

Uncertain how to feel, she looked at the doctor, who was waiting at the door. She said, "Zachary has that book."

ZAC WAS SITTING on the edge of his bed in socks, blue jeans and a faded black T-shirt when Grace arrived for a visit. He stood up and kissed her, taking advantage of the minutes till Leif or one of the others looked in the door. They checked on him constantly, and when Grace was around they were even more vigilant.

Sitting down on the bed with him, Grace reached up to touch his face. "You shaved."

"Under supervision. I mustn't have 'sharps.'" Zac felt demeaned by the rule. He would never kill himself. Or anyone else.

But he'd never thought he would spit on people, either.

Grace thought of the *DSM-IV* she'd found in Zac's room. Dr. Holyoak had listened to her theory that Zac must have guessed the seriousness of his breakdown in New York and tried to discover what caused it. But the psychiatrist had said little in response, and Grace knew he suspected other possibilities. That Zac knew more about his condition than he'd ever said.

More than he'd ever told her, his wife.

Now she said, "Zac, I saw the *DSM-IV* in your room. I was collecting your laundry, and I didn't know what it was at the time." After explaining about noticing a copy in the psychiatrist's office, she asked, "Did you suspect you were sick?"

Zac knew the complex implications of the question and of any answer he might give—knew because he'd thought

of little else during the past year. This was the green card
again, only worse. He had to explain. "Yes. But listen,
Grace..." God, it would have been so much easier if he'd
told her earlier, when his mind was functioning properly.
Now, even finding the words was difficult, and saying
them was harder. He made himself try.

"At first, I thought it was something ghastly, like
schizophrenia. But my symptoms had lasted just one
month. I concluded it was a brief psychotic episode,
nothing more. But I wanted to make sure I was really all
right, so I stayed away from you for a year. If this had
happened again, I wouldn't have come back."

Grace couldn't believe her ears. "You tried to diag-
nose this yourself? Didn't you see a doctor?"

"No. I was afraid of the INS. They don't want aliens
with mental health problems, because they can become a
burden to the state. I thought a doctor might report me.
And by the time I felt secure about my green card, the
episode was far in the past. When you and I started...
When we became lovers again, I decided to see a doctor,
but I didn't have a chance before this happened. If there
was something seriously wrong, I wouldn't have kept it
from you."

Their eyes met. Obviously there was something seriously wrong.

Grace's mind reeled. Reminding herself he was ill, she
held her temper in check. But she felt betrayed. It was too
much like Valentine's Day. Like hearing him say, *Don't do
this, Grace. I need that green card.*

Not once in his narrative at the Anasazi Palace had he
used the word "psychotic." Now she knew the omission
was deliberate. Her accusation came out before she could
stop it. "My God, Zac. How can I ever trust you?"

"I didn't want to worry you needlessly."

Grace pressed her lips shut. She didn't believe that for a minute. He'd been afraid. Of losing his green card.

But she saw a subtle difference this time.

This time, he had feared losing *her*.

THREE DAYS LATER Dr. Holyoak came to see Zac in his room prior to discharging him. While Grace and Zac sat in chairs near the foot of the bed, the psychiatrist perched on a stool, saying, "Zac, I think you've been experiencing a brief reactive psychosis—a brief psychotic episode triggered by a stressful event—in this case, the accident on the river. The last time this happened was just after Grace left. Also a traumatic time.

"But I have to say, my diagnosis is provisional. I'm troubled, because this has happened twice, and that's rare. We need to make sure this isn't a more serious recurrent disorder." Meeting Zac's eyes, he said, "Your mother's condition has made me wonder."

Zac's face was impassive, but Grace knew he was afraid. A recurrent condition could mean he would be on medication indefinitely. And already Grace had noticed something disturbing, something she was sure Zac noticed, too. The drug that was taming his psychotic symptoms had begun to exact its toll. Side effects...

Dr. Holyoak said, "Grace, I'd like to speak to Zac alone for a moment."

Curious but understanding, she got up and left.

When she was gone, the psychiatrist rolled his stool closer to Zac. "Look, I'd like you to talk to someone, get started in psychotherapy. There are mental illnesses for which drugs alone are the best therapy, but I think because of the nature of what's happened to you—and frankly, because of your family background—you would benefit by talking to someone. Sometimes things that happened to us when we were young affect our ability to handle similar situations as adults."

Zac drew back slightly. Medications with grim side effects were bad enough. He didn't need to talk to a stranger about his childhood. Anyhow, he'd had a good childhood. He said, "I wasn't abused." As he spoke he heard and felt the difference in his speech. Anxiety filled him.

Dr. Holyoak said, "It could be that something happened to you when you were young, something that had a painful effect on you—something you don't even recall. Or that you've never acknowledged was painful. It's possible something like that could make it difficult for you to confront traumatic incidents." The psychiatrist sat back in his chair. As though sensing Zac's resistance, he said, "It's possible that in a couple of weeks you'll be well and this will be no more than a bad memory. But twice, you've responded to threatened loss with psychotic symptoms. I think it could happen again. Wouldn't you like to do all you can to see that it doesn't?"

"Of course." But Zac's mind was spinning. *When you were young...* Keeping his counsel, he said, "You sound as though you think the cause is some trauma in my childhood. Is that it? Or is there something physically wrong with me? Which is it?"

"Well, I think it's safe to assume you have some kind of physical predisposition for this kind of episode. Perhaps some depression, in fact. It can manifest in many ways, and if that's all there is to it, medication can help. But the stressors that triggered both of your psychotic episodes were very similar. It makes me suspect that your childhood experiences might play a role, as well. So, to answer your question, my guess would be both."

Zac's chest felt tight. "You think it's genetic."

"In part. It's not clear how these things work. According to what your parents told me on the phone, your mother has had severe major depressive episodes with psychotic features."

His mother had been psychotic? Zac started to protest, but then he realized what the doctor had said. *According to your parents . . .* How could they not have told him?

"However," said Dr. Holyoak, "there are other issues at play here." He looked at Zachary. "You grew up with a mother who was often suicidal. That's a formidable burden for a child."

Zac stared. None of them ever discussed that with people outside the family. Even amongst themselves they avoided the details. *Your mum's having a spell.* His father would never have told . . .

But he had. And if his father had said that much, he would have said more. He would have told everything. Resigning himself to discussing it, at least briefly, Zac said, "Look, I remember finding her after the overdose, but it wasn't a suicide attempt. It was an accident. I'm sure you think it cruel that I was made to start prep school the next day, but that was my choice. My father had enough on his hands." Like Grace now. "I kept my chin up, and I was fine. Aside from the occasional bad dream, I've never had a moment's trouble coping with it."

The psychiatrist's ironic expression was eloquent. "Loss?"

Zac tightened inside, seeing the obvious. He had become psychotic. That wasn't coping. "I didn't lose my mother."

"You didn't lose your wife in the river. But I imagine that in both cases you thought you had." The psychiatrist changed gears. "There are good counselors at the mental-health clinic in Moab. I'll give you some names. The process will take time, but I think you'll find it's worth it."

"How much time?" He needed to get back to the set. *God. The film.*

"Psychotherapy can go on for months or years. Not always continuously, but it's a long process."

Months or years?

Thinking of *Kah-Puh-Rats,* Zac changed the subject, asking what had been on his mind all morning. "Can you reduce my medication? I can't work when—" He closed his mouth. The psychiatrist could see and hear.

He was slurring his words.

Dr. Holyoak sat back with a small sigh. His eyes were penetrating, and Zac knew exactly what he was thinking, exactly what was happening.

No, Zachary thought. *Don't say I can't.*

But the psychiatrist said only, "Let's wait for this to go away first, all right? If it's a brief reactive psychosis, you should feel better soon."

And if it's not? Zac thought. *What then?*

DAY AND NICK had brought the Austin-Healey to Grand Junction for Grace, and she used it to drive Zac back to Moab.

They put up the top to reduce the noise so they could talk. Zac's mind felt slow and he hated the sound of his own speech, altered by the medication, but he wanted to tell her about the conversation with Dr. Holyoak. When he did Grace seemed almost as shocked as he was.

"Your parents never told you your mother was that ill?"

"They must have assumed I knew. She was often depressed, but it was never discussed as an illness." He paused. "She used to threaten to kill herself."

Staring through the sunny windshield at the road ahead, Grace tried to hide her horror. "Your mother is suicidal?"

"Not anymore."

Grace remembered his nightmares. People he loved killing themselves.

She glanced at him in the confined space of the sports car, then returned her gaze to the road as Zac said, "I found her after she'd overdosed on sleeping pills. It was an accident, not a suicide attempt, but... well, of course I thought she was dead." Relating the story, he felt little. It was a dim twenty-year-old memory. Should he feel something?

Grace barely breathed. "You never told me that." There was a lot he hadn't told her. The green card. Suspicions he was mentally ill.

"It's not my favorite subject. But, anyhow, I'm supposed to go talk to someone about it." He'd rather have a root canal.

"Does Dr. Holyoak think it might make you better?"

"Well, obviously he thinks I'm screwed up." Again Zac heard his own words slurring, felt the slowed pace of his thoughts. He *was* screwed up. Royally. And he needed to tell Grace the rest. "He thinks it's genetic, too."

"A predisposition. Yes, I know that."

Zac said, "You want children." So did he.

"Did he say we shouldn't have children?"

"No." And Zac knew that brief reactive psychosis was not a chronic mental disorder, was not that serious in the long run. Recurrent episodes like his were rare. But was that all he had? His mother...

The rest of the drive home was quiet. When the car turned off the River Inn Road and down the drive lined with tamarisk, Zac felt a sense of dislocation and lost time. It had been only about two weeks since he'd been at the house, but since then the vegetation had come into bloom, the river had gone down, and the weather had become torrid.

The inn, however, was unchanged. When he saw the gables and chimneys, the French doors and curved balcony railings, Zac knew he was home. Here was the lady with her shoes off on the shore of the river.

As Grace parked under the cottonwoods, he heard barking and saw the silhouette of the dog jumping up against the screen door. Day had known they were coming. She must have brought Ninochka home. Eager to see the puppy, Zac told Grace, "Leave the bags. I'll get them later."

He got out of the car and went up the steps to unfasten the latch. Ninochka bounded toward him, jumping up.

"Down." He crouched to her level, petting her, ruffling her fur, playing. Her tongue slathered across his nose and her madly wagging tail whipped his face as she jumped about, wriggling with excitement, beside herself. Zac said, "Look how big you are. You're the most beautiful dog in the world." Her markings had darkened since he'd last seen her, and her double-layered coat was thick and healthy. Grace joined him on the steps, and they sat there together, throwing an old pink Frisbee for the ecstatic dog.

Then Zac collected the bags from the car. Though he and Grace had been sleeping together in her room upstairs before they'd left for Cataract Canyon, he still kept his clothes in her father's old room. As Grace followed him and the husky into the downstairs bedroom, he said, "You need to go to work, don't you?"

Grace shook her head. "I'm out of a job. Nick and I are closing on Rapid Riggers this weekend. All I need to do is pack up my desk." Everything was changing at once.

She told Zac, "I'm going to make dinner. What do you want?"

Zac thought, *I want my life back. I want to be normal.* He forgot to answer.

Grace understood. Leaving him to his thoughts, she went out to the kitchen to see what was in the refrigerator. She needed to make a trip to the farmers' market to buy vegetables, but Zac... In the hospital, they'd taken away even his shoelaces. Nobody had said he was suicidal, but Grace didn't want to leave him alone at the house. Not after what he'd said about his mother. Not knowing what must be going on his mind. Genetic abnormalities. Slurred words. His career.

Grace worked in the kitchen for an hour, starting a loaf of bread and soup for dinner. Then she went down the hall and through the parlor to look in the door of Zac's room.

The French doors were open, and he was gone.

Trying to stay calm, Grace put on her sandals and went out onto the stone patio and into the heat. Zac was down by the river, near the boiler from the *Moab Princess*, throwing the Frisbee to Nina. Grace walked alongside the house and toward the shore to join them. She stepped on a twig as she approached, and Zac looked up.

Seeing her, he knew she didn't trust him to be alone. Angry—at his illness—he scooped up the Frisbee Ninochka had dropped and tossed it again. As the husky took off running, Grace reached him. She was wearing red cutoffs and a denim vest, and the sight of her body stirred him. At least he wasn't impotent, despite the meds. But there was a chasm between him and Grace, and he knew what it was.

Doubt. Every kind.

Ninochka bounded back with the disk, dropped it and stood waiting, poised to go again. Zac picked up the disc and threw it. Then he glanced at Grace. Her expression was probing and compassionate, but she seemed to know he wanted to be alone. She clasped his fingers briefly and turned to go back into the house.

Zac wanted her so badly the touch felt like fire. He watched her walk away, and when Ninochka brought back the Frisbee again, he said, "Enough, girl," and went to sit on a boulder near the shore. The husky came to sit beside him, and he scratched her ears and combed her fur with his fingers and accepted all her sweet affection. But it wasn't what he most wanted.

He hungered for his wife.

DINNER WAS QUIET. Afterward Zac helped Grace wash the dishes, but it took him a long time to think to offer. As they worked together, with him washing and her drying, Grace noticed his hands trembling, and she knew he saw it, too. Finally he put down the dishrag and said, "Excuse me," and left the room.

Grace finished the dishes alone, then went into her father's old room. Zac had gone outside again, but she could see him through the French doors. He sat on the patio steps watching the last colors of the sunset leave the sky.

Grace opened the screen door and walked out.

Hearing her, Zac was glad when her long legs settled beside him on the steps. In the dim blue light of disappeared day, his hand slid into hers, and he looked down, saw the difference between the two. His hand was muscular, long-fingered, big-knuckled, wood-colored. A man's hand. Hers was Graceful, paler. His fingers interlocked with hers.

Grace breathed shallowly. She wanted things to be as they'd been before Cataract. But everything had changed—just as it had when she'd left him.

Ninochka, who'd been snooping around near the foundation of the house, came up the steps and lay beside Zac. With his free hand, he petted her.

Grace waited, thinking, *Touch me.* She wanted more than holding hands. *Touch me like a lover, Zachary. Let me know you're really back.*

He might have read her thoughts. His hand slid from hers, and she felt it traveling up her spine, his fingers beneath her hair, stroking the back of her neck.

Grace looked at him, and that was enough. In the dusk that was turning to twilight, he brought his face near hers, looked into her eyes. Their mouths touched. Lips opened. Grace clung to his shoulders through his T-shirt, and then her hands wandered, too, to slide through his hair, to reach down the front of his body.

The low rasp of his breath reached her ears as she touched him through his sweat pants. Hard. Blood racing, she slipped her hand under the waistband, against his skin, reached down, and wrapped her fingers around him, felt his blood coursing. Zac grabbed her, pressed his mouth to her neck, fumbled open the buttons on her vest. Moments later they got up and walked the few feet to the door. In the downstairs bedroom, they pulled back the purple patchwork quilt and the blanket and top sheet and got in bed.

As they tossed their clothes to the floor, Grace whispered, "I missed you so much. I love you, Zachary."

He clasped her to him in a stanglehold. "I love you." He covered her mouth, kissed her with his tongue, felt her body pushing against his as their legs intertwined. Her love for him had never felt so tangible. So good.

Grace rolled over to slide open the night stand drawer. Aware of what she was doing, Zac lay motionless, sober, remembering what he'd managed briefly to forget. Mental illness. *Genes...*

He sat up, and took the packet from her, and she said, "Zac—"

Zac, let me do it.

Their eyes caught in the darkness, and Grace threw herself into his arms. Zac didn't recognize the sound that came from his throat, didn't understand the fierce trembling of his body. It was more than arousal or need. It was love so strong it hurt.

Grace said, "Oh, Zac, I don't know what I'd do without you. I've never loved anyone so much."

Stoking the fire further was out of the question. Together, they hurriedly dealt with the condom and came together almost frantically, wishing there was some way to be even closer to each other. And never part.

Neither noticed when the husky jumped up on the mattress and lay down to sleep, and in the middle of the night Zac barely stirred when the dog moved over beside him and rested her head on his arm.

THE NEXT MORNING Grace and Zachary went for a run with the dog, and afterward Grace went to the farmers' market and the grocery store. She had finished her shopping at City Market and was heading out to the convertible with two bags of groceries when she noticed the flyer. It was posted on a message board outside the store, and she might have walked past had the largest words on the paper not stood out so boldly.

LOST: SIBERIAN HUSKY

Almost dizzy, Grace paused beside the board and read the entire flyer. A four-month-old gray husky pup named Jasmine had been lost on the Poison Spider Mesa Trail at the end of March. A reward was offered for her return, and two numbers were listed, one local, one with an unfamiliar area code.

Poison Spider Mesa, Grace thought. The Jeep trail led from the River Inn Road up onto the plateau into a world of Navaho sandstone dunes. It was a popular place for mountain biking and hiking, but on top it was precipitous and desolate. No place for a puppy.

Still, her conscience smarted as she turned away from the notice. Ninochka must be the husky of the ad, and her owners cared enough to offer a reward. They'd probably be relieved to know that she was all right, that she'd found a good home. Maybe they'd let Zac buy the dog from them.

Maybe they wouldn't.

Grace stole another glance at the flyer. Without wanting to, she saw the local telephone number. It was easy to remember. Too easy.

Turning away fast, she strode across the parking lot in the hot morning sun. Ninochka was Zac's dog. They'd established a bond, and they needed each other. God, how he needed her now.

CHAPTER FIFTEEN

WHEN SHE GOT HOME, Zac was outside tilling a patch of ground near the carriage house. Ninochka lay nearby chewing a rawhide bone.

Turning off the tiller, Zac came to kiss Grace. In the slightly slurred voiced to which she was growing accustomed, he said, "I thought we should have a kitchen garden."

Grace's gaze lingered on his eyes. The sun was shining in them now, turning them the color of jade. Thick black lashes. Grace said, "I'm so glad I married you." However it had happened. Whatever else had happened.

Zac's smile faded. It was as though smoke had spread over the sky, dulling everything. They were standing very near each other as he said, "What if we can't have children?"

"If we decide we shouldn't, we won't." She kept her eyes on his. "But it's a choice. Let's make it when you're well."

Zac knew she was right. But he remembered what it was like when his mother wouldn't get out of bed. His father encouraging her, pleading with her, shaming her and finally lifting her just so that he could change the sheets. He'd never asked the servants to help. *If I get that sick...*

Turning away, he stared out toward the river. He didn't want to tell Grace he'd tried to sand the floor upstairs and had gouged the wood with the sanding machine. He didn't want to admit that he'd tried to work on the porch at the northeast corner of the house but that his hands shook too badly to hammer a nail. He didn't want to say that he couldn't even play "Chopsticks" on the piano but could only sit and stare at Hamlet's mad girlfriend who'd drowned herself in the lily pond.

Instead, he told himself he would get better as he had in New York. Then he'd be able to do the things he always had.

At last he said, "May I use your boat this afternoon?"

Grace looked toward the Colorado. Clouds were reflected in the water. "You can't drive anywhere." Not on so much medication.

"I'll put in here. I can row upstream and back down. I thought I'd see if Ninochka would go."

The dog lifted her head at the sound of her name. Her tail flopped from one side to the other.

Grace said, "Okay."

Later that afternoon they put the dory in the river, and Ninochka eagerly joined Zac in it. Zachary had water for both of them and a dish for Nina, and Grace was glad the dog was going with him. As they rowed off, she returned to the house, trying not to think of the flyer or the phone number she couldn't forget.

TWO DAYS LATER they drove to Grand Junction for Zac to see Dr. Holyoak. He was so much better that the psychiatrist reduced his medication and said he could return to work whenever he felt able. He also reminded Zac about starting psychotherapy, and Zac promised to make an appointment as soon as the film was wrapped. Until then he had enough on his mind.

Though the producers had cut most of his remaining scenes, there were still several to be shot. Zac was glad the role had been shortened. The side effects of the medication were not disappearing as quickly as he'd hoped, and he dreaded returning to the set. The inn was his refuge. He'd begun working on the upstairs again...thinking.

Dr. Holyoak had warned him about avoiding stress and getting adequate sleep, and Zac knew that the career, the ambition that had owned him most of his adult life, was stressful. And it had caused him to make some bad choices. Marrying Grace hadn't been one of them, but how it happened was. Now, *Leaving Hong Kong* was only a memory—a bad one. But he and Grace had to live with the knowledge that he'd married her for a green card. Zac knew it ate at her. It ate at him.

He had done it for his career. And now, for the first time in his life, he wondered...

Was his career worth it?

THE NEXT MORNING a production assistant drove out to the River Inn to bring him a call sheet. At ten that night they would shoot the camp fire scene in which the Howland brothers and William Dunn decide to leave the Powell expedition. Zac was to report to the set at eight.

He and Grace left at seven-thirty in the Austin-Healey to drive to the base camp at Big Bend, upstream from Moab on the river road. It was a silent drive, and when Zac saw the trailers and the people, he was glad of Grace's presence. And ashamed of how badly he wanted her there.

As they got out of the car and crew members walked past, smiling at him awkwardly, Zac reflected on all Grace had done for him in the past weeks. Looking after him in Cataract Canyon. Visiting him in the hospital.

As he often had in the past few days, he thought about his parents—especially what they'd been like years earlier, when things were worse. His mother crying behind the door. His father beseeching, soothing...caring. Becoming angry and fed up. But always, ultimately, being there beside her.

Why don't you leave her, Dad? Pip had asked.

Zac had been about eight at the time, and he remembered his own paralyzing fear at his older brother's suggestion—and his relief when he'd seen his father's surprised expression. The earl had said, *Well, Pip, I love your mother. And she counts on me to take care of her.*

But Zac never wanted Grace taking care of him that way.

He could hardly stand the thought.

SENECA HOWLAND'S character had three lines in the camp-fire scene. Though Zac had repeated them a hundred times that day, he couldn't say them without slurring. Inevitably, when it came time to film, Meshach noticed.

The first retake didn't surprise Zac, but the second made him anxious. The third made him afraid. That time he knew he had enunciated more clearly than he had all day. And it wasn't good enough.

They changed lines.

They cut a line.

In the end the script doctor suggested giving him a flask and having him sip from it during the other parts of the scene, after which he was to appear drunk. That required retaking the part of the scene that *had* worked, the part during which he didn't have to speak.

Meshach said, "We'll make it work, Zac."

Zac was not comforted. He was trapped in a body that had become a demon. The body he'd always taken for granted. The body he'd always been able to control perfectly.

When he lifted the flask to his mouth, his hand shook.

Watching from a seat on a boulder some distance behind the cameras, Grace felt her heart clench and unclench. Why was he putting himself through this?

But she knew. Acting. He loved it and he needed it. The revelations that had come with his illness had made her understand how much. It was probably a way to deal with his emotions, especially pain.

Grace doubted it was the right way. Maybe if he found a better way, he would have no more psychotic episodes.

On the other hand, perhaps that was denial on her part.

Leaves crunched on the ground near her, and she looked up to discover Hal Markley slapping a mosquito on his neck. She hadn't known the producer was on the set. Smiling, he came over to lean casually against the boulder where she sat. He was dressed in duck trousers and a polo shirt, but at the moment he seemed surprisingly at home in the outdoors.

Nodding in Zac's direction, he asked Grace, "How's it going?"

Grace knew he didn't mean the filming. She was surprised by the inquiry, but she supposed the producers did have an interest in Zac's health. Particularly given his difficulties tonight.

Not wanting to say anything that could jeopardize Zac's career, she replied, "He's getting better." It was true. But he wasn't off medication yet.

Markley nodded and stood there in silence for some time. Grace wondered why he didn't leave until he said, "Look, I want you to tell Zac we'll get this film wrapped one way or another. Don't let him sweat what's going on tonight. We see worse things on movie sets. Drugs. Tempers. Zac's a pro. If we have to shoot his scenes on the soundstage in a few weeks, we will. But I think he can finish this, and I'd like to see him do it."

Touched by the producer's kindness, Grace said, "Thanks. I will tell him."

With a faint sigh Markley said, "Yeah, everyone's bipolar in my family. Manic-depressive." Behind his horn-rimmed glasses, his eyes regarded Grace with empathy. "I know what you're going through."

She tried to hide her surprise, but he saw it and said, "Hey, there's a lot of people like Zac out there. And a lot of people worse off. Let me know if there's anything I can do for either of you. If you need any resources, I can give you some numbers. Legal information. Support networks. You're not alone."

You're not alone.

But despite Hal Markley's solicitude, Grace felt very much alone as she drove Zac home at two in the morning, after sixteen takes.

She told him what the producer had said, but he seemed not to hear. Grace knew he was preoccupied by his poor performance.

When they reached the River Inn, she went to bed in his room, where they'd been sleeping since his return from the hospital, but Zac didn't join her. He kissed her goodnight, then went upstairs and walked through the halls with Ninochka.

As he contemplated the repairs still needed on the second floor, he thought about what had happened on the set and about the producer who had manic-depressive relatives, who was perhaps bipolar himself. He thought about the Ben Rogan ads and being on "The JoAnn Carroll Show" and being naked with Ingrid Dolk. He thought about running with Ninochka in the mornings and rowing the dory in the afternoons and about Grace working over her hot stove and coming to him in the night, her hair swinging against his face as she laid her body over his and moved against him like the river.

He thought of his parents.

He walked around and around the upstairs, thinking and thinking, and he felt shaken to the foundation of who he was.

THE NIGHTMARE CAME that night—with a difference. The paneled Tudor door became the reinforced door of the seclusion room. He couldn't kick it in, but he remembered the window, and he looked through...

A dog tongue slurped across his face. Paws pressed down on his chest. Jolting awake, heart racing, Zac immediately noticed the sweat-soaked sheets. *The dream.* Behind Ninochka, Grace was sitting up, her hair a sexy, uncombed silhouette against the starlight, her diamond earring flashing in the dark. Summoning the husky, she said, "Here, Nina. It's all right."

The dog looked at Zac, then moved and lay down on another part of the bed.

Zachary sat up and reached for Grace, folding her into his embrace, drawing strength from her presence. After a moment he said, "Go get in bed upstairs and go back to sleep. I'll change these sheets and join you."

Grace heard the steadiness of his voice under the words he couldn't utter with precision. She felt the strength of his body holding her. A tender embrace for her, not comfort for him.

She said, "Why don't you take a shower? I'll change the sheets."

Zac withdrew. "No."

He got out of bed, and Grace watched him pull on some sweatpants and leave the room. Hearing the door of the linen cabinet open and shut, she stood and began stripping the damp sheets from the bed.

Nightmares...

She started. Zac stood in the doorway. Even in the darkness, she sensed he was angry. "I'll do it, Grace."

She dropped the sheet and deliberately stepped back from the bed. Taking a seat in the rocker, she watched him change the sheets.

"Would you like some tea?" she asked.

"I can take care of myself, Grace."

She remembered earlier that night, when she'd had to drive him to the set. He couldn't take care of himself. Not completely. Not now. He certainly hadn't been able to take care of himself in Cataract Canyon. She said carefully, "Not that I think you can't get yourself a cup of tea, but what would be so awful about my taking care of you?"

He turned and stared at her in the dark, then tossed a pillow onto the bed. "Nothing." Everything.

"Isn't that what we do for each other?"

Zac didn't answer.

She sensed his strain but pressed, "Isn't that part of being married?"

Zac sat down on the corner of the mattress. She was still naked, and she looked beautiful there in the rocking chair. Strong. Womanly. He said, "I don't want you to be my keeper. You're my wife."

Grace stared at his broad shoulders, the silhouette of his body that was itself a definition of masculinity. She answered, "Helpmate? Friend? In sickness and in health?"

He tensed.

Grace thought of the times he'd met her after work at Jean-Michel's and ridden the subway with her. The labor he'd put into her house. How he'd saved her life on the river. They did take care of each other. Quashing a vision of her father's casket over his grave, she said, "I love you. You're the keeper, Zac."

Keeper. He'd heard her use the word that way in the past, once when she was talking to Ninochka. She'd called the dog a keeper, too. A good one, worth keeping. Grace loved him.

Like his father had loved his mother. Unconditionally. Zac said fiercely, "You don't understand how bad it is. You don't know what you're saying."

Her eyes pierced his in the dark blue starlight. "Who do you think got in that dory with you in Cataract, Zachary? Who listened to you screaming while they medicated you and took you away? I think I understand how bad it is."

"*No. You don't.*"

Grace sensed he wasn't talking about himself but about his mother. "Zac, I didn't marry you expecting it to be a piece of cake." She *had* expected it to be for love, but that was moot now. There was love between them, and they were joined for life.

"You know, Zac, my dad used to tell me this. He said life is a river. There are calm stretches and rapids. Smiling holes and frowning holes. Those you can run and the ones that stop you. And the river wouldn't be as beautiful or interesting if it was all calm water."

Smiling holes and frowning holes, thought Zac. He remembered the past Christmas, his mother laughing. Laughing hard over some absurdity of Pip's. They'd all laughed. All been happy. That night, her mood had crashed. A medium-low—crying, but not as bad as she'd once been.

Yes, he understood smiling holes and frowning holes. Acknowledging, even celebrating, those extremes and the whole spectrum of human experience was what attracted him to drama. Comedy and Tragedy. But the last thing he wanted was for his marriage with Grace to become a vehicle worthy of the ancient Greeks.

Aware that he was on the verge of blurting out things too intimate to share even with her, he said, "I'm not obtuse. I know those things, Grace. I'll make the tea." Seeing her expression, a shell trying to hide the fact that he'd wounded her, Zac rebuked himself for deriding Sam Sutter's philosophy. He paused at the door and looked down at her. "Your father was wise."

In the kitchen, he filled the kettle and put it on the stove. Then he threaded his way to the living room in the dark, keeping the lights off so he couldn't see the painting of Ophelia. As he heard Ninochka coming across the floor and felt her settling near the foot pedals, he tried to steady his trembling fingers sufficiently to hit the right keys.

He played a shaky Chopin étude, then switched to blues, struggling through melodies as disturbing and dark as madness. He tried Cole Porter next. Rodgers and Hart. Gershwin. He started to play *that* song, but his chest felt too hot, and his eyes dropped to his shaking hands, to his wedding ring.

Abruptly he saw Grace watching him in the dark from the arched door to the foyer. She said, "The tea's ready."

Zac hadn't heard the whistle. *He didn't need a keeper.* But Grace said *he* was a keeper. Someone to keep. Someone worth keeping. Standing, he closed the cover on the keys. Careful not to let his gaze touch the woman over the mantel, he joined Grace. She had put on one of his T-shirts, and it hung around her thighs.

He pulled her against him. "I love you." They kissed with their tongues in each other's mouths, there under the arch. Her touch, and the things she'd said earlier, drew words from him. Confessions.

"My mother... she wouldn't even have a bath. It was as though she had no dignity—but she couldn't help it...." More spilled out in between, the uglier things. "She told my father she wanted to end it. I used to listen through the door. The door was always locked. I stayed outside and listened, because I was afraid she was killing herself. I wasn't supposed to do that, lurk outside her room. Pip showed me how to pick the locks. We weren't supposed to..."

Listening to his whispered words in the dark, Grace knew he was telling secrets. His secrets and those of his family. In her mind she saw a little boy hearing his mother threaten to abandon him in the most final way. Finding her asleep in her bed. Unable to wake her. Certain she was dead. Not supposed to talk about it.

"She must have become depressed because I was going to school. I was her youngest. It happened the night before I was supposed to leave. They were to take me up early in the morning, and she took the pills so she could sleep that night. It was an accident."

Although she heard no uncertainty in his voice, Grace recognized an unspoken question. Had his mother really tried to kill herself?

"She's much better, now. I suppose she has better psychiatric help. Better medication. Things have changed in twenty years."

His voice trailed off, and Grace imagined what he must be thinking. Trying to understand how his mum could have wanted to kill herself when she had two sons. When she had him. He would never know for sure if she'd really tried that night.

Grace realized that his dilemma, though larger and more painful, was like one of her own—a question that had plagued her for more than a year. Had Zac married her for love or a green card?

Like him, she had to rely on the clues of her experience and the testimony of another—him. She must find the answer in her heart. Or learn to accept her doubt.

HE WAS OFF medication in a week, and the film was wrapped in two. As the studio pulled out of town, everything returned to normal, and Grace knew she and Zac had come to a crossroads. California. She knew that before they left she must call the owners of the dog.

Just as she knew that, if the owners had Ninochka's papers, their right to the husky was indisputable. They could take her from Zac.

As the days wore on, she expected him to mention moving, but he never brought it up. Instead, he spent his time gardening, rowing and working on the upstairs of the house, and he made an appointment at the mental health clinic to talk to a counselor. He had two sessions in one week—the first with a psychologist, the second with a men's group. When he came home from the last, Grace found him in the kitchen with his shirt off. It was 105 degrees out, scorching summer. As he nodded hello to Grace, he lifted a beer bottle to his mouth with an unsteady hand.

Grace hadn't noticed his hands shaking for days, and the slurring had disappeared. She'd thought he was well. He looked well. She asked, "What's up?"

Zac took another drink and watched her, trying to block out the memory of the session. He hadn't spoken at all, but hearing other men discuss appalling traumas they'd suffered had been excruciating. He wasn't sure he could go back. But he knew intuitively that the pain was why he was supposed to go.

He told Grace, "Well, it was a difficult afternoon." It came out sharply, which he hadn't intended.

Grace responded to his tone. Impatient with keeping her distance, with letting him have his space, she said, "Zac, what are we doing? Are we going to California? I need to know what to expect from my life."

Energy shuddered through him. The tower shaking. Change. Instinct overwhelmed him. He knew it was the instinct he'd been fighting since the end of April, when he'd first come back to her, when he'd first seen this place. He said, "No. We're not going to California."

Grace's heart thundered. "What are we going to do?"

Zac swallowed some more beer so that he wouldn't say something sarcastic. Wouldn't say, *Well, dear, I'm giving you your way.* Because it wasn't her decision. It was his.

And it hurt.

"I don't know what we're going to do. Right now I'm planning to go rowing."

Grace eyed him suspiciously. Not going to California. Not, apparently, going anywhere. "Zachary, are you contemplating a career change?"

He met her eyes, and his looked like those of a person who'd lost a loved one. "Yes."

"Don't do it on my account."

He gave her a cold look and opened the refrigerator to get another beer.

"I never asked you to give it up."

"Shut up!" He slammed his hand against his face, took a breath and left the room. The dog, who'd been lying in the corner panting, got up and followed him.

Grace stood stricken in the middle of the kitchen, thinking of what she'd said. She knew she was wrong. She *had* asked him to give it up. In a hundred ways.

And it was the wrong thing.

Her emotions whirled. They had to go to California. If Zachary sacrificed his career for her, he would never forgive her. It would drive them apart. Anyhow, acting was the biggest part of him. She didn't want him to change. And *that* was one of the most startling revelations of her life.

California...

The dog.

She made herself do it.

As she dialed the number that had been on the flyer, she knew it was the right choice, but she felt as though she was betraying Zac in the cruelest way. She should at least break it to him first. But perhaps she could surprise him with Ninochka's papers, instead.

When she heard a woman's voice on the other end of the line, she almost hung up.

"I saw your ad about a lost husky."

"The dog? Have you found her?" The woman sounded genuinely excited.

Wondering if she was the owner, Grace forced herself to continue. "Yes. We found her about six weeks ago." Six long weeks. "We'd like to buy her." Zac would be thrilled. Surely he worried about the owners sometimes.

"Oh, I know she doesn't want to sell her. But she'd love to give you a reward. Where are you calling from?"

Grace's heart pounded. The owner wouldn't give up the dog. She thought of Zachary being wrenched from Ninochka.

Loss.

"Are you there?" said the woman. "I didn't get your name."

Shaking, Grace placed the receiver back in the cradle.

ZAC RETURNED in the dory at six o'clock, and Grace went down to the shore as he pulled the boat onto the beach. He looked suntanned and sexy, but Grace could hardly meet his eyes. She shouldn't have made that call.

As Ninochka made a beeline for the shade, Zac abandoned the boat and joined Grace. His arms circled her, his chest came toward her, and she felt his head against her hair as he said, "I'm sorry I yelled."

The phone call had almost made her forget the scene in the kitchen. She told Zac, "I'm sorry I made you want to quit being an actor."

He pulled back so they could see each other's eyes. "You haven't. I'll always be an actor. I just want to do things differently." His hands went to her face, and he smoothed strands of hair into her braid as he searched her eyes. "Grace, would you like to turn this place back into a hotel?"

Grace opened her mouth but didn't speak.

"Tell me."

"Yes."

He kissed her. "Then that's what we'll do. I'd like it, too. Do you know you and I have always lived in hotels? Even our place in New York was a hotel once."

Was he giving up film acting? "What about your agent? I know he's been sending you scripts."

Zac kept his arm around her as he steered her toward the house. He spoke low, his head near hers. "I'll keep modeling. But no films right now. The psychotherapy is important. Our marriage is, too. Let's see if we can make this inn something special, all right?"

Grace felt as though she was dreaming. Her heart was racing, but she knew it wasn't just because Zac was holding her, saying those things. It was because of what she'd done while he was on the river. The phone call.

"Come this way." He led her around the side of the house toward the stone patio. His hand was on the small of her back, his fingers slipping into the waistband of her shorts. Subtle signs. He was going to get her into the shower with him, make love to her. Leisurely dinner, perhaps a movie on video afterward. Sweet companionship. Best friend.

She'd betrayed him.

As they walked around the corner of the house, he pointed and said, "Do you think we could have a croquet pitch there?"

Ninochka bounded past them, chasing a butterfly.

Grace said, "I found her owner."

"What?"

He stopped walking, turned and stared at her.

"There was a flyer at City Market." Grace repeated the contents of the ad.

Zac listened grimly.

"I called the number."

Zac felt his breath becoming strange, too shallow. He didn't know how to react. "Tell me."

She did, and afterward she said, "I'm sorry. I should never have called."

"Calling was the right thing to do. But you should have told me. Why didn't you?" When he saw her eyes, he knew. He was sick, and she'd been protecting him.

Taking care of him.

Across the slope, Ninochka investigated an animal burrow near the carriage house. Zac and Grace stood in the heat watching the dog.

"I'm going to phone her back," he said.

"The owner won't sell."

His expression made hers callow by comparison. "Of course she will. We just have to offer enough."

WHILE ZAC PHONED the woman in Moab that night, Grace sat at the kitchen table petting Ninochka and listening. What she could grasp from Zac's conversation was that the Moab woman was the owner's aunt and that the owner was from out of town.

As the conversation wore on, Grace saw Zachary's face change subtly, saw him swallow, as though he'd heard something distressing.

When he hung up he looked at Grace for a few seconds before he said, "The good news is that the owner lives in Alaska and may not be able to come down here for some time to get her dog. The bad news is—" Briefly he stopped speaking, but then he went on as though his words were nothing of import. "She's a sled-dog racer. And she wants this dog back."

TWO MONTHS PASSED. They worked on the inn by day and made love at night. Zac went out of town three times on modeling assignments, and Grace occasionally filled in when Day and Nick needed an extra guide to row the Daily.

That was where she was the day the green Jeep Wagoneer came down the sandy driveway. Zac was working upstairs, in one of the rooms on the east side of the house. At the sound of the car, Ninochka trotted out onto the balcony to see who was coming. Zac followed.

The first thing he saw was two mountain bikes on a rack on the roof. The second was the Alaska license plate on the front of the vehicle. GTMUSHY. Zac's stomach rolled. He'd been dreading this visit all summer.

From the passenger door emerged a strongly built woman with a strawberry blond ponytail and a deep suntan that was peeling from her nose. Her sunglasses hung on a strap from her neck, so Zac could see her eyes as she squinted up at the balcony. She looked about his age, and so did the driver. He was big, with curly dark hair. Both wore shorts, tank tops and heavy hiking boots.

The woman nodded up at the balcony and said, "Hi. I think that's my dog."

Zac felt like he'd eaten lead. "I'll be right down."

As he slipped back through the French doors, Zac resisted the impulse to close Ninochka in the room to keep her from coming with him. There wouldn't be a problem. He could persuade the woman to sell.

And if he couldn't . . . Nina was hers.

Downstairs, he invited the visitors up to the screened porch. The woman was very interested in Ninochka and said to her companion, "She looks just like Tamar, doesn't she?"

"I'll say." The man crouched near Ninochka, touching her nose with his finger. "You're a pretty girl."

The woman asked, "What have you been calling her?"

Zac told her and watched as she tried out the name. Ninochka responded. The couple liked dogs.

Zachary wasn't sure what he'd expected. What he'd read about mushers at the library had been damning, and he'd gone back to read more when the Moab woman he'd called about the lost husky ad had told him the name of her niece, the owner. Betsy Jason was someone in dog-sled racing. But over the years, she'd lost more than one dog during races. Running them to death.

To victory.

Now, meeting her was like seeing a part of himself—the part he'd recently discarded. Ambition. Or in Betsy's case, competitiveness.

They sat around a table Zac had salvaged from the carriage house weeks earlier. After inspecting the new-comers, Ninochka lay at Zachary's feet.

Betsy's boyfriend, Dan, remained silent while she said, "Look, I've brought you a reward, and I'd also like to reimburse you for vet bills, dog food, whatever you spent on her. It looks like you've taken good care of her, and I'm just thrilled to get her back."

Zac said, "I'd like to buy her from you."

Betsy exchanged a regretful look with Dan. Then she said, "My aunt told me that. I can't do it."

Zac felt it would be crass to name a figure so soon, so he said, "I'll pay whatever she's worth to you."

"Money doesn't matter. I have seventy-six dogs I've raised from pups. Ninochka's mother was one of the best. I lost her last year."

In a race. Zac was sure of it. But he was impressed with how readily Betsy had begun using Ninochka's name. Undoubtedly she knew it would be a step backward for the dog's training to do anything else.

Zac said, "She's been spayed."

Betsy shrugged. "That was probably a good thing for you to do." Her words implied she might have done something different.

Zac felt his way. Panic rose inside him, and he squelched it. "How did you lose Ninochka?"

Betsy threw Dan a killing glare.

Her boyfriend spoke. "*Mea culpa.* I took her mountain biking. We got separated."

Zac's hand slid down beside his chair and his fingers touched coarse hair, then downy undercoat. Ninochka licked his fingers. Meeting Betsy's eyes, hoping he could make her see, he said, "This dog and I have a relationship. She's the only pet my wife and I have. You have seventy-six other dogs."

"Seventy-five. This one is number seventy-six. And I assure you, I have a close relationship with every one of those animals."

Like an Indy driver has with the cylinders of his car, Zac thought. He said, "I'll give you five thousand dollars."

Betsy's expression was compassionate. She said, "I'm glad Ninochka has been in the hands of someone who loved her. But I loved her mother. And I'm taking her back to Alaska. If you object, we'll have to call the sheriff."

There was nothing to do.

They were going to take his dog.

Betsy Jason's sled dog.

Zac looked at Betsy and said, "I'd appreciate it if you could leave her here now and come back tonight. She's my wife's dog, too. I know Grace would like to say goodbye."

CHAPTER SIXTEEN

HE SPENT THE HOURS till Grace came home playing with Ninochka, fighting feelings behind his face and his eyes, watery feelings. He felt dazed and frightened, aware of what was happening.

Loss.

It had set him off before. He had to keep it together this time. He had to stay sane for Grace.

Through the blistering afternoon, he played in the shallows of the river with the husky, then took her inside, where it was cool, and played with her there. He lay down with her on the bed, and Ninochka, smart Nina, knew something was wrong and kept licking his nose, giving him that "What's wrong?" look.

He told her.

THAT EVENING, Grace watched him gather Ninochka's things. Toys. Brush. The blanket from her bed. The dog knew. Her tail drooped. She lay down on the floor and watched them with worried eyes.

Grace was afraid.

What would this do to Zac?

His jaw was very tight, his movements deliberate but oddly relaxed. Almost rehearsed. Seeing him that way, seeing him pack the dog's things in a box, reminded her of another time he'd helped pack. Memories rushed at her. Leaving him.

Now Grace saw Zac through clear eyes. His emotion-less features, the way he could walk around so casually when his world was falling apart, did not mean that he didn't love. Rather that he'd never learned how to show his pain—perhaps even how to feel it—and he loved too much to know what to do.

He had always loved her.

At seven, they heard the car outside. In the kitchen, Grace looked at Ninochka, then up at Zac.

His features even, he said, "Let's go, girl." He picked up the box, and Grace opened the door. They went out, but Zac had to call Ninochka three times before she would follow.

OUTSIDE, WHERE THE SUNSET made shadows shaped like cottonwoods, Betsy Jason removed Nina's collar and handed it to Zac.

He took it, not knowing what to do with it.

Betsy met his eyes. "She'll be happy. Really. These dogs are never happier than when they're running."

Zac held his tongue with effort.

Dan opened the back door of the Wagoneer. "Here, Ninochka. Here, girl. Come on! Come on!"

Ninochka looked at Zac anxiously and tucked her tail between her legs. After a moment Zachary started to walk to the Wagoneer to coax her inside, but Betsy held up her hand. "No. It's better if you don't. She should get used to my voice."

She walked to the car and said, *"Ninochka. Come."*

Again the hesitation.

Betsy repeated her command.

The husky looked at Zachary. He looked at the ground, at the cottonwoods, anywhere else. He heard Betsy call her again, and he turned toward the river and watched the flow of the water. *Ninochka...*

When he looked back the dog was in the car. Betsy was praising her, petting her.

Taking her.

The doors shut, and Zac saw Ninochka looking at him through the window. As the engine started, Grace's hand slid into his, then her arm went around him. Dust choked the air as the Jeep turned and drove out.

Through the hazy orange light of the sunset, they watched the road resettle against the tamarisk, and then Zac turned to his wife, who was still there. Grace, whose brown eyes were frightened. Grace, who must be wondering if he would now go mad. She said, "I'm going to make some tea."

Taking care of him. Zac said, "Thank you." They went into the kitchen and he sat down at the table and stared at Ninochka's collar, still in his hand. After a moment he set it on the table, separating himself. It was going to be okay. He was just a little numb. Trying to think of other things, he asked Grace, "When we build the restaurant kitchen beside the Princess Room, how about if we put the sink against the west wall? Let me tell you what I'm thinking...."

At the stove Grace listened to his plan and tried to find an appropriate way to respond. She thought of their quarters, which would include the parlor, her father's old room and two others in the lower northwest corner of the building. She thought of the dog who had gone. There was nothing to say, and before the kettle whistled Zac suddenly got up and left the room. After the water had boiled and she'd poured it into the teapot, Grace went to find him.

He was in the living room, standing before the hearth, staring at the Waterhouse print in the dusk. He asked Grace, "Does this picture mean anything to you? Do you care about it?"

Ophelia.

Grace actually rather liked it, but it was just something she'd gotten at a garage sale. Nothing her family had owned. "It doesn't matter."

"'There's rosemary, that's for remembrance. Pray you, love, remember.'" Zac reached up and jerked the frame off the wall so hard the picture hanger flew across the room. "'And there is pansies, that's for thoughts.'" Holding the frame, he strode to the front door, opened it and went out. When the screen door banged behind him, Grace followed, onto the shadowy porch and down the steps.

He was headed for the river, but he stopped before he reached the shore. As Grace made her way toward him in the darkness under the cottonwoods, he turned the frame on its side and, with his man's strength, hurled it like a Frisbee out into the river.

It landed with a splash in the middle of the current, the glass winking its last in the falling light. Zachary yelled, "'Poor Ophelia! Divided from herself and her fair judgment, Without the which we are pictures or mere beasts.'" Still turned toward the river, he shouted, "'Your sister's drowned, Laertes!' Drowned! She should have taken her meds! She should have had some psychotherapy!"

But then he fell to his knees in the dirt and put his hands over his face. Grace went to him and knelt beside him.

"Gracie." He turned to her, hugging her, and she combed his hair with her fingers, rubbed her cheek against the beard stubble on his.

He was shaking, and Grace held him tighter in the dark, in the night while mosquitoes whined in her ears. Hearing his quiet, gasping breaths, feeling wetness against her neck, she hugged harder, her head against his. "Shh, shh. It's all right. It's all right. I love you."

Zac could feel her soft skin and hair and smell the lemongrass, and it was comforting, but it made him feel more. This was what it was like to feel. Warm woman in his arms. Pain that wouldn't stop.

Holding him, Grace felt his sobs and caught the choked, almost unintelligible words of grief, words it hurt even to hear. "I want her back.... I want her back."

SUMMER BURNED ON, and he did not go mad.

His family came out for two weeks in late July, around the time of his birthday. While his father helped install ceiling fans on the screened porch, his mother visited with Grace, and Pip flirted with Day.

Day was a frequent visitor at the River Inn. The last time she'd come, to share the five-course dinner Grace had made for his family before they returned to England, she'd brought a yellow flyer, which now hung on the refrigerator:

AUDITIONS!
for a Moab Players production of
Suddenly Last Summer
by
Tennessee Williams

The auditions were in two weeks. Zac was glad. He wanted the distraction. The house kept him busy, but he knew he was mourning the loss of his dog. His dog, who was running somewhere on the tundra, maybe running too hard, running her heart out.

On a Monday in the second week of August, he and Grace awoke before dawn, took a long run, then came home and worked outside in the garden. Zachary wanted to expand the plot next year, perhaps landscape the periphery, but at least now they had fresh vegetables every night.

At 6:30 a.m., it was not yet too warm, and weeding the rows together was peaceful.

As Grace bent over, picking a pest from a squash vine, Zac watched her pale hair and her long legs. Since Ninochka had gone, the relationship between him and Grace had strengthened. Clicked. Zac knew he had simply loved the dog, but he also knew there was a part of himself he'd been afraid to show Grace. A vulnerable part it had been safe to feel with the husky, who would never reject him.

Straightening up, Grace said, "Don't you think it would look nice if we grew morning glories against the carriage house?"

"Would you like to get married?"

"What?" Grace stared at him.

She knew it was not a confused question. Zac was steady these days.

Grace understood him better than she ever had—both who he'd always been and who he had become. That he knew when to let the river steer the boat. When to push on the oars. When to pull. He'd been spending the summer learning how to stay out of holes, but they both knew the river was wild and unpredictable and it could catch him and keep him again.

He crossed the garden toward her, a muscular man in a pair of cotton rugby shorts and a tattered Oxford T-shirt. He needed a haircut and a shave, and he still made her heart stop whenever she saw him. His face near hers, he repeated softly, "I said would you like to get married? Would you like to marry me?"

Grace's heart quavered. "We are married. What are you talking about?"

His mouth hovered near hers. "I married you for a green card." He paused, watching her eyes. "I want to marry you for love."

Grace touched her lip with her tongue. Her gaze caressed his face. His chin. His mouth.

He said, "I'm so in love with you. I always was, but I really think we should fix this. I wasn't thinking of getting divorced first. Just getting married. Again. Will you marry me?"

Grace nodded. "I'd marry you again a hundred times, Zachary." Into her mind flashed the memory of his face when he'd been packing Ninochka's toys. When he'd been helping pack *her* things. She said, "I'd marry you a hundred times for a green card."

He lowered his face to hers and kissed her gently, then slipped closer, his mouth opening against hers. His arousal rose with the sun, and for a while they behaved like two people living in the middle of nowhere, not yet running a hotel. But eventually the ants, starting their day, began crawling on them.

As they stood up and adjusted their clothes, Zac said, "It's up to you of course, but my idea was to pack sleeping bags and a tent, go down the river to somewhere secluded and make our promises to each other. Have a private celebration. Or if you like, we can invite Nick and Day. They'll have to bring their own boat."

"And find their own beach," Grace said, thinking of the sounds she and Zac made in the night.

They talked about their plans as they went inside. While Grace sliced peaches for a cobbler and rolled out dough for scones, Zac played the piano they'd finally had tuned. He was playing "Love Is Here to Stay" when the phone rang. Grace grabbed the receiver at once before he could stop the song.

"Hello?"

It was a woman on the line, and Grace listened carefully, her heart racing. She glanced through the dining room as she responded. Zac was still playing the song. "Yes... Oh, of course. That would be wonderful. Um...a plane ticket. That's no problem, but I think we might like to come and get her, instead. May I have your number? I'll call you back when I know how we want to do it, but yes, yes, we do. Definitely. Thank you so much."

She took down the phone number the woman gave her, promised to call back soon and replaced the receiver. Then she hurried out through the dining room and up the stairs.

ZAC WAS JUST STARTING a polonaise when Grace appeared beside him and set something on the piano's music stand. Still playing, Zac squinted at it. An airplane cocktail napkin. He ceased the song and reached for the napkin.

The honeymoon coupon he'd given her when they'd flown to New York together.

Grace said, "Since we're getting married, I thought we should have a honeymoon."

"Yes." He smiled and turned to straddle the bench, then pulled her down beside him. "Where would you like to go?"

Grace sighed. "It's so hot this time of year. I'd like to go somewhere *cold*. Like... Nome, Alaska." She met Zachary's eyes, and his face was tense. She knew he was afraid.

His brow furrowed slightly as he said, "Why there?" Then, softly, "Who was on the phone?"

"A sled-dog racer named Betsy, who wants to give you back your dog. She said Nina misses you, and...she wants to give you Ninochka and her papers. She said if we sent a ticket she'd put her on the plane, but I've always wanted to visit Alaska, and I thought if we could get married soon..."

Zac's arms slipped around her. "I'd be happy to honeymoon somewhere cold. You're all the warm I need."

And all the Grace.

EPILOGUE

Two years later
Love is here to stay...

ZAC OPENED the backstage door. Nick was outside in the shadows.

"Is everything ready?"

Nick nodded. "Aye-aye. How soon will you be out of here?"

"Thirty minutes."

"Okay. See you then. By the way, nice duds."

"Thank you. They're Siamese." Zac shut the door and slipped through the dark hall and back into the wings. He was on next.

GRACE SAT in the fifth row, her eyes glowing as she watched the musical rising to its climax. Day's sweet soprano blended beautifully with Zac's voice, and they played off each other well, always leaving the audience laughing.

Beside her Fast Susan whispered, "They gave him that part because of how he looks in those clothes. That little vest and no shirt. Does he dress up like the king at home?"

"He is the king at home. And I'm the queen. Shh," Grace said. "I love this song." She loved seeing Zac on stage. Every time. What he did as an actor was beautiful, and Grace realized that Zachary had made her perceive what drama, at its best, could accomplish. It could reflect life in a way that made those in the audience cherish their humanity.

With a smile in her heart, she watched and listened as Anna invited the King of Siam to dance.

AFTER THE FINAL CURTAIN call Grace went out the side door. She and Zac caught each other as he emerged from the back of the theater. He was sweaty and smelled like the stage. Framing her face in his hands, he kissed her on the mouth and said, "Give me five minutes to get out of this. Those flowers aren't for me, are they?"

"Of course not. They're for my sister. I have something else for you."

"Yes, you do." In the shadows against the brick wall of the theater, his hand slid to her breast. His tongue wandered in her mouth. . . .

Five minutes later they were in the Austin-Healey, the warm spring night blowing through their hair as Zac drove toward the Moab Bridge.

Grace was eager to be home. She wanted to be alone with him so badly, to make love the way they did at night when the dishes in the restaurant kitchen were washed and the guests were in their rooms. They had good employees at the River Inn, trustworthy enough to manage dinner and guests so that Grace and Zac could slip out together for an occasional date. Or for her to see a performance, like tonight.

But being home was best. And lately lovemaking had become something more. Zac had been well for two years. Long enough. They were both good boatmen, and each knew when to bail for the other. They'd decided to try the rapids.

To try to conceive a child.

The sound of the tires changed as they crossed over the Colorado on the bridge. Then Zac slowed the car.

"What are you doing?"

"Stopping at Rapid Riggers."

Grace pulled her hair out of her face and looked toward the office. It was dark except for the security light. Why was Zac stopping here?

As he pulled into the lot, her eyes swept toward the river. The night was moonless, but she could see a large black shape on the water. Almost like a small barge. "What's that?"

Zac stepped out of the car and walked around to open her door. He was wearing his grizzly-bear shirt, and Grace touched him as she got out.

Taking her hand, he led her across the lot toward the river.

Grace could see the shape more clearly now. She could see the railing. The cabin. The paddle wheel.

Her heels were sinking into the mud, and Zac put his arms behind her and picked her up. Grace kept her eyes on the riverboat and saw the moment the lights went on. White lights surrounding the canopy. She could see that the craft had been specially designed to navigate the Colorado, and as Zac carried her out onto the concrete launch ramp, she read the name on the bow.

Sam Sutter.

She couldn't talk, only look up at Zachary. He'd been waiting to see her eyes. Then he kissed her, and the kisses continued when they'd climbed aboard, after they'd shared a champagne toast with Nick and Day, their partners in the riverboat venture, after Nick and Day had vanished into the wheelhouse.

The sound of the engine changed, and Nick, the captain, headed the boat downstream. As the *Sam Sutter* carried them home to the River Inn, Zac stood with Grace in the shadows. He sang to her, held her, whispered things that excited them both. Bowed his head over her breasts where they curved above the sweetheart neckline of the taffeta slip-dress he'd bought her in New York more than two years earlier.

As the lights of the inn neared, they saw their home from the water. Seeing the familiar details of the structure, Zac felt a sense of belonging that he'd never experienced anywhere else, even at Oakhurst. He and Grace had made the River Inn theirs. Zac hoped someday one of their children would want to run it, to keep it lovely.

After saying good-night to Nick and Day, who would take the boat back up the river to Rapid Riggers, Zachary and Grace walked down the gangplank to the boat ramp. When they reached the shore, two dogs rushed at them, tails wagging. Ninochka dropped a Frisbee at Zac's feet.

"Not now." He crouched and petted her. "Coupon, don't jump on Grace."

Kicking off her shoes to walk up the sandy bank, Grace petted the second dog, a short-legged one-eared mottled-brown mutt whose face looked as though it had been hit by a frying pan. "Hello, Coupon." When she'd first seen the dog, she'd told Zac, *If you want to keep it, you'll need to use a coupon.* Now Coupon slept on her side of the bed at night. He was a darling.

She and Zac held hands as they avoided the front door and walked around to the stone patio. Grace poked her head into the restaurant kitchen beside the Princess Room. Jill, her sous-chef, saw her and said, "Everything's cool. Great night."

Zac was tugging on her fingers. Grace stepped back out into the night. Accompanied by their dogs, they slipped along the patio and through the French doors into their bedroom, and Zac closed the blinds in case any guests were out roaming.

He turned to her, his lips slightly parted, his eyes like coal. Grace lifted her face, reached for his shoulders . . .

The Romeo and Juliet bed was massive, made of cherry wood with panels on the sides and on the headboard and a wide ledge all around. Zachary had made it with love for her, aware every minute of what they would do on it, that it was the bed of their marriage. Lovemaking and sleeping and dreaming and a shared future. A life raft.

Now, on the bed, he made love to her, watching her, loving her, going in deep, with his heart and his body and his seed. Aware of what they both hoped would happen. A baby. Made in love. Grace clung to him, shuddering, and Zac felt her squeezing him, taking him with her as the walls of their private quarters absorbed their cries of love.

Afterward, as she lay in his arms and the dogs staked out their spots on the king-size mattress, Grace said, "You were so good in the play, Zac. I know you could be a star. A big star. I always knew it. If you ever want to leave here and be a professional actor again, it's all right with me. As long as I can go with you of course."

Listening to her, Zac remembered the praise he'd received for *Kah-Puh-Rats*. He thought of who he'd been when he'd married Grace for a green card. The changes in him were deeper than she knew. It was enough to do what he loved, as he had tonight. Look out on the audience. See faces smiling, laughing or simply responding to the performance, to whatever spoke to them. Now he saw greater peace and wealth in the home they'd built together and in the tradition they'd restored. In standing outside in the desert night. Here the air was thin and clear, and the ancient lights in the sky seemed only a moment away.

He held his wife closer, kissed her hair, watched Coupon snuggled against her leg on top of the sheets. He said,

"Why would I want to be a star when I can be an ordinary man and hold heaven in my arms?"

Grace smiled. Zac would never be ordinary.

He was a keeper.

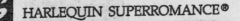

HARLEQUIN SUPERROMANCE®

WOMEN WHO DARE
They take chances, make changes
and follow their hearts!

Christmas Star
by Roz Denny Fox
Harlequin Superromance #672

Since her childhood, Starr Lederman has always wished on
what her mother called the Christmas star—the first star out
on those December nights just before Christmas. Now her
adopted daughter, SeLi, does the same thing.

But SeLi isn't wishing for toys or video games. She's
out for the serious stuff—a dad for herself. Which
means a husband for Starr. And SeLi's got a man all
picked out. Clay McLeod, rancher.

Clay's not looking for a wife, though. Especially not a woman
as independent and daring as Starr. A woman *he* believes is
having an affair with his brother. His married brother.

But at Christmastime, things have a way of sorting
themselves out....

Available in December, wherever
Harlequin books are sold.

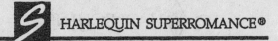

HARLEQUIN SUPERROMANCE®

a heartwarming trilogy by *Peg Sutherland*

*Meet old friends and new ones on a trip to
Sweetbranch, Alabama—where the most unexpected
things can happen...*

Harlequin Superromance #673 *Double Wedding Ring* (Book 1)

Susan Hovis is suffering from amnesia.

She's also got an overprotective mother and a demanding
physiotherapist. Then there's her college-age daughter—and
Susan also seems to have a young son she can't really
remember. Enter Tag, a man who claims to have been her
teenage lover, and the confusion intensifies.

Soon, everything's in place for a Christmas wedding.
But whose?

Don't miss *Double Wedding Ring* in December,
wherever Harlequin books are sold. And watch for
Addy's Angels and *Queen of the Dixie Drive-In*
(Books 2 and 3 of Peg Sutherland's trilogy)
this coming January and February!

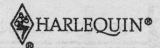